THE
SUMMER
CHILDREN

ALSO BY
DOT HUTCHISON

A Wounded Name

The Butterfly Garden

The Roses of May

THE SUMMER CHILDREN

Book 3 in the Collector Series

DOT HUTCHISON

Text copyright © 2018 by Dot Hutchison

Published by Thomas & Mercer, Seattle

www.apub.com

Amazon, the Amazon logo, and Thomas & Mercer are trademarks of Amazon.com, Inc., or its affiliates.

ISBN-13: 9781542049887
ISBN-10: 1542049881

Cover design by Damon Freeman

Printed in the United States of America

To C. V. Wyk—
Look at us! We did it!

Once upon a time, there was a little girl who was scared of the dark.

Which was silly, even she knew that. There was nothing in the dark to hurt you that wasn't also in the light. You just couldn't see it coming.

So maybe that was what she hated, that blindness and helplessness.

Always helpless.

But things did get worse in the dark, didn't they? People are always more honest when no one can see them.

In the light, her mama would only sigh and sniffle her sadness, blinking away tears, but in the darkness her sobs would become living things, fleeing her bedroom to tuck away in the drafty corners of the house and wail so everyone could hear them. Sometimes screams would stalk after them, but even in the dark her mama was rarely brave enough for that.

And her daddy . . .

In the light, her daddy was always sorry, always apologizing to her and her mama.

I'm sorry, baby, I didn't mean that.

I'm sorry, baby, I just lost my temper.

Look what you made me do, baby, I'm sorry.

I'm sorry, baby, but this is for your own good.

Every pinch and punch, every slap and slam, every curse and insult, he was always sorry. But sorry was only for in the light.

In the dark, he was Daddy, entirely and honestly himself.

So maybe she wasn't silly after all, because wasn't it a lot smarter to be afraid of true things? If you were afraid of something in the light, wasn't it just good sense to be more afraid of it in the dark?

1

The roads around DC are rarely quiet at any time of day, but a little after midnight on a hot summer Thursday, I-66 is sparsely populated, especially once you pass Chantilly. Beside me, Siobhan babbles contentedly about the jazz club we just left, the singer we went especially to see and how wonderful she'd been, and I nod and hum in the pauses. Jazz isn't really my thing—I tend to prefer more structure—but Siobhan loves it, and I planned the evening as a bit of an apology for having to work through a handful of date nights recently. The mothers—my last set of foster parents—always told me relationships took conscious effort. Back then, I didn't realize how much effort they meant.

My job doesn't lend itself to standard date nights, but I do try. Siobhan is also an FBI agent and should theoretically understand the up-and-go constraints, but she works translations in Counterterrorism Monday through Friday, eight to four-thirty, and doesn't always remember that my job in Crimes Against Children is nothing like that. We've been on rocky ground the past six months or so, but I can sit through an evening of music I don't care for if it will make her happy.

Her steady stream of chatter shifts to work, and my hums get a little more absentminded. We talk about her work all the time—not the details of what she's translating, but her coworkers, deadlines, the sort of thing that doesn't bring Internal Affairs around asking about security leaks—but we never talk about mine. Siobhan doesn't want to hear about the horrible things people do to children, or the horrible people that do them. I can talk about my teammates, our unit chief and his family, but it even unnerves her to hear about the pranks we pull on each other at the office when our desks bear folders full of horrors.

I'm used to this disparity in our relationship after three years, but I'm always aware of it.

"Mercedes!"

My hands clench on the wheel at the sudden spike in volume, eyes flicking to the dark road around us, but I'm too well trained to let my flinch make the car swerve. "What? What is it?"

"Were you even listening?" she asks wryly, back to her normal volume.

That would be no, but I'm not about to admit that. "Your bosses are ignorant assholes who wouldn't know Pashto from Farsi if their lives depended on it, and they need to get off your ass or learn to do it themselves."

"I complain about them far too much if that's your safe guess."

"Am I wrong?"

"No, but that doesn't mean you were listening."

"Sorry," I sigh. "It's been a long day, and waking up early is going to suck."

"Why are we waking up early?"

"I have that seminar in the morning."

"Oh. You and Eddison being you and Eddison."

That's one way of putting it. Mostly accurate too.

Because apparently it's inappropriate, when your partner/team leader asks after a specific report, to tell him not to get his nuts in a vise. And it's definitely inappropriate for said partner/team leader's automatic response to be "Calm your tits, *hermana*." And it's *especially* inappropriate if the section chief happens to be walking through the bullpen and hears the exchange.

I'm honestly not sure who laughed harder over it later: Sterling, our junior partner, who witnessed everything and got to duck down behind the safety of a cubicle partition to hide her giggles, or Vic, our former partner/leader and now unit chief, standing beside the section chief and lying his ass off to assure him that this was a one-off occurrence.

Not sure if the sec-chief believed him or not, but both Eddison and I were assigned to the next quarterly sexual harassment seminar. Again. I mean, we're not Agent Anderson, who has his name on the back of a chair and a first-name relationship with the roster of instructors, but the two of us are there far too often.

"Is there still a pool on whether or not you two are dating?" Siobhan asks.

"Several," I snicker, "and at least one to guess the date our latent sexual tension finally overwhelms us."

"So one of these days I should expect a text apologizing for jumping him?"

"I think I just threw up in my mouth a little."

She laughs and reaches up to pull the clips from her hair, her wild red curls spilling around her. "If you're going to be up and about earlier than usual, do you need to take me back to Fairfax tonight?"

"How would you get to work? I drove us straight from the office."

"Oh, right. But the question stands."

"I'd like you to stay over," I tell her, taking a hand off the wheel so I can tug one of her curls, "as long as you don't mind sleeping."

"I like sleeping," she replies dryly. "I try to do it every night, if I can."

I respond with dignity and maturity: I stick out my tongue. She laughs again and bats my hand away.

I live in a quiet neighborhood on the outskirts of Manassas, Virginia, about an hour southwest of DC, and almost as soon as we pull off the interstate, we become the only car on the road for minutes at a time. Siobhan sits up straighter when we pass Vic's neighborhood.

"Did I tell you Marlene offered to make me a raspberry trifle for my birthday?"

"I was there when she made the offer."

"Marlene Hanoverian's raspberry trifle," she says dreamily. "I'd marry her if she swung that way."

"And if she didn't have fifty-plus years on you?"

"Those fifty-plus years have taught her to make the best goddamn pistachio cannoli ever. I am all sorts of good with those extra decades."

I pull onto my street, most of the houses dark at this time of night. We have a mix of young professionals in starter houses and empty nesters and retirees who've downsized. The houses are more cottage than anything, only one or two rooms, set like single blooms in decently sized lawns. I can't keep a plant alive to save my life—I'm not allowed to touch the numerous plants in Siobhan's apartment—but my next-door neighbor, Jason, tends my lawn and the shared garden that stretches between our houses in exchange for helping him with his laundry and mending. He's a nice older man, still active and a little lonely since his wife died, and I think we both enjoy the trade.

The driveway is on the left side of the house, extending a full car's length beyond the back wall, and as I cut the engine, I automatically check that the back porch with its sliding glass door looks undisturbed. There's a certain amount of personal paranoia that comes with the job, and on the good days, when we've saved kids and gotten them safely home, it feels like an okay cost.

Nothing seems out of place, so I open the car door. Siobhan grabs our messenger bags from the backseat and skips ahead of me on the curving walk to the front porch. "Do you think Vic will bring in something from his mother tomorrow?"

"Today? Chances are good."

"Mmm, I could really go for some Danish. Or, ooh! Those berry-and-cream-cheese pinwheel puffs."

"She's offered to teach you how to bake, you know."

"But Marlene is so much better at it." She passes the motion sensor, and the porch light flickers on as she grins over her shoulder at me. "Besides, it would never survive to the baking part if I tried to do it, I'd eat—Oh my God!"

I drop my purse, gun in hand with my finger stretched along the side of the trigger guard before I can put thought to it. In the bright glare of the porch light, a shadow sits on the bench swing. I inch forward past Siobhan, gun aimed down, until I can see more clearly through the rails. When my eyes finally adjust, I damn near drop the gun.

Madre de Dios, there is a child sitting on my porch, and it is covered in blood.

Instinct says, *Race for the child, take him or her in my arms and shield them from the world, check them over for hurts.* Training says, *Wait, ask the questions, don't disturb the evidence that will help find whatever asshole did this to them.* Sometimes being a good agent feels a lot like being a heartless person, and it's hard to convince yourself otherwise.

Training wins, though. It usually does.

"Are you hurt?" I ask, still inching forward. "Are you alone?"

The child lifts its head, face a horrific mask streaked in blood, tears, and crusting snot. It sniffles, thin shoulders shaking. "Are you Mercedes?"

He knows my name. He's on my porch, and he knows my name. How?

"Are you hurt?" I ask again, to give myself time to process.

The kid just looks back at me, eyes huge and haunted. He—fairly sure it's a he, though it's hard to tell from here—is in pajamas, a giant blue T-shirt and striped cotton pants, all spattered thickly with blood, and he hunches around something, clutching it. He sits up more as I get closer, up the three steps of the porch, and I can make it out: a teddy bear, white where blood hasn't rubbed, rust and red, into its fur, with a heart-shaped nose and crinkly gold wings and a halo.

Jesus.

The spray patterns on his shirt are alarming—somehow even more than the rest of this—because they're thick stripes, far too reminiscent of arterial spray. It can't be his, which is almost comforting, but it's still someone's. He's the kind of fine-boned small that suggests he's probably older than he looks; my guess is ten or eleven. Beneath the blood and the shocky pallor, he looks bruised.

"Sweetheart, can you tell me your name?"

"Ronnie," he mumbles. "Are you Mercedes? She said you'd come."

"She?"

"She said Mercedes would come and I'll be safe."

"Who is 'she,' Ronnie?"

"The angel who killed my parents."

2

A shrill whine suddenly reminds me that hi, yes, Siobhan is right behind me, Siobhan who doesn't like to hear about what I do and can't watch a help-us-feed-children-in-Africa commercial without bawling. "Siobhan? Can you get our phones out, please?"

"Mercedes!"

"Please? All three phones? And hand me my work phone?"

She doesn't hand it to me so much as throw it at me, and I fumble to catch it against my side with my left hand. I can't put the gun away until I know the area is clear, and I can't prowl around the house to check because it would leave Siobhan and Ronnie unprotected. Siobhan doesn't carry a gun.

"Thank you," I say, using the Soothing Agent Voice and hoping she doesn't punch me for it later. She thinks it's manipulative; I think it's better than letting someone freak out. "On my phone, can you pull up the notepad? Type Ronnie's name in, and get ready for an address. Once you have that, call 911, give them both our names, tell them we're FBI agents."

"I'm not a field agent."

"I know, they just need to know we're law enforcement. Hang on, let me try to get the rest of what they'll need." I study Ronnie, who's damn near hugging the stuffing out of the bear. He hasn't moved from his spot on the bench swing, and there are no bloody footprints around him or on the steps. There's blood dried on his bare feet, but no footprints. "Ronnie, do you know your address? Your parents' names?"

It takes a few minutes to get their names, Sandra and Daniel Wilkins, and enough of their address to be useful, and I can still hear Siobhan whimpering as she types it into my phone. "Call emergency," I tell her.

She nods shakily and walks quickly down the curve of the path with her phone to her ear, my personal cell lit up in her trembling hand so she can read out the information. She's briefly out of sight where the path meets the drive, but then I can see her head down the driveway to stop at the curb, just within the cone of light from the streetlamp. Good enough, even if I'd rather she was closer. I can't protect her from here.

"Ronnie? Are you hurt?"

He looks up at me, confused, but flickers away from eye contact half a second later. Oh, I know that body language.

"Is any of that blood yours?" I clarify, because there are a lot of ways a child can be hurt.

He shakes his head. "The angel made me watch. She said I'd be safe."

"Were you not safe before? Before the angel came?"

He lifts one shoulder in a half shrug, eyes fixed on the floorboards.

"Ronnie, I have to step away so I can call my partner at work, okay? He's going to help me make sure you're safe. I'll stay right where you can see me, all right?"

"And I'm safe?"

"Ronnie, I promise you, as long as you're here, no one is going to touch you without your consent. No one."

I'm not sure he trusts it, or that he gets it—I don't think consent is something his parents have ever taught him—but he nods, hunching back into himself over the teddy bear, and watches me through his sandy fringe of hair as I walk to the curve of the path, where I can see both him and Siobhan clearly. Keeping the gun pointed at the ground, I wake up the phone and tap "2" to dial Eddison.

He picks up on the third ring. "I can't get us out of the seminar; I already tried."

"There's a bloody little boy on my porch. An angel made him watch her kill his parents, then brought him here to wait for me."

There's a long silence, and in the background I can hear what sounds like a post–baseball game analysis on the television. "Wow," he says finally. "You really don't want to go to that seminar."

I bite my lip, not quite fast enough to hold in the strangled laugh. "Siobhan's calling emergency."

"Is he hurt?"

"That's a complicated kind of question."

"Our kind of complicated?"

"Smart bet."

"I'll be there in fifteen."

The call ends, and for lack of a pocket in my little black dress, I slide the phone under my right bra strap where I can grab it without letting go of the gun. I walk back to the porch, sitting down on the top step. After a moment, I angle my body so I can see both him and the end of the driveway, my back against the rail post. "Help will be here soon, Ronnie. Can you tell me about the angel?"

He shakes his head again, and clutches the bear a little tighter. There's something about the bear, something that . . . oh. The blood on the fur isn't spray. It's castoff, from his arms, from his face, probably the bear's back is coated, but he wasn't holding it when his parents were attacked.

"Ronnie, did the angel give you that bear?"

He glances up, meets my eyes for a heartbeat, and then fixes his gaze back on the floor, but after a moment, he nods.

¡Me lleva la chingada! Our team gives teddy bears to victims, or their friends and siblings, when we have to interview them, because it's a bit of comfort, something to hold or squeeze—or in the case of one

twelve-year-old, throw at Eddison's head. But to give a bear to a kid after you've murdered his parents in front of him?

And he said "she." That's so fucking rare, if he's right.

Eddison drives up, parking at the curb several houses down to keep out of the way of the emergency vehicles that should be arriving very shortly. Eddison and I live a fifteen-minute drive apart; a glance at the phone says it's been just under ten since the call ended. I'm not even going to ask how many traffic laws he just broke. He's still in jeans, his feet jammed into untied sneakers, but he's got his badge clipped to his belt and an FBI windbreaker to lend him the authority his Nationals T-shirt leeches out. His hand is on his holstered gun as he approaches, stopping briefly to check in with Siobhan. They're not, and probably never will be, friends, but they're friendly enough given that their only points of commonality are me and the Bureau.

When he reaches the driveway side of the walk, he touches next to his eye, then twirls his finger. I shake my head, tilting my gun so he can see it still in my hands. He nods and draws his weapon and pocket flashlight, disappearing around the side of the house. After several minutes, he comes back into view and reholsters his gun. I stretch and hook my heel into my purse strap, pulling it toward me so I can put my own sidearm away, finally. I hate having a drawn gun near kids.

Before we get a chance to say so much as hello, an ambulance and a police car, followed by an unmarked sedan that is definitely also a police car, pull onto the street, sirens off but lights flashing. Fortunately, they cut the lights as soon as they park. Some of the neighbors get nervous enough living near an FBI agent; not waking anyone up with this would be preferable.

I actually recognize the plainclothes walking toward us. We worked a missing kids case together two years ago, and found the kids safe and sound in Maryland. Terrible as it sounds, I'm suddenly grateful for the experience, or this meeting would be a lot more awkward. Detective

Holmes comes straight to the porch, one of the uniformed officers and both paramedics walking behind her. The other officer stays at the end of the drive to talk to Siobhan. "Agent Ramirez," Holmes greets me. "Long time."

"*Sí.* Detective Holmes, this is SSAIC Brandon Eddison, and this," I continue, taking a deep breath and gesturing to the porch swing, "is Ronnie Wilkins."

"Have you checked him over?"

"No. He said he wasn't injured, so it seemed best left to you. Agent Eddison did a circuit around the house to check for others, but aside from that, there's been movement only at the car, along the paved path, and where I'm sitting."

"Agent Eddison? Anything of note?"

He shakes his head. "No visible blood trails, no signs of attempted entry around the windows or back door, no blood or dirt or debris on the back porch. No one in wait, no obvious footprints."

"How much has he said?"

"I've tried not to ask him much," I admit, but I relay what he's told me.

She listens intently, tapping her fingers against a small notebook sticking up out of her pocket. "All right. I hope you know I mean nothing personal by this—"

"Where do you need us to stand?"

Her lips twitch in a smile, and she nods. "Curve of the path? I'd like you in sight, for his sake, but some space would be good. If you don't mind introducing us?"

"Absolutely."

Eddison offers me a hand up, and I turn to face the child watching from the porch swing. "Ronnie? This is Detective Holmes. She's going to ask you some questions about what happened tonight, okay? Can you talk to her?"

"I . . ." He looks between me and the detective, drops his gaze to the holstered gun at her hip, then shudders and stares at the floor. "Okay," he whispers.

Holmes frowns thoughtfully. "I might need—"

"Just call out." I poke Eddison in the shoulder blade to get him moving, and we walk down the path until we're just short of disappearing around the edge of the house. "I haven't told Vic yet."

"I called him on the way," he replies, his knuckles scraping the coarse stubble on his jaw. "He said to keep him updated, and not to bother Sterling with it tonight. We'll tell her in the morning."

"It's not a Bureau case."

"Exactly." He glances over my shoulder to the end of the drive. "Siobhan doesn't look happy."

"I can't understand why; we had a romantic date and came home to a blood-covered child on the doorstep. What's to be unhappy about?"

"Ronnie Wilkins. Does the name ring any bells?"

"No, but there's almost certainly a Social Services file on him." I watch the paramedics and officer check Ronnie over, gathering samples and evidence. They pause between each step, checking in with him for permission. He looks confused by it. Not their touching him, just that they ask. Holmes leans against the front rail a couple of feet away, making sure not to crowd him or loom over him. They let him keep hold of the teddy bear, occasionally asking him to move it to his other hand but never touching it themselves. It's good to see.

"Why you?"

"I really hope we find out, because I haven't a clue."

"Technically we don't have authority to see his file, but I'll ask Holmes once the kid is settled. Maybe something in his history will jump out." He crouches down to tie his shoes properly. "My couch is open, by the way."

"Oh?"

Despite the hour, sweat beads along his hairline. The sight makes me unpleasantly aware of how my dress is clinging damply to my back. Summer in Virginia. He gives me a lopsided smile and shifts position to tie the second shoe. "You're not going to be able to stay here, and Siobhan does not look in the mood to have you trail into her place at some obscene hour of the morning."

This is true. "Thanks," I sigh. "As long as one of the officers precedes me inside, I should be able to grab some fresh clothing and such, rather than break into a go bag."

"*Lo que quieras.*"

On the porch, one of the paramedics unfolds a crinkly silver blanket and tucks it gently around Ronnie. They must be getting ready to move him. Holmes is on her phone, listening more than talking, it looks like; her face doesn't give away much. She has a kid around Ronnie's age, if I remember correctly. After she hangs up, she says something to the officer and heads down the steps to join us.

"Social Services is going to meet us at the hospital," she informs us. "Agent Ramirez, they're asking that you not be there, at least at first. They want to see if your absence will help him remember anything else the killer might have said about you."

"His parents are definitely dead, then?"

She glances down at her phone and whistles. "Oh, yeah. Detective Mignone is in charge of the scene. He says if you two want to check it out, he'll get your names down."

"Really?" asks Eddison, and he sounds more doubtful than he probably intended.

"We all know that this isn't a Bureau case, but it could well become one. Piss jurisdictions, I'd rather keep you up to date before it's an issue."

"Appreciate it."

"Agent Ryan can head on home." I'd forgotten about Siobhan for a minute. "We may call with more questions at some point, but there's no reason to keep her here. Agent Ramirez, do you need anything from inside before we put the tape up?"

My stomach sinks at the mention of the tape. Obviously I was never going to be able to keep it entirely from my neighbors, but the tape is going to make it a bit conspicuous. "Please," I answer. I nod encouragingly at Ronnie as the paramedics and officer walk him past, the smaller paramedic keeping one hand flat against the boy's shoulder.

Ronnie twists around to look at me, his eyes wide and wounded.

"He's going to be okay," Holmes says softly.

Eddison snorts. "For certain definitions of okay."

This isn't something you can go through without scars, deep and always a little raw. No matter how Ronnie ultimately stitches himself back together, he'll see the seams, and so will anyone else who knows those scars on their own soul.

"I'll let you give the news to Agent Ryan."

I pull my keys from my purse and waggle them at Eddison. "I'm going to let her take my car, if she feels okay to drive. Hers is in the garage at work, so getting it back won't be a problem."

"*Buena suerte.*"

When I head down to the end of the drive, Siobhan has shifted from shocked to spitting mad, pacing in tight circles with her hair bouncing around her. She looks glorious, and I am not about to tell her that. "The detective says you're free to go. Are you okay to drive or do you want me to drop you off?"

"Is this one of your cases?" she asks instead of answering. "Did it follow you home?"

"We don't know what this is. As far as we know he's not connected to any cases we've worked on or been asked to consult on. We'll dig in today to find out for sure."

"He was brought to your house, Mercedes! He was given your name!"

"I know."

"Then why are you so fucking calm?" she hisses.

I'm not, but then, there aren't many who would realize that. I can't really blame her for not being one of them. My hands aren't shaking, my voice is even, but there's a frisson of electricity arcing through me that makes everything seem like it's going a million miles an hour. "I've seen worse," I say eventually.

Which might have been the wrong answer. She snatches the keys from my hand, gouging my palm. "I'll text you the garage level in the morning." She stalks up to the car, not even seeming to notice when Eddison opens the passenger door to put her bag inside. I step back onto the grass about two seconds ahead of her slamming the gas and nearly backing over me.

"So that went well," Eddison notes.

"Asshole," I mutter.

"Whatever you say, *mija*. Go on, get your gear. I'll text Vic."

The officer who had been with Siobhan accompanies me inside. It's bizarre; there's absolutely no sign that whoever dropped off Ronnie made any attempt to enter the house. I grab a bag and shove in clothes and toiletries, as well as one of the books of logic puzzles I keep beside the bed. There's a choked sound from the officer standing in the bedroom doorway.

When I glance over, he just points up.

Okay, I can see how that might be a little discomfiting in light of the evening's events.

A long shelf runs along all four walls in the bedroom, about a foot and a half from the ceiling, and it's entirely covered with teddy bears. In the corners, small cloth net hammocks hang down to allow the largest and smallest bears to be seen. One sits alone on the nightstand on my side of the bed, a faded black-velvet creature with a red-and-white houndstooth bow tie. The fact that most of them are from after I aged out of foster care . . . well, there's no way for the officer to know that.

"The one Ronnie was holding? Not one of mine," I tell him.

"Are you sure?"

"Yes." I study the bears along the shelf, checking each one against my memory of when and where I got it, or who gave it to me. "None of mine are missing or moved, and none have been added."

"I'll, uh . . . I'll let Detective Holmes know."

Just to be on the better side of caution, I check the gun safe set into the floor under the bed, but both of my personal handguns are there, the ammo still in the lockbox in the closet by my shoes.

"I need to change, but I know you have to keep me in sight. Any chance you could keep your eyes on my feet?"

"Yes, ma'am."

I change quickly, leaving the dress on the bed. Despite the hour, I pull on something suitably professional, in case we end up going straight to the office from the Wilkinses' house. We still have that damn seminar in the morning, and I don't think the experience needs to be compounded with a reminder of the dress code.

In the kitchen, I climb onto the counter next to the fridge and reach into the short cabinet over the appliance, scraping my fingers along the side until I find the spare keys I've taped to the wood. Vic, Eddison, Sterling, and Siobhan all have keys of their own, but it seemed a good idea to have an extra set. Hopping down, I hold them out to the officer so he can see the dots of nail polish. "Yellow is top dead bolt, green is lower dead bolt, blue is the doorknob. The orange one unlocks the glass over the screen door in back."

"Agents and cops," he agrees. "Windows?"

"Basic switch locks, no keys needed." When I gave Siobhan her set, she had a panic attack over how many locks there were. She feels four is excessive. As a result of that conversation, it's actually written down on a Post-it somewhere that I am not allowed to ask her landlord to put more on her door.

The officer locks the door behind us, and I have to stand still and breathe against a deep churning in my gut. This is my *home*, the thing that's always mine, and here I am being chased out of it for something I can't understand yet.

Eddison grabs my bag, because his reaction to female distress is gentlemanly awkwardness. The ratio of *gentleman* to *awkward* varies depending on the person provoking the response. He even holds the car door open for me, so I do the only sensible thing.

I smack the back of his head, the blow cushioned by the dark curls starting to get a little too fluffy and shaggy. *"¡Basta!"*

"¡Mantén la calma!" he retorts, and leaves me to close the door myself.

Poor Eddison. With the exception of Vic, he's doomed to spend his life surrounded by strong, prickly, opinionated women, and he wouldn't have it any other way. I've never really been sure what he did to deserve such glorious distress.

3

Sandra and Daniel Wilkins live on the north side of Manassas in a solidly middle-class neighborhood, maybe a little past its prime and starting to get run down. Every house was built from one of three blueprints, with different paint jobs in the same palette to give a sense of variety, but everything sags a little and most of the cars are older models, many with mismatched panels replaced because of accidents or rust. The ambulance we pass is on its way out, lights and sirens off, and the medical examiner's van in one of the driveways is a good hint as to why there's no particular sense of urgency. Two patrol cars and an unmarked sedan that probably belongs to Detective Mignone flank the driveway.

There are a few neighbors out on their driveways, watching the illuminated house, but mostly the neighborhood is still asleep. Eddison parks halfway down the street to make sure we aren't in the way of the cars or van, or blocking any of the residents in. I move my holster from my purse to my belt, slip my credentials into my back pocket, and finally shift my work cell from my bra to my pocket, because I forgot to do it while changing.

"Finished primping?" Eddison asks.

"I do like to look my best," I retort.

He grins and opens his door, and we walk up to the house. When we present our credentials to the uniform at the door, he marks the time off on his clipboard. "There's a box of booties outside the main bedroom," he advises. "Careful where you step."

That's encouraging.

There's no blood obvious on the white painted steps to the second story, or on the tan carpet down the hallway. "Detective Mignone?" Eddison calls out. "Agents Eddison and Ramirez; Holmes sent us over."

"Bootie up and come on in," answers a male voice from inside the bedroom. There's a low murmur of other voices.

We bend down to pull the thin paper booties on over our shoes. It isn't just to protect our shoes, but also to minimize impact on the evidence, to avoid things like dragging blood or putting fresh shoe prints on the surfaces. I pull on a second pair over the first, and after a moment's thought, so does Eddison.

Ronnie had an awful lot of blood on him; the room has to be a god-awful mess.

I probably should have guessed it from the ME's van outside, but it somehow comes as a surprise that the Wilkinses are still in bed. The covers are in disarray, and there is blood pretty damn near everywhere. I can track a few spots that are clearly arterial spray—it's a very distinctive pattern—and several that seem more likely to be cast off, probably from a knife. After that, it gets more chaotic where different blood patterns cross and drip. There are dual negative spaces on the carpet on either side of the bed. One on each side is most likely where the killer—Ronnie's angel—stood, but the others . . .

When he said she made him watch, I didn't imagine he meant this closely.

Two sets of bloody footprints track around the bed and to the door, but they stop there. There was zero blood in the hall. The killer could have carried Ronnie—probably carried Ronnie, as an extra measure of control—but she had to have had something to cover her feet. Booties? Bags? Another pair of shoes? The larger pair of bloody prints shows shoe treads, at any rate.

"Kid's really okay?" asks the suited detective. Mignone appears to be in his fifties, his skin weathered by sun, with close-cropped hair and a bristling salt-and-pepper moustache.

"Traumatized, but physically unhurt," I tell him. "Unless you count old wounds."

"Don't know if Holmes mentioned it: patrol knows this house pretty well. Their neighbors usually make a point of being uncurious, but there are still a couple calls a month for domestic disturbance. We'll get a copy of the full file on your desks tomorrow." He nods at both of us, then gestures to the bodies on the bed. "Hell of a thing."

That's one way to put it.

Daniel Wilkins is on the left side of the bed, a broad-shouldered man with a layer of beer fat over muscle. What he looked like before the attack is impossible to gauge: his face isn't just bloody, it's been slashed and stabbed, along with his torso.

"Twenty-nine separate knife wounds on him," says the medical examiner, looking up from the other side of the bed. "Plus two gunshot wounds to the chest. Those weren't immediately fatal, but he wasn't moving around with them, either."

"Any shots on her?"

The ME shakes her head. "Probably intended as a subduing measure. Near as we can tell before autopsy, the shots on him came first. Then she was attacked, and the killer went back to him. Spent a bit more time on him. She's only got seventeen knife wounds, all on the torso."

Seventeen and twenty-nine . . . that's a lot of rage.

"Physically fit killer," Eddison says, carefully stepping between two arcs of blood on the carpet so he can get closer. "Frenzies like this are tiring, but they also carried Ronnie down the stairs and to a vehicle, then up to Ramirez's porch."

"And you really have no idea why?" asks Mignone.

I am going to get very tired of repeating no. Fortunately, Eddison does it for me this time.

I come around to Sandra Wilkins's side of the bed, standing next to one of the ME's assistants. "Probably hard to tell, given the mess, but does she show signs of abuse?"

"Besides the black eye and swollen cheek? She's got some bruising, and it wouldn't be any surprise to find a few broken bones on the X-rays. We'll know better once we get her cleaned up."

"And some of her hospital records are in the file," adds Mignone. "Entrance into the house looks pretty straightforward. Porch light was unscrewed just enough to not connect, not far enough to fall and shatter."

"That's it?"

"Didn't need to be any more sophisticated than that; it did the trick. Didn't have to pick the lock because it's been broken for a while. Mrs. Wilkins locked her husband out of the house during a fight so he broke the lock, never replaced it."

"Was that in a police report?"

"Yes, few months ago. No blood in or around the kid's room. Looks like the killer woke him up, brought him here, started to work."

"Matches what Ronnie said."

"I'm guessing she never pressed charges?" Eddison says.

"Gee, it's almost like you've seen this before." Mignone straightens his tie, an incongruously cheerful thing with giant sunflowers all over it. "In the morning, we'll get on the horn with CPS, get copies of their files. I'll make sure one gets to you. Ronnie's got a couple inches, at least."

"Police file, hospital records, Child Protective Services file . . . that's a lot of eyes and hands on this kind of information," I say. "That's not even counting family members, neighbors, friends, teachers, church members, or any other groups they might be part of. If the murders are connected to the abuse, that is way too many people to sift through."

The second assistant clears his throat, blushing as we all turn to look at him. "Sorry, this is only my second, ah . . . murder? But am I allowed to ask a question?"

The ME rolls her eyes but looks provisionally impressed rather than irritated. "It is how we learn. Try to make it a good one."

"If this is about the abuse, Mrs. Wilkins was probably abused too: Why would the killer attack her as well?"

"Remind me when we get to the van. That earns you a lollipop."

Morbid humor: not just an agent thing.

"*If* this is about the abuse," Eddison answers, "and we are still spit-balling that, but if it is, then killers of this kind generally consider the mother complicit, even if she is herself a victim. She didn't protect her child. She had to have known about it but didn't stop it, either because she didn't think she could, or because she chose not to in order to relieve some of the burden on herself."

"When I go to my parents' on Sundays, my mom asks me if I've learned anything new over the week," the assistant says. "I need to start lying."

"Fact of the day calendar," Eddison tells him. "Seriously."

"Saw some of the neighbors outside," I note. "Any of them mention hearing gunshots?"

The detective shakes his head. "We'll know better once the bullets are out, but there seems to have been some kind of silencer. A potato, probably, from debris in the wound tracks. Neighbors mentioned screams, but that's pretty commonplace for this house."

"A child's screams?"

Eddison gives me a slightly jaundiced look. "You think Ronnie stood and watched his parents get murdered and *didn't* scream?"

"He didn't move off my porch. After the killer left him there, he could have gone to any other house and asked for help, but he stayed exactly where he was put. And look at the carpet: Is there any sign of a struggle around where he must have stood?"

"If he'd ever admitted to Social Services what was happening to him, he likely wouldn't have been returned to the home." Eddison rubs at his jaw. "So he's probably pretty conditioned to protect his father by keeping silent. Anyone suitably authoritative is someone he'd probably obey, so long as it didn't mean talking about the abuse."

"Poor kid's got years of therapy ahead of him," the ME observes.

"Does the scene remind you of any of your cases? Or things that have come across your desk that didn't become your cases?" asks Mignone.

"Not a one," Eddison says. "We'll go back through, just in case, and let you know if we find anything."

"Does it echo any of yours?" I ask, and get looks from both Eddison and Mignone. "Ignoring the blood, this is a clean scene. Simple, efficient entry and exit, with the child. Clear planning, awareness of the character of the neighborhood. This doesn't feel like a first time, and if it is, what the hell comes next?"

Mignone blinks at me, his moustache twitching. "Thanks, this night wasn't nightmare enough already."

"The mothers taught me how to share."

True to Eddison's prediction, it's almost four in the morning before we walk out of the house, our booties placed in evidence bags with one of the officers just in case and our time of departure marked on the scene log. The neighborhood is still quiet, the areas beyond the house dimly lit by isolated porch lights and a couple of streetlights. A thick cluster of trees runs behind the houses on the other side of the street, and I'm tired enough that my skin crawls at the sight of them.

There are reasons my street has big lawns and no woods.

Eddison nudges my shoulder with his. "Come on. Marlene will be up in half an hour; we can keep her company."

"We're going to invade Vic's kitchen—"

"Vic's house, Marlene's kitchen."

"—and keep his mother company before he wakes up?"

"That is exactly my plan. What do you think she's making?"

Doesn't matter what it is, it'll be amazing, and dinner was a very long time ago. I lean against the top of the car, looking out at the dark fringe of woods. I can't hear anything from them, and it seems strange, to finally find trees that are silent. Strange and frightening. "You know, Siobhan got me craving those cream-cheese-and-berry puff pastry pinwheels."

He smirks at me over the roof and unlocks the doors with a beep and the soft clunk of the latches releasing. "Come on, *hermana*. We'll go drink all the coffee before Vic wakes up."

"That seems an excellent way to end up dead."

Unwillingly, we both glance back at the illuminated house, the Wilkins adults still inside, their son at the hospital, terrified and traumatized and in the company of strangers.

"We'll leave one cup. Three-quarters of a cup."

"Deal." I slide into the car, buckle in, and close my eyes until we turn back onto the main road, where the trees don't crowd so close.

Once upon a time, there was a little girl who was scared of the night.

It wasn't the same as the dark. A dark closet, a dark room, a dark tool-shed, those were things that would change in an instant. You could make it not-dark, or at least try.

Night, though. Night you just had to grit your teeth and wait out, no matter what was happening.

Her daddy started coming to her in the night, and it was different. He didn't hit, not unless she struggled or told him no. He'd kiss the bruises he left on her during the day, call her his good girl, his beautiful girl. He'd ask if she wanted to make him happy, make Daddy proud.

She could hear her mama crying down the hall. In that house, everyone could hear everything, no matter where they were.

So she thought her mama must have been able to hear, when her daddy groaned and shouted and talked and talked like he couldn't keep the words in.

Her mama must have been able to hear.

But she never saw her mama at night.

She only saw Daddy.

4

"Well, you're all here disgustingly early."

I flap a hand toward Sterling's voice, too tired to lift my head up from the conference table and look at her. After a moment, hands curl my fingers around a sturdy paper cup with heat bleeding through.

Okay, that might be worth lifting my head for.

And it's good coffee, too, with vanilla creamer, not the utter crap made in the kitchenette of the break room or the cafeteria. This is not Bureau-funded coffee. I let the smell and taste pull me upright and see Eddison gulping his own cup of jet fuel. Sterling watches, a wry smile tugging her lips, and then hands him another one. Vic gets one that smells of the hazelnut creamer he loves but won't use at work because real agents drink coffee black, or some such nonsense.

Sterling's been with us for eight months, a transplant from the Denver field office, but somehow we're still caught in that weird transition where we simultaneously can't imagine the team without her and are still figuring out how the team works with her in it. She absolutely belongs here, both in skill set and in temperament, but it's . . . well. Strange.

Vic sits back in his chair with a sigh, absently moving through a series of stretches with his left arm to help keep some flexibility around the giant fucking scar in his chest, also known as the reason Sterling joined our team. It's been a year since he got shot defending a child murderer we'd just arrested. Vic got shot, my hands were covered in blood trying to keep pressure on the wound until the ambulance got there, and Eddison had to arrest a grieving father for shooting a federal agent.

It was a very bad day.

Things for Vic were touch and go for longer than any of us like to recall, and the brass used the long recovery to finally force him to accept the promotion to unit chief. It was either that or retire, and whatever his wife's secret hopes, Vic isn't ready for that yet. Fortunately for everyone's sanity, he used that extra authority to get Eddison and me out of the seminar this morning so we could research the Wilkins family.

Pulling up another chair, Sterling settles in with her giant cup of tea. "So what happened and how can I help?"

For the next couple of hours, the only sounds in the conference room are the click of laptop keys, the squeak of chairs, and the slurp of disappearing coffee. Sterling eventually stands, stretches, and heads back into the bullpen. When she comes back, walking in her strangely silent way, she holds the Keurig from Vic's office, the box of K-Cups dangling precariously from one crooked finger. Padding up behind Eddison, she waits until he turns the page he's on.

"Give me a hand?" she asks suddenly.

Eddison yelps and jerks forward, midsection slamming into the edge of the table.

Vic rolls his eyes and shakes his head.

"Bells," mutters Eddison. "I'm putting goddamn bells on you."

She grins and drops the box of K-Cups in front of him. "You're a peach," she says cheerfully, and comes back around the table to set the machine on the counter. She plugs it in and sets it to work.

As far as we can tell, the FBI has never had a reason to register the Wilkinses' existence. There are no outstanding warrants, no nefarious backgrounds, nothing that would bring them to the attention of a federal entity. Their extensive law enforcement history seems to be on a purely local level. So why was Ronnie brought to my home?

As my stomach starts complaining that I've had too much caffeine in the hours since breakfast, I send Siobhan a text to check in with her, see how she's doing now that some of the shock might have worn off. Inviting her out to lunch at least makes it look less like I'm hovering, and more like apologizing.

She texts back the location of my car and that my keys are with the front desk.

"Lunch with Siobhan?" asks Sterling.

"Not unless I want it frozen."

She winces in sympathy. "Delivery it is, then."

A quick rock-paper-scissors tournament twenty-five minutes later leaves Eddison with the job of going down to meet the delivery guy, but he's no more than stood up when one of the trainee agents on front-desk duty hip checks her way into the conference room overburdened with bags and a large cardboard file box. Eddison helps her get the bags of food safely onto the table before everything topples over.

"Thanks," she says, blushing a little.

Sterling and I look at each other, and she rolls her eyes heavenward. Vic just looks resigned. There is something about Eddison that is catnip to the female baby agents. He's prickly and damaged and fiercely protective and respectful of the women in his life, and that combination seems to be a siren call. As far as I can tell, it's not even anything he says or does; simply by existing in the same room, he can make them blush and stammer. The best part is, he genuinely doesn't notice. He has no clue.

Vic won't let us tell him.

With a polite thank-you for bringing us the files, Vic gets up and firmly shoos the young woman from the room, physically inserting himself between her and Eddison in order to get her moving out the door.

A snicker escapes from Sterling.

Eddison glances up from untying the knots on the plastic bags. "What?"

Sterling loses it, which sets me off, and even Vic is chuckling and shaking his head as he closes the door.

"What's so funny?"

"Can you please pass the chopsticks?" Sterling asks sweetly. When he does so, she flutters her eyelashes. "Thanks," she says, exaggerating the baby agent's starstruck tone.

Vic chokes a little but doesn't comment, just hands me my food and a fork, because I'm too damn hungry for chopsticks.

That's the thing about Sterling, really. She's twenty-seven but looks maybe seventeen, all big blue eyes and blonde prettiness. Despite the badge and the gun and the severe black-and-white work attire, never any color to soften or flatter, she routinely gets asked if she's here to visit her father. She's never going to pull off more than sweet and innocent, so she doesn't try, just perfects that harmless appearance so everyone underestimates her.

It's beautiful.

She also came to us immune to the Eddison catnip. Her very first day in Quantico, she silently walked up behind us and scared the hell out of him by saying hello, and while he was trying to unclench his fingers from the edge of his desk, she met my eyes and winked.

It made me feel so much better about having someone new on a team that hadn't changed for almost ten years.

We eat quickly and clean up so we don't get food on the files. I open the box sent over by Mignone and cringe. *"Mierda,"* I sigh. "This is a lot of paper for a ten-year-old."

From her seat, Sterling sits up very, very straight and cranes her neck to see. "That whole thing?"

"No. It's also got the police reports from the domestic disturbances and the mom's hospital records. Still." I haul out the two folders marked with Ronnie's name, both so large they have to be clipped shut with the most massive binder clips I have ever seen, and drop them on the table. They land with a significant whump. "That's Ronnie."

She leans closer, reading the top of one of the folders. "They named him Ronnie."

"Well, yeah, that's why—"

"No, I mean, they *named* him Ronnie. Not Ron or Ronald and call him Ronnie. They named him Ronnie."

"That's an unfortunate thing to do to a child," mutters Eddison.

I look up at him, lift the stack a couple of inches, and let it drop again.

"Fair point."

Sterling takes the folders with Sandra Wilkins's hospital records, and Vic and Eddison split the substantial pile of police reports between them, leaving me with the Social Services file.

There's a point in this job when you expect things to become less heartbreaking. You struggle through your first cases, expecting that at some point in the misty future, you'll become inured to it all the way your partners are, that what you see and read will affect you less. One day, you'll see a child who's suffered abuse they can't even name, and it won't shatter part of you.

It never happens.

You learn how to work through it, how to hide it, how to make it useful. You learn that your partners aren't inured to it; they just conceal it better than you do. You learn to let it motivate you, but it never stops wounding. And the thing is, you know better than almost anyone else, *because* it's your job, that the system isn't perfect, but it tries its best.

Dios mío, it tries its best.

And then there are times, like now, when you realize its best is nowhere near good enough.

Four times. Four times Ronnie Wilkins was removed from his home by Social Services because of physical abuse, and *every time* he was returned. The first time he was given back because his mother left his father, and Ronnie was taken to her at her mother's. Except two months later, she went back to her husband and brought Ronnie with her. The second time was because his parents submitted paperwork showing that his father was undergoing counseling and anger management, sessions that stopped as soon as they had Ronnie back. The third time, his grandmother had to drop the custody suit because Daniel Wilkins came over with a baseball bat, beat the hell out of her car, and once again, just a few weeks ago, because Ronnie simply couldn't admit to the abuse, wouldn't tell the social worker how he got so badly hurt he had to be hospitalized.

This poor child kept getting delivered straight back to hell.

We chase Vic out of the office at six, but the rest of us stay until nine-thirty to finish scanning the last of the Wilkinses' records, by which point I'm seriously contemplating opening a K-Cup and drinking the sludge for pure caffeine, and I stay slumped and half-dozing in my chair as Sterling and Eddison clean up around me. It's not remotely fair of me; Eddison has been awake as long as I have. When I try to help, though, he snaps my hand with a rubber band.

Eddison drives me to his place, and we bicker the entire time in order to keep me awake. We're frequently short on sleep, especially during a case, and we've learned tricks to keep ourselves going. Still, it's a relief to pull up to his building.

Eddison's apartment is mostly bland, even a little sterile. You have to hunt for the things that make it look lived-in: the worn patches on the black leather couch, the small divot in the coffee table where he kicked too hard while watching a baseball game. Honestly, the things that make it look almost like a home are all gifts. Priya gave him the dining room table, after she made him help her rescue it from a closing Mexican restaurant. The brightly, chaotically painted tiles on top give the space its only burst of color. She also took the pictures that surround the large television, portraits of Special Agent Ken in his travels.

And by Special Agent Ken, I mean a Ken doll in a tiny FBI windbreaker. The photos are excellent in and of themselves, black-and-white compositions with beautiful attention to detail and light, but it's definitely a Ken doll, and I love it.

We met Priya Sravasti eight years ago, when her older sister was murdered by a serial killer whose victim count ultimately hit sixteen girls. Three years ago, Priya was nearly the seventeenth. She lives in Paris now, attending university, but somewhere over the years our team simply adopted her, and she became family. She also became Eddison's best friend; despite their age difference, they bonded over being prickly and angry and missing their sisters.

No matter how long it's been since Faith got kidnapped, Eddison will never stop missing his little sister. There are no photos of her displayed, but there aren't photos of anyone except Special Agent Ken out where people can see them. Eddison protects the people he loves by hiding their pictures away, where he can look at them when he wants but no one else is likely to find them. Only at work does he keep a picture of Faith, right next to a picture of Priya, and they're his reminder of why he does this job, why it means so much to him.

Vic has his daughters; Eddison has his sisters, even if he still struggles with naming Priya that way.

I change for sleep, boxers and a T-shirt I accidentally stole from Eddison during a case and declined to return, while he digs through his linen closet. Together, we put sheets and a blanket on the couch. He waves a yawning goodbye and disappears into his room, where I can hear him moving about for a few more minutes as I brush my teeth and scrub off two days of makeup at the kitchen sink.

I'm bone-deep tired, the kind of exhaustion where my eyes hurt even when they're closed, but despite the comfort of the couch I've slept on countless times, I can't seem to fall asleep. I keep seeing Ronnie, his eyes so shattered and wounded within a mask of blood. I shift positions, hugging one of the pillows to my chest, and try to settle.

Eddison's snores rumble through the silence, courtesy of a long-ago broken nose that he couldn't be bothered to get set properly. They're not loud, his snores, it's never been a problem to share a hotel room with him, but they're reassuringly familiar. I can feel my bones getting heavier, the stress gathering and slipping away in rhythm with the soft sounds.

Then one of my phones rings.

Groaning and cursing, I roll over and grab it, squinting at the overly bright display. Oh *mierda*, it's my *tía*. I know exactly why she's calling. Fuck. I don't want to talk to her right now.

Ever, really, but especially not now.

But if I don't, she'll keep calling, and the voice mails will get increasingly shrill. Snarling a little, I accept the call. "You already knew I wasn't going to call," I say instead of hello, keeping my voice down so I don't bother my partner.

"Mercedes, *niña*—"

"You already knew I wasn't going to call. If you pass over the phone or put it on speaker, I'm going to hang up, and if you keep calling after what has really been a hell of a day, I'm going to change my number. Again."

"But it's her birthday."

"*Sí*, I know." I close my eyes and burrow back into the pillows, wishing the conversation was just a part of a nightmare. "It changes nothing. I don't want to talk to her. I don't want to talk to you either, *Tía*. You're just more aggressively stubborn than she is."

"Someone has to be stubborn as you," she retorts. Her voice is surrounded by chaos, the kind of noise you can only get at a birthday party where "immediate family" still means some hundred or so people. The bits of speech I can make out are mostly in Spanish, because the *madres* and *tías* and *abuelas* have rules about using English at home if it's not for schoolwork. "We never hear from you!"

"Well, it's hard to be estranged from people if you give them regular updates."

"*Tu pobre mamá—*"

"*Mi pobre mamá* should know better, and so should you."

"Your nieces and nephews want to know you."

"My nieces and nephews should be grateful their *abuelo* is still in prison, and if they're very lucky, none of the other men will take after him. Stop stealing my contact info from Esperanza, and stop calling. I am not interested in forgiving the family, and I am sure as fuck not interested in the family forgiving me. Just. Stop."

I hang up, and spend the next several minutes declining her repeated calls.

"You know," rumbles a sleepy voice from the bedroom doorway. I look up to see Eddison leaning against the frame, his boxers and hair both sleep rumpled. "That's your personal phone. You can shut that off as long as you keep your work one on. She, uh . . . she doesn't have your work number, does she?"

"No." And if I weren't so fucking tired, I'd have thought of that myself. I always remember that there's a difference between my two phones; I just tend to forget why that difference is important. After double-checking that it's my personal phone—identical to my work phone, except for the Hufflepuff case—I turn it off and feel a palpable sense of relief. "Sorry for waking you."

"Was it anything specific?"

"It's my mother's birthday."

He winces. "How did she even get your number? You just changed it a year ago."

"Esperanza. She keeps my number under a different name, but I'm the only person she knows with an East Coast area code, so her mother always snoops and finds it. She just can't make up her mind whether she should be haranguing me to come back to the family, or haranguing me for leaving it in the first place."

"Your dad's still locked up, right?"

"Yes, my great sin as a daughter." I shake my head, hair falling in my face. "Sorry."

"I forgive you," he says sententiously.

I throw a pillow at him, and immediately regret it despite his goofy, confused blinking. Now I have to get up and retrieve it unless I want it thwacked back in my face.

Instead, he picks it up and offers his free hand. "Come on."

"*¿Qué?*"

"You're never going to get any sleep now. You're just going to lie there and brood."

"*You're* going to accuse *me* of brooding?"

"Yes. Come on."

I take his hand and let him pull me up, and he uses it to tow me into the bedroom. He steers me to the left side of the bed, because he doesn't really care which side he's on as long as it's the one farther from the door. A minute later, he returns with my gun, which I'd put under the couch where I could easily reach it, and puts it into the holster nailed to the side of the left nightstand. He gets under the covers first, sliding over rather than walking because he's tired and lazy and I really can't blame him, and for a moment it's all shuffling linens as we settle in comfortably.

"You don't have to feel guilty for it," he says suddenly.

"For what, Ronnie showing up?"

"For not forgiving them." He reaches out in the darkness, finds a handful of my hair, and uses it to find my face so he can tap the parallel scars that run down my left cheek from just below my eye. "You don't owe them that."

"Okay."

"It's not right for them to ask it of you."

"I know."

"Okay."

A few minutes later, he's fast asleep and snoring again, his hand still splayed across my face.

I honestly can't imagine how half the Bureau thinks Eddison and I are hot for each other.

5

Saturday is spent back at the office, catching up on what was supposed to be yesterday's work. After several months of so many back-to-back cases that we were barely home long enough to change go bags before being sent out again, Vic put us on desk rotation for a few weeks so we could catch our breath. Basically that means paperwork, and a lot of it.

I spend Sunday on Eddison's couch with a stack of logic puzzles to get my brain off worrying about Ronnie, while Eddison has the Nationals game up on his insanely large television. His laptop is open on the coffee table, Skype running to show Priya stretched out on the bed at Inara and Victoria-Bliss's New York apartment. She's got the game streaming on another computer at her side, so they can watch the game together across two hundred fifty or so miles. She set up in the bedroom so as not to disturb her summer hosts, neither of whom give two shits about baseball, but they both drifted in anyway, sprawling over her, each other, and the bed in equal measure with their own projects.

Inara and Victoria-Bliss we met during what may be our most infamous case. Certainly it was one of the most bizarre. They were among the many girls kidnapped by a man over three decades and kept in the Garden, a massive greenhouse on his private land, some of whom he killed to preserve their beauty. Tattooed with intricate butterfly wings, the Butterflies were his prized collection, in both life and death. After the Garden, with the wounds still fresh and the trials looming, Vic connected them to Priya. The three became fast friends, and whenever Priya was back in the States, she managed to spend at least a few days in New York in the warehouse apartment they had shared with half a dozen other girls.

They have their own place now, the massive bed covered in a quilt made of Shakespeare lithographs. Neither of them are in black, the color the Gardener gave them, neither of them have their backs bared the way he insisted was necessary. Victoria-Bliss is, in fact, in an eye-smarting shade of orange even brighter than a traffic cone, both front and back emblazoned with the name of the animal shelter she volunteers at. It's healthy, and it's good, and it's wonderful to see the three of them so close. And possibly a little terrifying; they're indomitable young women, and could probably take over the world if they were so inclined.

"How are the pictures going?" Eddison asks during a commercial break.

"Going well," Priya answers. "Next week or two, I'll head down to Baltimore to talk to Keely's parents. They want to see some of the finished photos before they and Keely decide whether or not to participate in the project."

"Think they will?"

Priya's knee gently nudges Inara's hip, and the other girl looks up from her tablet, pen bouncing against the pad beside it. Inara shrugs at the webcam. "I think they will," she says. Keely is the youngest of the Garden survivors, brought in only in the Garden's last days, and Inara has always watched out for her very closely. "We've talked to them about it several times since Priya and I came up with it, making sure they know it's not prurient or sensational, that it really is about healing. I don't blame them for wanting reassurance."

"Speaking of others." Victoria-Bliss frowns down at her fingers, streaked with cranberry-colored castoff from her clay. "It's been a few weeks since any of us have heard from Ravenna. Pretty much since we did the photo session with her. She and her mother got in a huge fight about it and now no one knows where she is."

Her mother, Senator Kingsley, can't understand why her daughter still struggles to separate Ravenna, the Butterfly in the Garden, from Patrice, the politician's perfect daughter. It's precisely because of the senator that the young woman is having such difficulty. As public and newsworthy as the discovery of the Garden and the subsequent trials were, the senator's position means her daughter's attempts at recovery have been scrutinized. How is anyone supposed to heal like that?

"She came to see me," I tell them, and Victoria-Bliss's frown clears. Except for Inara and Victoria-Bliss, who got adopted by the team in general, I'm the one still in touch with most of the Butterflies. I was the one in the hospital with them, the one who initiated most of the contact for interviews. "She stayed with me a couple nights and then continued on to a family friend while she gets her head on straight from the fight with her mother. I don't have a name or location, but if you send an email and tell her you're concerned, I'm sure she'll respond eventually."

Inara nods absently, probably already composing the message in her head.

"She said it helped," I add. "Whatever you guys are doing, she said it really helped."

All three girls smile.

"So when do we get to see the photos?" asks Eddison.

"When I decide to let you," Priya tells him dryly. Behind her, Victoria-Bliss snickers into a handful of polymer clay she's softening. Priya scowls suddenly, brows crinkling in toward the blue crystal and silver bindi. "The fuck was that, Fouquette? The ball decides to float majestically into your glove and you drop it?"

"He needs to be traded to an American League team," Eddison says. "Let him be a designated hitter for some idiot pitcher, and get him the hell out of the outfield."

"Or send him back to the minors to get some basic skills."

"I don't know," Victoria-Bliss drawls, and Eddison braces himself. "I kind of like the chants of 'fuck-it, fuck-it' because of all the dumb asses who can't manage his name. I mean, the networks have to blur the sound of the crowd, that's kind of amazing."

Eddison grimaces, but doesn't argue.

I'm not sure what it says about us that this is our normal.

On Monday, I text Siobhan an invite for coffee before work—even if that means dragging my sorry ass to Quantico much earlier than usual—and get back a frankly snippy instruction to let her decide when she's ready to talk to me again. When the mothers said relationships take effort, I don't think they intended me to run straight at brick walls.

Tuesday afternoon I leave work early, driving my car for the first time in nearly a week, to meet Detective Holmes at my house. She's sitting on the front step waiting for me when I get there. All the crime scene tape is gone, and someone even went to the trouble to clean the blood off the porch swing.

"We're nowhere," she greets me grumpily. I drop my messenger bag and the go bag desperately in need of replenishment on the swing and sit next to her. "We have nothing to go on."

"How is Ronnie doing?"

"The doctors didn't find any signs of sexual abuse. Physically, he'll heal pretty quickly. God bless his grandmother, she's already got him connected with a therapist. Without going into details, obviously, the therapist says Ronnie doesn't seem ready to talk yet, but he's apparently willing to listen. Long road ahead of him."

"So he hasn't said anything about the angel?"

"Female, taller than him but not as tall as his dad. Dressed all in white. Couldn't really tell us anything about her voice. He said her hair was blonde and in a long braid. He said he held on to it while she was carrying him."

"Police sketch?"

"A white mask. He couldn't give particulars." She sighs and leans against the post that ends the railing. The circles under her eyes are deeper than they were on Thursday. "Have you ever given any thought to putting up cameras?"

"Sterling's going to help," I answer. "One aimed on the porch steps and swing, and one on the mailbox to see the car. Hopefully."

"Good." She hands me the ring of keys I gave the uniformed officer. "There's been no sign of anyone coming back. Your immediate neighbor was a bit disgruntled he wasn't allowed to work on the lawn."

"Jason likes green things. I'll talk to him."

"The case we worked two years ago, you gave teddy bears to every kid we talked to. Is that SOP for your team?"

Nodding, I lean forward to brace my elbows against my knees. "Vic and his first partner Finney started it. I took it over after I joined the team. The bears are pretty cheap, plain, come in huge boxes with an assortment of colors. We give them to victims and young siblings, friends, if we talk to other kids. It's comforting, calming, helps them settle into an interview."

"And your collection?"

"Started when I was ten. I'd do odd jobs to earn money for them, and as long as they could all fit in a bag with my clothes, I could keep them with me when I was moved to a new foster home."

She gives me a sidelong look. "Were you ever adopted?"

"No. I was in the last home for a little over four years, and I'm still in touch with the mothers. They offered, but . . ." I shake my head. "I wasn't ready to have family again."

"Well, there's no reason not to let you come home. We've got a patrol coming through a couple times a night. If you get a case out of town, will you let me know?"

"Absolutely. For right now, we've got a conference out in California that we're leaving for Thursday morning. We'll be back sometime on Sunday." Crap. Sunday. It was supposed to be a very big day for Sterling, but will likely be a painful one instead. Eddison and I need to think of something good to do for her. "It'll be next week before we get the cameras up."

"All right." Putting a hand on my shoulder, Holmes levers herself to standing. "I'll let you know if we learn anything."

My cozy little home looks the same, which feels odd. It should feel different, shouldn't it, knowing what happened the other night? Everything is just slightly out of place, moved and moved back by officers looking to see if the killer entered and left something behind, but it doesn't really account for the sense of change that isn't. There's probably a word for that, German or Portuguese or Japanese or something. Not English or Spanish, anyway, or what little is left from my high school Italian. How can you be homesick when you're home?

But that's what it feels like, a longing for the moment just before, when this was still my sanctuary, the place that was mine and mine alone unless I specifically invited someone over. The place I could lock out the rest of the world for a few hours, my little paradise with its green open spaces and no woods till several streets over.

By the time I've marched myself through a succession of chores and repacked my bags, I am beyond ready to leave again. I've sometimes run to work, or to Siobhan's or Vic's or a date, but it's always been running to, not running from. I can't stand feeling like I need to run away from my home.

Picking up the bear on the nightstand, I run my thumbs over his worn, fading velvet nap, the nubby bow tie, the plastic eyes that have been sewn back on many times. I remember when he was given to me, and by whom, and all the comfort I've gained from him over the years. What kind of comfort is Ronnie going to get from the bear the killing angel brought him? After a minute, I put him back down and walk away, locking the handful of locks behind me.

Once upon a time, there was a little girl who was scared of doctors.

It wasn't the shots that worried her, unlike most of the kids in the waiting room. She was in so much pain every day she barely noticed the pinprick of the clean slide of the needle into her arm.

No, she was scared of doctors because they lied.

They told her she was perfectly healthy, that everything was wonderful. Daddy was more careful about leaving marks if she had an appointment coming up, but she wasn't sure it mattered. Even when there were bruises, the doctors would just cluck and tell her to be more careful when she was playing. They asked how she felt but didn't listen when she told them everything hurt.

Her left arm, all the way up near the shoulder, had a bruise that refused to heal, because her daddy grabbed her there and squeezed, over and over and over. They told her mama to be careful of shirts with elastic bands in the sleeves while she was growing, that they could cut off circulation and leave lasting bruises.

Once, and only once, she decided to be brave and tell the whole truth. The doctor was young and pretty, and had the kindest eyes. She wanted to trust eyes that kind. So she told the doctor everything, or tried to—until her mama cut her off and scolded her for watching the wrong kinds of TV and getting confused. The doctor nodded along and laughed about fertile imaginations.

Mama told Daddy as soon as he got home.

For two weeks, his temper prowled like a tiger through the house, but he didn't touch either of them, just in case someone was coming. The little girl was scared out of her mind, but they were the best two weeks. Even her arm started to heal.

But no one came. No one was coming.

6

I stay at Eddison's on Tuesday because my house still feels unsettling, and Siobhan still isn't talking to me. For all our fights over the past three years, and there have been many, we've never had this cold silence.

I stay at Eddison's again on Wednesday because we have to be on our way to the airport at half past fuck it's morning. Sterling joins us for the second sleepover, stretching out on the couch in leggings and a giant navy blue T-shirt that says "Female Body Inspector" in tall yellow blocks. Eddison stares at the lettering, blinks, opens his mouth . . . and then buries his face in his hands with a pained groan before disappearing back into his bedroom.

Sterling and I look at each other, and she shrugs before digging out five dollars from her purse. "You win. I thought for sure he'd say you should be wearing it," she admits, handing me the bill.

"Until he accidentally tells you to calm your tits, he isn't going to make any other sex-adjacent commentaries," I tell her, tucking the money behind my credentials and dropping the case back on top of my bag. "He's still feeling out boundaries, so to speak, and he's under pretty strict orders not to break you."

"Vic?"

"Priya."

She grins and shakes the ponytail kink from her hair. "She's a good kid."

"Need anything?"

"Nah, should be good."

I've already brushed my teeth and scrubbed off my makeup, so I crawl in next to Eddison, flick out the lights, and shift until I've found a comfortable position. Several minutes later, he turns onto his side. "We should both get that shirt," he says.

"I have that shirt."

"Really?"

"The mothers gave it to me for my birthday a few years back. I wear it running."

"I need that shirt."

"You don't need that shirt."

"But—"

"You have never seen you in a bar. You don't need that shirt."

The sound of giggling seeps through the closed door, followed by a thump and more giggling, which I'm pretty sure was Sterling laughing herself off the couch.

"I always forget the door is that thin," Eddison sighs.

"I don't."

The sheets rustle as he brings up one leg, plants his foot firmly against my ass, and shoves me off the bed.

Sterling's giggling gains some hiccups.

The flights out to California pass mostly in a stupor of sleepiness and paperwork, as much as we can manage on our tiny trays, at any rate. The three-day conference is focused on making sure local police departments know when and how they can avail themselves of federal resources, and which agency they should call for which kinds of problems. In between presentations, there's a lot of reassuring worried or belligerent local cops from across the country and shit-talking with reps from other agencies. It's the closest thing to a working vacation we'll ever have.

We get back to Eddison's apartment a little past three on Sunday morning, because God knows the Bureau isn't going to pay for hotel rooms one more night than absolutely necessary, and Eddison ends up on the couch this time. There may have been some collapsing involved, the inevitable crash that comes of cramming him full of sugar on the second half of the second flight to make sure he was hyper enough to drive us safely back from the airport. Between the two of us, Sterling and I manage to strip him down to boxers and undershirt and get him tucked into the couch in a way that should keep him from falling off but will probably confuse him in the morning.

"Go on in," I tell Sterling, hip checking her toward the bedroom. "I just have to dig clothes out."

After she closes the door to change, Eddison makes a remarkable recovery and looks up at me. "You've got her?"

"I've got her."

Because today was supposed to be Eliza Sterling's wedding day, and being a team—being family—means she'll be lucky to piss in peace because we're not leaving her alone. I turn off her personal cell and switch her work cell to silent, leaving both with Eddison. Having a grumpy bastard screen calls is remarkably effective, really. After changing into pajamas, I brush my teeth and scrub off my makeup at the kitchen sink, then check the locks and turn off all the lights on my way into the bedroom.

Sterling sits on the bed, back in her shirt and leggings with her hair fluffed all around her, holding Eddison's alarm clock in her lap, with a stricken expression on her face. The soft click of the door closing behind me makes her look up, and her eyes are glassy with tears. "I thought today was still yesterday," she whispers.

Working in the Bureau—or any law enforcement, really—has a cost. For Sterling, the chance to advance and join a prestigious team came at the cost of her engagement. From what little she's said about it, there wasn't a chance in hell of him following her to Virginia. When she came home bubbling over with news of a promotion, he didn't understand why she thought she'd be working after they got married.

Even when something's wrong, the ending of the thing hurts.

Gently prying the clock from her hands, I put it back on the nightstand, flick off the lights, and nudge her under the covers. She doesn't make any objection when I press up beside her, and while I have the uncomfortable feeling our hair will get knotted together at some point in the night (it's happened before), I'm not about to move away. Her mother exploded when the engagement was broken, so she can't go home to Denver for hugs, and while both Jenny and Marlene Hanoverian would be only too happy to mother her as much as she'll let them, we're not going to wake them up at three-thirty on a Sunday morning.

So I'm here to give her as many hugs as she needs, and unlike Eddison, I won't feel a whit self-conscious. And if she happens to cry a couple of times during what's left of the night . . . well. She's in pain, and I sure as hell won't judge her for it.

Late in the morning, we're both woken up by the smell of bacon frying, and it only takes a few minutes to untangle our hair enough to get out of bed and shuffle out to investigate. Eddison does not cook. Eddison gets bored of anything that takes more attention than toast. But it's Vic who stands at the stove, giving us a salute with the greasy tongs, while Eddison scowls down at the pile of potatoes and the large grater Vic must have brought with him, because it's certainly nothing Eddison's going to bother keeping in his own kitchen.

Sterling gives the guys a sleepy smile, though she's pale and her eyes are still pink and puffy. "Thanks," she says softly.

"I didn't get a single call from another agency about you three starting a blood feud with other teams," he replies, and it's sort of an acknowledgment. As much as he's going to give, anyway, when the conversation pains her so.

"You don't say?" She drifts over to the table and sits on top of it, where she can see over the counter into the kitchen. "Nice to know they didn't snitch."

"Don't scare them at all, or scare them so much they're afraid to talk." He flips the bacon, reaching for a turkey baster to siphon off some of the extra grease. "Anything in the middle is asking for trouble."

Sterling may or may not realize that he's purposefully distracting her, giving her something to say without making it have weight. Ordinarily she would, but Vic does this for all of us when we're hurting. It's one of his gifts: let me distract you, let me fill the silence for you, until you decide there's something you need to say.

We eat brunch, and when Vic heads back home to work on some chores around the house, the three of us go for a run and then take turns in the shower, using up all the hot water. We kidnapped Sterling straight from work on Wednesday, so she's not surprised when we grab our bags and chivvy her out to Eddison's car.

During the drive, my phone buzzes with a text, and I flinch. Fortunately, the message is from Priya, not Holmes. *You've got Eliza?*

Yeah, we've got her.

Thank you.

Three years ago, when Priya was being stalked by the bastard who murdered her sister, Sterling was on the team from the Denver field office—along with Vic's old partner, Finney, and the third member of their team, Agent Archer—that checked in on Priya and pursued the stalker. Partly because of choices made during that sequence of events, mostly because of repeating those mistakes in another case, Archer is no longer an agent with the FBI. In spite of Archer, maybe even because of him, Priya and Sterling bonded and kept in touch after the case was resolved.

Priya was delighted when Vic and Finney conspired to steal Sterling for our team. It doesn't shock me that she knows what it cost, or that she's worried today. As Sterling said, Priya's a good kid.

Sterling gives us a lopsided smile when the car pulls up in front of a bar a few minutes after it opens for the day. It's one of the quieter bars in town, the kind where groups of friends gather to nurse a drink or two over hours of laughter and conversation, rather than have to shout over pulsing music or the din of crowds of other people. I steer Sterling to a semi-private booth in a corner while Eddison goes up to order the first round and let the bartenders know that we'll be driving her home.

"I don't even know why I'm sad," she says suddenly, somewhere into hour three. "I wasn't even happy with him."

"Then why were you going to marry him?" Eddison asks, picking at the damp, peeling label of his beer.

"My mom was over the moon when he asked. He did it in front of both sets of parents, the whole restaurant looking on because it was this giant spectacle . . ." She scowls at the bright blue shot in her hand, and knocks it back without a wince. "I didn't feel like I could say no that publicly, you know? And then our mothers were so happy, and so full of plans, and every time I tried to talk about it, they said it was just nerves, that it was natural for a bride to be anxious, and I just . . . Everyone else seemed so happy, and I thought maybe I was just wrong."

The next round of shots and beers comes with three glasses of water, too, because we're trying to get her drunk, not dead.

"He said if I came to Virginia, I was coming alone, and I was so *relieved*," she continues a little while later, like twenty or so minutes of companionable silence didn't happen. "Like there was finally this tangible thing that I could point to and say *this, this* is why, and no one could tell me it was in my head."

"But then they thought you should stay and make it work?" I surmise, and she nods miserably.

"But why am I sad?"

Because the first time the price is high—the first time this job asks for too large a piece of ourselves and we feel the bleed for weeks and months—is always sad. "Because doors close," I say instead, "and we can still miss what was on the other side even if we choose to walk away."

"I still have the dress. He insisted I had to get it right away."

"If you've already spent thousands of dollars on a dress, you're less likely to call it off," Eddison offers quietly. "He knew you weren't happy."

"Do I burn it?"

Eddison scratches at his scalp, the curls in his dark hair more obvious than usual. He really needs to get them trimmed. "I think you do whatever you want with it. Burn it, throw it away, keep it for the real deal."

Sterling gapes at him, looking properly scandalized for the first time since I've known her. "You don't keep a dress for another wedding!" she tries to whisper. The bartender looks over at us with raised eyebrows, so clearly that attempt didn't work.

"But isn't that one of the things you're supposed to look for? Making sure everyone can wear it again?"

"That's for bridesmaids' dresses!"

He lifts his fresh beer, the foam licking at his upper lip, and winks at me. That clever bastard. "Aren't those just identical to the wedding dress?"

"No, they're—well, they used to be, actually, but . . ." And off she goes, giving us a rambling but mostly coherent history of bridal attendant costumes and traditions around the world, the kind of champion-level nerdery she tries really, really hard not to show at work because it's difficult enough for her to get taken seriously by anyone outside the team. When she transitions to the soulless takeover by the bridal industry, Eddison discreetly replaces her empty pint glass with a fresh beer.

Somewhere around hour six, as the three of us are eating the scraps of an enormous appetizer platter, he points a chicken wing at me and Sterling, side by side on the opposite side of the booth. "We can all agree I've been behaving myself, so I finally get to ask: What the hell do the shirts mean?"

Sterling collapses into gales of bright, unrestrained laughter that make half the bar smile in response. I just grin and drink my gin and tonic. The shirts we're wearing are plain white cotton, with "I Survived Dinner with Guido and Sal" scrawled across the front, souvenirs from a meal that defies all explanation or retelling. Eddison should be forever sorry he skipped out on that dinner in New York at the beginning of summer.

Sterling has one small bout of tears around eight. It's six o'clock mountain time, and in another life, she'd be getting introduced as Mrs. Dickhead Umptysquat right about now. It's not him she's crying over, but rather, finally coming to grips with the fact that your life has taken an entirely different direction than the one you expected. You draw a map, you make a plan, and then it's all suddenly upended, and you're so caught up in the changes as they happen that it doesn't really sink in until further down the road. I wrap an arm around her shoulders, hugging her tight, and the distinctly uncomfortable Eddison silently excuses himself from the table.

And that's okay. Dealing with crying people will never be his strongest point, but he's supportive in other ways that matter just as much.

Like coming back with an overfull basket of fried mushrooms, which he can't stand but are Sterling's absolute favorite food. She accepts one with a sniffle and a tremulous smile, and we all politely ignore the faint blush seeping across Eddison's cheeks.

A little after ten, Eddison and I settle the bill between us, leaving Vic's contribution as a tip for the very discreet bartenders and waiters who have responded to our hand signals and otherwise left us alone. Sterling slumps against my side, sleepy eyed but curious, occasionally lapsing into soft giggles at nothing in particular. She's a very tame, happy kind of drunk, affectionate without being effusive.

At Eddison's, we transfer Sterling and our bags into my car, handing our adorably soused agent a bottle of water for the short trip. My job for the night is to give her as much water as she can manage without feeling sick, so she'll be more or less presentable for work in the morning. She struggles with the cap until Eddison opens it for her, then gives him a bright little chirp in thanks and chugs three-quarters of the bottle in one go.

Blinking, he opens another bottle and hands it to her.

As we drive, she leans her head against the window, watching the stores and neighborhoods as we pass. "Thank you," she says quietly.

"You're ours now," I answer, and there's something about the moment, or maybe just the many hours at the bar, that demands nothing above a murmur. "That undeserving bastard didn't know what a good thing he had in you, but we do. Thank you for letting us do this for you."

"My dad kept asking if I was sure. Said he didn't care if we lost money on deposits and dresses and things. Just wanted me to be sure." She sighs, tugging the band out of her ponytail to let her hair flop around her. "I should have told him. I just didn't want him to get in trouble with Mom."

I know something about keeping silent like that. Not exactly like that, but close enough to understand the impulse. I turn onto my street and try to decide if there's a response that doesn't start a conversation she is far too drunk to have.

"Mercedes?"

"Mm-hmm?"

"There are children on your porch."

I slam on the brake, and she hiccups as the seat belt catches, and when I look out her window, sure enough, there are three children on my porch, two sitting on the swing and one pacing back and forth in front of them, her motions keeping the light on, and even from this distance I can see the blood and the teddy bears.

7

I pull all the way up the driveway, because there's no sense in blocking the way for the emergency responders even as it feels deeply callous to just *drive past the children.* "Stay here until I call for you," I tell Sterling, pulling my gun and flashlight out of my purse.

"Because I'm drunk?"

"Because you're drunk."

"Okay." She nods quickly, both of her phones in her hand, and I can see Eddison's name on the screen as she starts slowly tapping out a text. Good girl.

Hands crossed at the wrist, so both the gun and the flashlight can point outward, I prowl around the back of my house to make sure no one is lying in wait. There's no sign that anyone has come this way in the past few hours, though there are some grass clippings that suggest Jason mowed as soon as the police gave him the okay. The back door is still locked, the glass intact, with no visible blood on the step or handle. Around the far side of the house, the edge of the porch slowly comes into relief, and then the children waiting there. I click off the flashlight and put it in my back pocket.

"My name is Mercedes Ramirez," I tell the children, and all three flinch. "This is my house."

"We're not trespassing," the middle child retorts defiantly. "The angel lady brought us here!"

"The angel lady?"

The oldest, a girl perhaps twelve or thirteen, still in the early stages of puberty, nods, keeping herself between the steps and the other two. "She killed our parents," she says bluntly. Blood streaks the sides of their faces, and a little down their arms, not nearly as much as was on Ronnie. She holds her bear—white, with crinkly gold wings and halo, just like Ronnie's—by one foot, smacking it against her thigh in agitation. The younger ones clutch theirs, seeking comfort she already knows isn't there. "She woke us up. Said we had to go to their room. She said . . . she said we had to see that we're safe now."

"Safe?"

"We were safe at home," the middle one says. She keeps her free arm around the youngest, a boy who can't be more than five. "Why did she hurt our parents?"

I glance at the older girl, and there are shadows in her eyes. Maybe the younger one was safe at home, but this one wasn't. She meets my eyes briefly, then looks away, reaching back for her sister. "They were dead," she says quietly. "She made us listen for heartbeats to be sure."

The blood on their cheeks.

"First things first, are any of you hurt?"

The girls shake their heads; the boy buries his in his sister's shoulder. "The lady had a gun, but she said she wasn't going to hurt us," the oldest answers. "Our parents were already dead, so . . . we . . ."

"Did what she said, and kept yourselves safe," I finish firmly. "What are your names?"

"I'm Sarah." The oldest girl reaches for her brother's shoulder. "Sammy. And Ashley."

"And your last name?"

"Carter. Sammy's a Wong, like his dad. Like our mom, after they got married."

"Can you tell me their first names? And your address?"

Sarah gives me the information, and I text it to Sterling. A few seconds later, I get a thumbs-up emoji. A text from Eddison follows. *On my way, so is Vic.* Okay.

Moving slowly, I sit on the top step. "Help is on the way," I tell them. "I work for the FBI, and one of my partners is in the car, calling the police. The others are on the way."

After giving me a long look, Sarah apparently decides that I'm not going to move any closer than I already have, and sits on the very edge of the swing to put an arm around her little brother, sandwiching him between her and her sister. "So what happens now?" asks Sarah. She's so tightly contained, despite the fear and the pain in her eyes, and it breaks my heart to think what she must have gone through to learn that self-control so young.

"The police are going to have questions for you about what happened, and they'll take you to the hospital to get you checked over and cleaned up. They'll make sure there are counselors available to you, when you need to talk. They'll look for family who can take you in."

"Our grandparents are out in California. They might not . . ." Sarah glances down at Sammy, still tucked sobbing into Ashley's side, and doesn't finish.

I can fill in that blank: they might not be willing to take Sammy. "I promise, the police are going to work really hard to make sure that whatever happens, it's the best possible thing for you." Unfortunately, it's the most I *can* promise. However much I want to, I can't promise they'll all stay together. That's never in my power.

Detective Holmes arrives on the tail of the ambulance, another car pulling up behind her a minute later. "Ramirez," she greets me quietly.

I nod in response.

She crouches down beside me, keeping her eye on the kids. "The woman who made the 911 call: Is she drunk?"

"She is; that's why she has remained in the car the entire time and made the call." I frown at Holmes's disapproving look. "It was supposed to be her wedding day. We took her out and got her drunk."

Holmes blinks at that, and doesn't seem to have anything to add.

"She's had zero contact with the children or the environment. She has literally not even opened the car door."

"All right. Sarah? Ashley? Sammy? My name is Detective Holmes. How are you guys doing?"

The girls eye her, from her shower-damp blonde hair to her heavy-duty work boots, and shift so close together Sammy can barely be seen.

It's harder this time to sit back and do nothing, to wait for Holmes to make decisions and issue orders to her officers and the paramedics. One of the officers, who has children of his own, takes charge of Ashley and Sammy, gently chivvying them into reluctant smiles as the paramedics look them over and escort them to the ambulance. Sarah watches them until they're out of sight in the vehicle, and even then seems reluctant to look away.

Holmes studies the girl for a minute or two, then catches my eye and tilts her head in Sarah's direction. She recognizes that darkness in her eyes as well. It's a different kind of bruising than Ronnie's, something that goes beyond painful, something sick and twisting. Getting to my feet, I walk carefully down the porch and hop onto the rail, facing the swing, so I can have proximity without infringing on Sarah's personal space.

"Sarah?" I say gently. "When did your stepdad start hurting you?"

She looks startled, then defensive, but when she sees neither of us is judging her, accusing her, her shoulders slump and her eyes fill with tears. "A little before Sammy was born," she whispers. "Mom was really sick all the time, and he said . . . he said she w-wouldn't m-m-mind, and that he needed it. But then he kept doing it. I wanted him to stop, and I was going to tell Mom, b-but h-h-he said if I w-wouldn't, he'd go to Ashley." The tears fall thick and heavy, and my arms ache with the need to hug her, be a shield from the rest of the world, even just for a few minutes. Instead, I clench my hands tightly around the rail. "I d-didn't t-tell," she continues, her voice starting to choke. "I never told."

"Oh, *mija* . . ."

Sarah kicks off from the swing and hurls herself at me, her skinny arms wrapping around my waist as she buries her face in my chest. With a muffled *oomph*, I hook a foot through the thin rail posts to keep myself from pitching off the porch. One arm against the girl's back, enough to comfort without making her feel trapped, I stroke her matted auburn hair with the other hand, crooning softly in Spanish.

Behind me, I can hear other cars approach, Eddison's and Vic's voices mingling with Sterling's as she updates them with what she can from my passenger seat. I tune them out, focused on the girl weeping against me. "I'm so sorry you had to go through that, Sarah," I murmur, timing the motion of my hand to my breathing. Gradually, Sarah starts to time her breaths to mine and calm. "You never should have had to, but you're such a good sister to protect Ashley that way. And you were looking out for them so well tonight, Ashley and Sammy both. I know that can't be easy."

"One of the girls in my class, her dad did the same thing," she mumbles into my T-shirt. Guido and Sal may never be the same. "She told our teacher and the school nurse. Her mom told everyone she was lying, that she was just trying to cause trouble."

"I'm so sorry, Sarah."

"I'm glad he's dead," she gasps, her tears gaining strength again. "I'm sorry, I know I shouldn't be, but I really am."

"Right now, Sarah, it's been a very long and scary night, and you're allowed to feel anything you want to feel." I squeeze her shoulder. "It doesn't make you a bad person."

"She knew. The angel, she knew what he did. I never told anyone, though."

"Has anyone asked you? Someone at school, maybe?"

Sarah stands up a little straighter, her arms still around my waist. "Um . . ." Her eyelashes are clumped together into little spikes, the pale red tear-darkened to brown. "We had scoliosis checks in PE a few months ago," she says after a minute. "The nurse and one of the lady coaches checked us in the coach's office. We had to lift our shirts. Fifth period, I got called to the office. My guidance counselor asked if everything was okay at home."

"Do you remember if she asked anything specific? Any hint what made them think something was wrong?"

Blushing fiercely, Sarah nods. "He . . . he grips hard. His hands leave bruises."

"Never again," I remind her. Holmes nods absently, her gaze on the small notepad in her hand. She looks pissed, but like she's trying to hide it for Sarah's sake. "He can't touch you ever again, and he will never touch Ashley." I wait until Sarah nods again. "What happened with the counselor?"

"I told her I fell off the counter putting dishes away, and that my stepdad caught me before I hit the floor. I know I shouldn't have lied, but . . ."

"But you were protecting yourself and your sister. I'm not trying to blame you for anything, Sarah. You did what you had to do, especially if you saw your classmate get in trouble for telling the truth."

"That was all I could think about," she admits. "She told the truth and everyone yelled at her, and what if . . ." She takes a deep breath and shakes her head. "A couple days later, I was pulled out of class again, and there was a social worker with the guidance counselor. I told her the same thing. She . . . she asked if they could see the bruises, and I . . . I told them no. There were fresh ones, and I knew they'd know, but I also knew they couldn't make me show them without my mom's permission."

"Sarah? Do you think your mom would have given permission?" asks Holmes.

Sarah starts shaking, and I hold her closer, sure enough of her now to wrap both arms around her for warmth and security. "I don't know," she whispers. "She really loves my stepdad. She always says she doesn't know what we'd do if something happened to him, she doesn't know how we'd live without him."

I close my eyes against her hair, consciously keeping my breathing even. Her mother knew.

"The social worker drove me home and told my mom everything. When he found out I didn't say anything, my stepdad bought me a bicycle. I've been wanting one for ages, but he always said no, and then he bought me exactly the one I wanted."

Abusers commonly reward their victims for staying silent or lying. I'm not about to tell her that, though, especially not when she already seems to know. Sarah seems so smart, and sweet, and so protective of her siblings. I'm not giving her any more to carry than I absolutely have to.

"Did the angel seem familiar at all? Her voice, or the way she moved?"

"No. She had a mask on, kind of like . . ." She trails off, frowning, then looks back up at me. "Not the Halloween masks. This is a fancy kind. Heavy. The kind artists paint on. My friend Julie collects the painted ones. She's got a whole wall of them, all different designs. Her mom writes the date she gets each one on the inside."

"I think I collected the same masks when I was a kid," Holmes notes. "My dad swore they were from Venice, and it took years before I realized he was lying. Still loved the masks, though."

"The angel's was bigger. It covered her whole face and wasn't painted at all. It was just white. And . . ." She shudders. "Blood. There was blood on it."

"Could you see her eyes? What color they were?"

Sarah shakes her head. "The eyeholes had mirrors. It was creepy."

I glance at Holmes. "One-way glass?"

"Would have to be, wouldn't it? Sarah, you've been saying *she* this whole time. How did you know the angel was a woman?"

"I . . ." Her mouth works soundlessly for a moment, then closes. A furrow creases her brow. "She had long blond hair. Light blonde, I think, and straight, and I don't know. I guess it just sounded like a lady. It wasn't a super high voice, so . . . I guess it could have been a guy. I don't know."

We continue to ask her questions, carefully spacing out where we push for extra information or clarification so we don't overwhelm her. Eventually, when we're out of questions for the moment and Holmes has called one of the paramedics back over, Sarah gives me a tremulous smile. "She said we'd be safe with you, that you'd help," she says, her voice soft and shy. "She was right. Thank you."

I hug her again, rather than try to answer.

Once upon a time, there was a little girl who was scared of cameras.

Cameras were entirely too honest; they didn't know how to lie. They could be made to lie, by a clever enough operator, but neither of her parents was that clever.

They showed how Daddy's fingers curled hard into her collarbone, into Mama's hip.

They showed how she and Mama both leaned away—from Daddy, from each other—and how Daddy pulled them in.

They showed her eyes.

They showed everything.

She hated seeing herself in pictures because her eyes always yelled the things she wasn't allowed to say, and still no one listened.

Then Daddy started bringing the camera with him at night.

He'd look through the photos whenever he wanted, even out in the living room like he was daring Mama to say anything.

She didn't. Of course she didn't.

And he'd bring them out for a select group of friends, men who all called her angel *and* pretty girl *and* beautiful. *They'd look through the pictures together, and any they really liked, Daddy would print them copies. But he'd never let them forget that he was in control, that he had what they wanted. No matter how much he gave them, he could take it all away again.*

8

Holmes lets me accompany them to the hospital this time, because Sarah's confession of the abuse means they have to do a pelvic exam. I don't know if it's because I was the one holding her or because mine was the name the killer gave her, but either way, Holmes agrees that my being there with her will probably help her stay calm.

Eddison and Vic are off to the Wong house to meet Mignone. Sterling comes with me, grave and silent in a corner of the ambulance with another bottle of water in her hands. She doesn't try to say anything to the children, though, or even to the officers and paramedics. She just watches and drinks her water.

At the hospital, Ashley and Sammy are bundled off together with a grandmotherly pediatrician whose slow, syrupy Tidewater drawl seems to fascinate and soothe them in equal measure. Sterling refills her bottle from a fountain and takes a seat in the emergency room with her phone. At this point, she's basically sober, but it wouldn't surprise me in the least if she asks the hospital to do a BAC test before she engages with the case in any way.

In a curtained-off exam room, I help a nurse and female officer change Sarah for the exam. Her pajamas are folded and placed in a bag that gets sealed and signed, and then the giant camera comes out. She gives me a startled look.

"It's okay," I tell her. "We have to have a record of any injuries you came in with. That camera has a kind of filter that helps them see bruises better. We can make sure the doctors know about it, and having that information in your file will help the social workers decide which counselors you need to talk to."

"Oh." She looks at the camera and steels herself with a breath. "Okay."

The bruises are terrible. Large handprints overlap on her hips and the inside of her thighs, and one side of her chest is almost uniformly indigo and yellow. Lighter bruising wraps around her neck, front and back, and brackets her face. Through the filter, we can see the shape of fingers.

"In a few minutes, the doctor is going to come in," I say, taking her hand as the officer packs the camera away. "Those metal things at the end of the bed that look kind of like bike pedals? Those are called stirrups, and she's going to ask you to put your feet in them so she can prop them up. You're going to feel uncomfortable, kind of like you're on display, but she is the only one who will see anything, I promise. No one is going to walk in, and even if someone tried, her sitting there between your legs will block everything from view."

"Do we have to?"

I wish I could give her a different answer, but I'm not going to lie to her. "Yes. This is something we have to do. If you need the doctor to stop, or explain something she's doing, just say so, okay? I know this sucks."

"Is it like getting a pap smear? Mom talks about that. She says when I get older I'll have to do those."

"It's pretty close. This is maybe a little more thorough, though."

"Why?"

"The doctor is going to make sure you don't have any injuries down there. When men hurt girls like this, things can tear, or get swollen, or infected. If those tears have been happening for a while, there could be scars that cause problems later on. So she has to make sure all the wounds are identified, so they can be treated."

"Oh."

I give her hand a squeeze. "Sarah, I was just a couple years younger than you when I had my first exam, and for the same reason."

Her hand spasms in response, fingers digging into mine. "Really?"

"Really. So I promise you, I *know* that this is going to be uncomfortable, but it really is important. We wouldn't ask you to do it if it wasn't."

"You said you're an FBI agent."

"I am."

"Do you . . ." She swallows hard, but when she looks back up at me, her eyes glitter fiercely. "Do you think I could be one someday?"

"Sweetheart, if you want to badly enough, and work hard enough, I genuinely believe you could be anything you want to be. FBI agent included."

"I want to protect people."

"You already do." My heart breaks a little at the confused tilt of her head. "Sarah, he would have gone after Ashley. You've been protecting your sister for years, and you've done such a good job of it, she didn't even know she was in danger."

The doctor comes in while she's chewing on that, a woman not much older than me with kind eyes and a gentle voice, and a way of explaining every step without making it overly technical or insultingly simple. In between parts of narration, she asks Sarah easy questions, things to get her talking without being too personal. Sarah squirms a little through the examination, and yelps once or twice when even the warning wasn't enough to prepare her, but the doc gives her a warm smile as she peels off her gloves.

"You did really well, Miss Carter."

"Is everything . . . is everything okay? You know, down . . . down there?"

"Mostly," the doc answers honestly, but she doesn't look worried. "You've got some inflammation, and it looks like some of the surface tissue has rubbed off pretty painfully, so we're going to give you some medications: antibiotics, to prevent infection, and some anti-inflammatories to help with the swelling and tenderness. Bad news—and it's not very bad, just sort of awkward—is that there's also a cream to help with it. After you've had a chance to rest and clean up a bit, one of my nurses will take you aside and teach you how to apply that. Think about your health class at school, add in a little more awkward, and you'll probably get the idea."

Sarah laughs, and looks a bit startled by it.

"We've got some pajamas on the way for you," the doc continues, "and once you've changed, the nurse is going to take you up a few floors. We've got you and your brother and sister all in one room tonight."

"And they're okay?"

"They are. Shaken up, scared, but physically they are just fine, and we're going to have nurses checking in on you through the night. There's a social worker up with them, too, and she's going to walk you through what will happen next. Do you need Agent Ramirez to go up with you, or can I borrow her for a minute?"

Sarah gives me a small smile. "I think I'll be okay. Thank you, Agent Ramirez."

"Mercedes," I tell her, and the smiles grows. "Before I leave, I'm going to give the social worker my contact info, and there'll be a card for you in there with my phone and email. If you need anything, Sarah, even if it's just to talk, please let me know. There's going to be a lot happening in the next few days and weeks, and it can be tough to deal with, especially if you feel like you have to be strong for your siblings. But you never have to be strong for me, okay? So if you need me, you call me."

She nods and squeezes my hand, then lets go so I can follow the doctor out of the room and down the hall to a charting station.

"Is it unprofessional if I want to find the bastard that's done this to her and twist his dick off?" the doc asks conversationally.

"Desecrating a corpse may be a crime in the Commonwealth of Virginia. I'd have to check, though."

"Corpse?" She considers that a moment, then nods sharply. "I'll accept that as good enough."

"So is her condition worse than you told her?"

"No, physically she'll heal fully with time and care. I'm simply of the opinion that anyone who commits rape should be castrated, and if they rape a child, the punishment should be as painful and damaging as possible."

"I like that opinion."

"We put a rush on your partner's blood work, and she's under the legal limit now. I don't imagine your team is going to get much sleep tonight."

"No, not so much. Thank you, Doctor."

In the waiting room, Sterling is frowning down at her phone, a foam cup at her elbow steaming. "There's a coffee vending machine, if you want something," she informs me. "If their coffee is as bad as their tea, you might not want to risk it."

"I'm awake enough for now," I admit, dropping into the seat next to her. "I haven't turned my ringer back on yet; any word from the boys?"

"They said it's a similar scene to the Wilkins house. Father was subdued with a couple of gunshots, mother was hacked to death, father was *really* hacked to death. Unlike Daniel Wilkins, Samuel Wong has a number of stab wounds on and around his groin."

"Ronnie Wilkins wasn't sexually abused, Sarah Carter was, so that makes sense, I guess."

"They live in one of the neighborhoods on the edge of town, where the houses each have a couple of acres. No neighbors close enough to hear or see anything." She looks up from her phone. "Vic said the mirrors in Sarah's room and bathroom were covered over."

"That's not uncommon for someone who's been hurt that way."

"CSU is going over the scene, but so far nothing really stands out. A lot of people in that neighborhood don't lock their doors at night."

"A safe neighborhood."

"I'm sure they feel safe now." She sighs and drops the phone facedown in her lap. "Did she make them watch?"

"No. Three would be much harder to control than one, especially since two of them weren't abused. She woke them up after and made them go in to listen for heartbeats."

"Holy God."

We sit in silence for several minutes. I try to decide which is better: telling Siobhan myself, despite her little edict about letting her initiate contact when and only when she's ready to do so, or leaving her to hear it through the grapevine at work. I should email the analyst pool so they can start running cross-checks as soon as they get into the office, finding anything and everything that links Sarah to Ronnie. One point in space is generally next to useless, but two points, two points can make a commonality, the beginning of a pattern. Two points can make a line. I wish Yvonne, our team's dedicated analyst, was back from maternity leave. She's good at finding those hidden threads between A and B.

"Do you think Eddison's bed is big enough for three people?"

"What?"

Sterling leans her head on my shoulder. She scraped her hair back into a ponytail at some point, and stray strands tickle the back of my neck. "Mine's not big enough, and yours is probably taped off. None of us should be alone tonight."

I reach across and tug lightly on her ear. "You're still a little bit drunk, aren't you?"

"Just a little."

"None of us get to sleep this morning, but tonight?" I tilt my head against hers and just breathe. "If Eddison's bed isn't big enough, we'll all go crash on the floor of Vic's living room."

"Deal."

The silence resumes, broken by distant conversations and the occasional intercom call. After a while, a handful of doctors in scrubs and paper trauma gowns race past us to the ambulance bay, and a few minutes later we hear the whine of approaching sirens. Sterling's phone buzzes and chirps with a series of texts delivered in swift succession. We take one more breath, one more moment, and then she picks up her phone, opens up the message, and starts reading the new texts out loud.

9

"They're saying more kids were taken to your door."

Siobhan is at my desk, and I have no idea what time it is right now, but she's obviously been to her desk already this morning (still morning?) because she's got her hideous sweater on. There's a vent right over her desk, and whatever thermostat it's attached to seems to be permanently set on freezing. The fact that my brain is stuck on her sweater, rather than her presence at my desk, does not bode well for the conversation that's sure to follow.

I lean back in my chair, trying not to rub at my face because my makeup is the only thing keeping me looking semi-human at the moment. "I left you a voice mail," I say after a moment. "Asked you to call me back."

"Yes, and then I got to my desk, and Heather was waiting there to tell me all about my girlfriend getting more bloodied children delivered to her door."

"It's not like I'm ordering them off Amazon."

"Mercedes!"

"What do you want me to say, Siobhan? Yes, there were children at my door. Yes, their parents were killed. Yes, it was terrible."

"What's going to happen to them?"

"I don't know," I sigh. I've been on the phone with the on-call social worker. Sarah and Ashley's grandparents in California are willing to take the girls, but they're apparently fervent racists and won't take "the half-breed," and Sarah has already announced that if she's sent anywhere without both her siblings, she'll run away. Which, you know, good for her, but still. The girls' father is in prison for a white-collar crime, his parents have been dead for years, and Sammy's grandparents haven't been located. There aren't any uncles or aunts, and it's hard to find fosters willing to take in a trio and keep them together. "For right now they're at the hospital until they're sure the oldest one is okay, and then they'll be taken to a group home while it's being figured out."

"And you're all kinds of fine with this."

"Are you just here to yell at me?"

She looks abashed at that. Tired, too, her eyes washed pink with exhaustion, and concealer can only cover the color of the shadows there, not the way the softer skin sags with fatigue. She hasn't been sleeping. "I miss you," she whispers.

"I miss you too, but you're the one who walked away."

"Bloodied children, Mercedes!"

"Victims, Siobhan, who certainly didn't ask for their parents to be murdered so they could inconvenience you."

"Wow." She sits—perches, really—on the edge of my desk and stares at her feet. "Normally when we fight, you're not this mean."

"Normally when we fight, it's over stupid shit." I dig through the mess of papers on my desk until I can find my phone, which tells me it's just shy of eight-thirty; I've been at my desk for almost five hours already. *Madre de Dios.* Swiveling my chair, I can see Sterling at her computer, typing rapidly, and Eddison at his obsessively neat desk nearby, feet up on the corner with a thick file opened across his lap. "Hey, *hermano*—" I say to him.

"Bring me back something."

"Got it." I grab my purse from the bottom drawer and head toward the elevator. A second later, a startled Siobhan follows suit.

"What's—was that a conversation? What was that?"

"We're getting coffee."

"I have work to do."

"Which is why you were at my desk?" I jab the call button harder than I really need to, and have to keep myself from doing it repeatedly. It's that kind of morning. "Come or don't."

"Mercedes . . ."

The elevator opens and I step in, turn around, and raise my eyebrows at her. With a muttered curse, she follows me.

"I don't have my wallet."

"Have your ID?"

"Yes."

"Then as long as you can get back to your desk later, I'm pretty sure I can spare the cost of a coffee, even yours."

"What's that supposed to mean?"

"That you order ridiculously complicated coffee."

"Oh. That's . . . that's true."

I'm tired and angry and confused, and more than a little hurt by her recent choices, so I'm well aware my current mood is set to bitchy. We head out of the building and down to one of the coffee shops. Despite how many there are in the area, they're all busy, feeding the addiction that keeps a large percentage of agents operating at something like capacity. A few blocks down, we manage to find one that's a bit quieter, with a little patio holding a handful of chairs and tiny tables, and no people. Some are sitting inside with the air-conditioning, and there are others getting cups to go, but we should get the patio to ourselves. No one wants to sit in this humid heat, no matter how early in the day it is.

Siobhan's order fills the side of her cup with arcane runes, and mine gets a quick smile from the barista for being so simple. I also grab a bagel and get a cannoli for Siobhan. It won't be as good as Marlene's, of course, but maybe it's good to remember that the longer she's pissed at me for something that isn't my fault, the longer it will be before she gets superlative baked goods again.

I'm not above bribery.

We wait in silence for the drinks. She plays with the cuffs of her giant ugly sweater, and I check the newest text from Holmes: *Why are so many of your neighbors in bed by ten?* By that, I'm guessing no one noticed a car driving up and off-loading children. People on the street are friendly, but they keep to themselves. The arrangement Jason and I have for lawn and laundry is an unusual degree of coexistence. There's not much reason to spend your time peeking through the curtains at the world outside when your life is inside.

Coffees and breakfast in hand, we retreat to the patio. She only picks at her cannoli, crumbling the thick shell between fingers and thumb. I am entirely too hungry to be delicate, and my bagel is gone in five bites. I maybe should have grabbed a second one.

"Mercedes? Why don't we live together?"

Her hair is so bright in the morning sun, fiery red corkscrew curls that fight any attempt to tame or contain them. She can't even use a hair band on it when it's dry; this morning, her ponytail is cinched by a giant pipe cleaner in a cheerful pink. I've gotten spoiled the past three years, being able to feel it against my skin, the weight of it in my hands.

"Mercedes."

"Because I don't like sharing space on a permanent basis," I say simply. "Because having my own space, having locks between me and everyone else, is important to me, and I'm not ready to give that up. Because I can't have my only safe space, my only private space, be a bedroom, even if it's converted to an office. Because I love you, but I can't live with anyone just yet."

"I stay over at yours, you stay over at mine, you and Eddison have sleepovers all the time. What's the difference?"

"The ability to say no."

"I don't—"

"My bedroom door didn't have a lock I could control, growing up. I went into foster care when I was ten, anywhere from two to six of us in a room, and if there was a lock, it was on the outside of the door, nothing we could touch. When my last set of fosters asked if I wanted to stay until I aged out, they did it by buying a lock and helping me install it on the inside of my door. They understood what that meant to me, how safe it made me feel, and that's why I stayed. It's the first space that was mine, not just because I was in it but because I could control who had access to it."

She sips her drink, watching the cars pass by. "You were in foster care?" she asks eventually.

"Eight years."

"You weren't adopted?"

"The last ones offered. I said no."

"Why?"

"Because family hurt me. I wasn't ready to try again. But I stayed with them for four years, and I'm still in touch with them. We get together a couple times a year."

"Three years, and you've never told me this?"

"You like to edit your world, Siobhan. You can't tell me you're not curious about why I went into foster care, but you'll get angry if I explain it. Because that's not what you want in your reality. Children don't get hurt in your little world."

"That isn't fair."

"No, it isn't, and I'm tired of pretending it's something I can do." My thumb taps against the scars on my cheek. I keep them covered most of the time, but not always. She's seen them, and she's never once asked how I got them. I used to be grateful for it until I better understood that she wasn't granting me privacy—she genuinely didn't want to know, because she suspected it might be something terrible. And it was, and it is, but still. "You constantly punish me for doing a job you think shouldn't be necessary, while refusing to admit that it is. I'm tired of feeling like I have to protect you from my history simply because you don't like that the world can be a horrible place."

"I'm not that naïve!" she protests, but I shake my head.

"You want to be. You're not, and you know you're not, but you *want* a world that simple, and you lash out at the people who remind you that it isn't."

Her hands are trembling. I watch her fingers tighten around the cup to try and stop it, and then she puts the cup down and hides her hands in her lap. "This sounds a lot like you breaking up with me."

"It isn't."

"Really?"

"I should have stopped pretending a long time ago. But you have to understand this, Siobhan: I'm not doing it anymore. You need to decide if you can be in a relationship with someone with a painful personal history, someone who needs to be able to talk about difficulties or triumphs with a job you hate. If you can, or think you can, wonderful. I really hope you do, and that we can figure out how to make this work going forward. If you can't, I can understand that, but that's your choice to end it."

"You're putting that on me."

"Yes." I drain the last of my coffee and stuff the trash into the cup. "Will you let me tell you something else about the children?"

Her expression says, *hell no*, but after a moment, she nods.

"They were hurt by their parents, and when this woman took them from their homes, she brought them to my house and told them they'd be safe. I would keep them safe. And yes, it's terrifying that she knows where I live and what I do, but she's also trusting me to keep these children safe. The history I have with my job, the reputation I've made with it, means these children aren't being left in the house with their dead parents. It's a small mercy, but a mercy nonetheless. She isn't hurting the kids, and she knows I won't either."

"I'm not sure I have anything to say to that," she replies shakily.

"That's okay. Just think on it while you're making your decision."

My phone buzzes with another text, this one from Detective Mignone. *Wong took pictures of his stepdaughter. In the photos, she doesn't seem to be aware of it. Social worker wants you there when they tell her.*

It might be close to an hour before I can get there, I reply.

That's fine. I'll let her know.

"I have to head to Manassas," I announce.

"You're going home? The day just started."

"My yesterday hasn't ended yet, and I'm going to the hospital to talk to one of the kids. Do you want to walk back with me or do you need some time?"

She looks at me for a long minute, and her shoulders slump. "I'll stay for a bit. I guess . . . I guess I'll talk to you . . . when?"

"Whenever you decide. You're at bat."

"At bat?"

"With a brother like Eddison, is it really so shocking baseball has crept into my vocabulary?" I stand and toss my trash, including the crumbled mess of her cannoli when she nods. I'm not sure she ate any of it, honestly. "I won't show up at your apartment or your desk, won't send you anything, won't text or call or email. I'm not going to pass notes like in grade school. This is up to you."

I hesitate, then decide what the hell and lean down to kiss her. However pissed at me she is, our bodies know each other, and she leans into me, her hand curling around my elbow. She tastes like raspberry and white chocolate and peppermint from that silly drink. There's a catcall from a passing driver, but I ignore that, focused on the feel of her lips on mine, the small sigh when my finger strokes along her jawline. This may be the last time we kiss, and it's frightening to realize that I've given up any say in that decision. Frightening, but right. When I pull away, it isn't far, our breaths mingling as my forehead rests against hers. *"Te amo y te extraño y espero que sea suficiente."*

Walking away feels like leaving a piece of me behind, but I don't look back. I head into the store instead, ordering drinks for Eddison, Sterling, and Vic, and a second one for myself. When I start back to the office, cups carefully slotted into a carrier, Siobhan isn't at the table anymore.

10

Sarah's sheer fury at learning her stepfather had cameras hidden around her room takes up pretty much the rest of the day. She's so angry and so hurt, but she also hasn't told her sister what happened, so all that rage spirals inward until we take her outside and let her scream. Nancy, a social worker with over thirty years of experience, expertly intercepts the running security guards to let them know what's going on, and I stay with the shrieking, sobbing preteen in the little garden space that's probably seen a lot of such things. She calms slowly, more a symptom of exhaustion than any actual calm, I think, and asks if she can see the pictures.

"Do you think it will help you?" Nancy asks evenly.

"They're pictures of *me*. How many other people are seeing them?"

"Detective Mignone found them when he was going through your stepfather's closet, and he immediately put them into an envelope and sealed them," I explain. "There will be one person who will have the job of cataloguing the pictures into evidence, along with a basic description of the contents, and then the new envelope will be sealed. Given that Mr. Wong is dead and cannot be brought up for trial, there's no reason for the pictures to ever see the inside of a courtroom. There's no reason for lawyers to request to review the evidence."

"What if Samuel showed them to someone else? Like to his friends or something, or shared them online?"

"Detective Holmes is asking her department to let her partner with the FBI cybercrimes division," I tell her. "We have people who specialize in tracking files and photos online. If he sent them to anyone using his computer, they'll find out. The police will also be talking to his coworkers and friends."

"So even if they didn't get pictures, they'll know there are pictures?"

"No. They won't mention the pictures specifically unless they're pretty sure they've got someone. They'll be very careful, Sarah. No one wants to see you hurt more."

"And if they do have pictures?"

"They'll be arrested and tried for possession of child pornography. Sarah, you are twelve years old. No one, and I mean *no one*, wants those photos out for anyone to see."

"But I have to *know*," she whispers, dropping to the bench like a puppet with severed strings.

"I can understand that." Nancy leans forward, not crowding Sarah but engaging a little more now that the yelling has stopped. "But they're trying to protect you. Those photographs are evidence of a crime, Sarah, and they're not simply going to give them to you, even if you are the one in them. They're not going to *give back* child pornography. Do I believe seeing them could help you? Possibly. Do I believe seeing them could hurt you? Probably. Sarah . . ."

Sarah, scratching at her wrist where the plastic hospital band is scraping her skin, waits for her to finish the thought, which is a good sign, I think.

"What your stepfather did to you, what he took from you, was extreme. Do you really want to see how much else he took?"

"I don't . . ." The girl blows out a frustrated breath. "I don't like other people seeing a piece of me I don't know. Samuel hurt me in private, but now these pieces of it are public."

"They're not public."

"But other people are seeing them, other people know they exist and why and how, and I don't get to see them."

Nancy considers her for a long moment, and I can almost see her running through options in her mind. "The only thing I can promise you is that we'll talk to the advocate about it once the court appoints someone. Beyond that it is completely out of my hands. I will promise that one piece, though. We'll see if there's any legal basis to request it. What I need from you in return is to prepare yourself for disappointment. If, and that's a big *if*, you're granted permission to see them, that has to be the unexpected outcome." She reaches out slowly, just two fingers extended, and touches Sarah's cheek lightly with the backs of her fingers. It's nonthreatening, a way to touch and reassure without implying the possibility of harm. "You cannot let those pictures be the thing you count on to heal you. You have to find your way without them. Can you work with me on that?"

"Do I have a choice?"

"Not a good one."

Sarah huffs out a laugh and looks surprised by it, and I think that's probably a good sign too.

When I leave them, they're still in the garden, talking over how best to tell Ashley what their stepfather did. From what Sarah says, Ashley liked Samuel, because he gave her pretty things. She's going to have a hard time understanding.

I head to Vic's, because that's what this team does when we don't know what to do, and Eddison and Sterling pull up a few minutes behind me. Marlene comes out to meet us, even though we all have keys, and wraps me in a tight hug, her slender arms digging into my back in a way that should be painful but is actually comforting. "How are you doing?" she asks softly.

I give her a crooked smile. "I'm doing."

"Well, that's something then, isn't it? And that poor girl?"

"Angry."

"Good."

It makes me laugh, and I hug her back, letting go only when Eddison and Sterling get within her hugging range.

Vic's daughters are all out for the evening, either working or catching up with friends, so there's only six of us sprawled across the back patio around the grill. Jenny put together what she calls *hobo dinners*, where you toss a bunch of things onto a square of aluminum foil, crunch it into a pouch, and throw it onto a covered grill or into an oven. She's got an entire book of handwritten recipes for them, and they are always delicious, provided Vic does his part and gets them off the grill before catastrophe happens.

"Priya sent me a thing today," Sterling tells me as we watch Marlene and Jenny play tug-of-war with Eddison's curls. Jenny's trying to convince him to cut them, or at least get a trim for God's sake, and Marlene is dramatically proclaiming he's allowed to do no such thing. Between them, Eddison is blushing and stammering and throwing us increasingly desperate looks for help. We stay a safe distance away with our beers.

"She does that sometimes. What did she send?"

She hands me her phone, which has a link in the message bubble. When I touch it, it takes me to a collection of De-Celebration photosets, where women celebrate a divorce or the end of an engagement with photo shoots of them destroying their wedding dresses in various ways. One woman and her collection of bridesmaids joyously shove their poufy dresses into a woodchipper. Another group is wearing their gowns and playing paintball. One woman, who looks to have torn her dress into strips and tied them together, is climbing down from a hotel window painted **BRIDAL SUITE—JUST MARRIED**.

"*¡¿Qué chingada?!*"

"Right? Look at . . . oh, which one was it . . . ah, this one."

I giggle, staring at the screen and its zombie bride and bridesmaid brigade. "That is definitely a creative use for a nonrefundable dress."

"She asked if I had any ideas."

"Do you?"

"Not yet." She takes a long sip of beer, then raises the bottle to Eddison in a salute when he yields his pride enough to run away from Marlene and Jenny. "But it's got me thinking."

God bless Priya.

After an amazing dinner of chicken and zucchini and marinara sauce, and mushrooms for those of us who like them, we talk for a while about the Hanoverian girls, and how strange it will be next year when Janey goes off to college like her sisters. When Marlene starts yawning, we clean up to head out, even though she calls us silly for it.

"You coming home with me?" Eddison asks.

Sterling answers before I can. "No, with me. You can have an estrogen-free evening for once."

"Y puede que la luna vaya a caer del cielo," he mutters.

"What was that?"

"Thank you, I appreciate it."

"Smooth," I whisper, and elbow him in the side. He rubs at his ribs with a scowl, but doesn't reply.

I text Holmes so she knows we're ready to install the cameras Sterling picked up on the way to Vic's, and by the time we reach the house, a uniformed officer is there to let us past the police tape. He greets us affably and watches us work. The cameras are small, mostly discreet and easy to hide, and Sterling's worked with them before. Which is good, because when I say we install it, I mean Sterling does, and I hand her things as she asks for them. It only takes her an hour to get them both up and properly networked, the video dumping to both an external hard drive and an online data cache. She's our tech guru whenever Yvonne is unavailable.

We thank the officer and hit the road to Sterling's apartment. She lives only a few streets down from Eddison, in a complex owned by the same company and which looks almost identical save for the buildings being pale orange rather than fawn-brown. She sorts through her mail at the box, dumping three-quarters of it straight into the trash can in the corner of the mail room. "Do companies actually bring in enough business from junk mail ads to be worth the money and waste?"

"Probably not, but why should that stop them?"

Her apartment is up on the second floor, and she pauses with her key in the lock. "It might be a little messy right now," she says apologetically. "I've been going through everything to pull donations."

"Is there a clear path?"

"Yes."

"Are there bugs?"

"No," she says more slowly, giving me a sideways stink-eye.

"Is anything growing?"

"No!"

"Then we're good."

"You have depressingly low standards," she sighs, and pushes the door open to flick on the entry light.

I follow her in, closing and locking the door behind me, and get my first-ever look at her place. "Holy fucking God, Eliza."

Startled, she drops her keys instead of hanging them on the hook she'd been reaching for. "You never call me Eliza."

"That's because I've never seen this before. I may never be able to call you Sterling again."

She blushes deeply and retrieves her keys, hanging them neatly on the small claw on the coatrack. "I'm never letting Eddison come here, am I?"

"Oh hell no, he will run screaming for the parking lot." I laugh, taking a few steps into the apartment. The walls are painted a delicate, icy sort of pink, with one wall a bolder pink for accent. The sliding glass door leading out to the tiny balcony is covered not only by vertical blinds to block the sun, but also by a sheer pink drape and bracketed by lavender and baby blue curtains, with one of those . . . what is it, a dust ruffle? A valance? The shorter thing that goes over the tops of the curtains, anyway, and like the curtains, it's trimmed in two lines of pink ribbon with tiny bows at intervals. Every single thing in the room looks perfectly coordinated, like a spread in *Martha Stewart Living*, possibly like Blessed Saint Martha of the Cupcakes came down herself and anointed it. The same is true in the kitchen, which has coordinating towel sets hanging from the drawer and oven handles.

The only mess I can see is around the dining room table with its pale yellow and mint green layers of tablecloths. Two of the chairs have masses of clothing draped over them, one has a half-full box open on the seat, and the other a mostly full trash bag.

"Holy fucking God, Eliza Sterling. I . . . I honestly can't remember the last time I saw so many ruffles. Or are those flounces?"

Her face is burning now, and she busies herself with hanging her purse just so next to her keys. "Please don't tell Eddison."

"I couldn't possibly spoil the surprise." I can't stop laughing, and the poor girl looks more embarrassed by the minute, so I drape myself over her shoulder in a kind of koala hug. "Why didn't you ever say you were so freaking girly outside of work?"

That at least gets me a crooked smile. "It's hard enough to get taken seriously. Can you imagine the guys finding out about this?"

"Hmm."

"What?"

I slump into her, digging my chin into her shoulder. "I'm trying to remember the last time you sparred with a man and it didn't end with him getting slammed repeatedly into the mats. You always kick their asses. It's why Eddison won't spar with you. When they can beat you sparring, then they can give you shit about the pink and frills."

She laughs and pushes me away. "Let me go change and I'll help you get the couch set up."

I change in the living room, into a T-shirt and boxers freshly liberated from Eddison's dresser because my other ones really need to be washed, and discover that the drawer of one of the end tables is actually a tiny gun safe. "Oh-two-one-four-two-nine," she announces when she comes back out and sees me looking at it. "I know it's stupid but I wanted something I didn't have to think about."

"Oh-two-one-four, that's what, Valentine's Day? Two-nine?"

"Saint Valentine's Day Massacre, 1929."

I digest that for a moment, looking around at all the ruffles and pastels and perfectly coordinated decorations. "You are a complicated person, Eliza Sterling."

"Aren't we all?"

"Oh, hell yes."

With her coffee table moved up against the entertainment center, there's enough room for the couch to pull out into a bed, which we finish off with *a complete bedding set* she grabs from the linen closet. She just rolls her eyes at my intermittent snickering.

"I can't help it," I insist. "It's just . . . you're so severe at work, you only wear black and white, you always have your hair back, you're so damn careful with your makeup, and then here it's this absolute fairy tale. I love it."

"You do?"

"Absolutely! It's just going to take my brain some time to reconcile the two. Anyway, you should have seen how long it took me to stop laughing the first time I saw Eddison's apartment."

"Really? But his apartment is exactly the way I'd picture it."

"If you were going to change it, to make it even more Eddison, what would you do?"

She ponders that while easing the pillows into the cases and fluffing them. "Take the pictures off the wall and change the table to something boring," she says eventually. "Those aren't his touches."

"Priya."

"I adore that girl."

We don't stay up to talk; it's been a long couple of days, after all. As tired as I am, sleep takes some time in coming. I haven't slept in my own bed in a couple of weeks now, and while the couch-bed is fairly comfortable as far as couch-beds go, it's still a couch-bed.

But that's not really what's keeping me awake. We live half our lives on the road, on the beds of whatever hotel we happen to land in. We've slept on couches in precincts and even sometimes on conference room floors when there wasn't time for more than a nap.

I keep thinking of Sarah, alone in her room at night, listening for footsteps down the hall, wondering if she'd be left alone for a night, or if her stepfather would enter. If he'd put a hand to her mouth and remind her in a whisper that she had to be quiet, she couldn't let her sister or mother hear. Sitting in the kitchen in the morning, aching and sick, staring at her mother and wondering if it was really possible she hadn't heard, that she didn't know.

It isn't impossible to heal from that, but it leaves scars. It changes the way you look at people, how far you can trust or let people in. It changes your habits, even your desires and dreams. It changes who you are, and no matter how much you struggle back toward that place, that person you started as, you never actually get there. Some change is irreversible.

My phone buzzes with a text.

It's from Priya.

Sterling says you're making fun of her apartment. You know I gave her some of that stuff, right?

And sometimes that change is good. Or leads to good, anyway.

11

Despite its beginning, the week continues fairly quiet. Sarah and I talk several times a day, and I get updates from both Holmes and Mignone. Sarah's able to give some useful descriptors of the woman who killed her parents: a few inches taller than Sarah but not tall, slender but strong—she'd carried Sammy to and from the car so the girls would follow along. She wore a white jumpsuit that covered her from neck to wrist to ankles, and white gloves, and she had a bag over her shoulder with multiple sets of plastic covers for her white sneakers. The white mask, with its suggestion of features and its mirrored-over eyes, she'd described before, but the blonde hairline came down over the top of the mask in such a way that it had to be a wig, the hair long and straight.

And that's where the discussions Eddison and I are having devolve into a long conversation about the distinction between *useful* and *helpful*, because none of these details are going to actually help us find the killer until we locate a person and happen to find those items on her. Mignone has already tried tracking purchases, but that's another thing that will be easier to do after the fact.

The police have also heard from Social Services: the files for Ronnie Wilkins and Sarah Carter both went through the Manassas CPS office, but none of the names on them matched. The one complaint filed by Sarah's school had been given to someone new to the office, whereas the same man had been handling Ronnie's file for several years.

I swing down to the FBI archives on Wednesday to submit a request. All of our case files, complete with our handwritten notes made during and after investigations, are preserved for posterity or auditing, whichever comes first. (Auditing. Always auditing.) Given that I've been in the Bureau for ten years, I've worked a lot of cases. Most of them have been with the team or done as consults, but I've occasionally been loaned out to other teams. We all have, really, if another team is missing people or there's a need for a particular specialty.

Agent Alceste, who works in the archives because it entails the least amount of human interaction, listens to the reasons for my request as she looks through the paperwork that is already filled out and waiting for her approval. Alceste doesn't like me—she doesn't actually like anyone—but she hates me less than most because I make sure if I absolutely have to bother her for something, I'm as prepared as possible.

Her husky voice still has a strong Quebecois inflection, probably because she doesn't talk with people often enough for it to smooth out. She tells me it will take a few days to copy over that much information. She's waiting for me to argue; most do.

I just thank her for the time and effort and leave her to the solitude of her office. I can access most of what I need from my computer, but getting all the files onto a drive will be a lot easier than searching for each case. Plus, this way I get to see Vic's and Eddison's case notes, not just mine. We work well as a team because we see different things; they may have noticed something on one of our cases that I didn't, something that may be relevant here.

I hope I'm giving myself a ridiculous amount of work for nothing, but I can't shake this niggling feeling that I might know why me. Why this killer gives the children my name and tells them they're safe now. That I'll keep them safe.

What if that's because I once told him or her the same thing?

That's what we tell them, the children we rescue. *You'll be okay. You're safe now.*

I think we're all dancing around the thought, not wanting to admit the possibility—or even the likelihood—that this killer has his or her origins somewhere in our case files. We're not ready to say it out loud yet, like the sound will give it too much meaning. It doesn't mean we get to keep hiding from it, though.

Late Friday morning, as Sterling and I sit on Eddison's desk to make him twitch while the three of us debate what to get for lunch, Vic comes through the bullpen, handing files and reports to various agents on his meandering way. "I'm supposed to tell you three to go home."

"What?"

"Independence Day is tomorrow. This is your observed day off for the federal holiday. You're not even supposed to be here."

"A lot of other people are here."

"Because they're either on the Monday rotation or they're as bad at the work-life separation as you three."

Ouch. Also a little hypocritical, given . . . well, everything.

Vic shakes his head. He's wearing a tie Priya, Inara, and Victoria-Bliss gave him last year for his birthday, stained-glass butterflies against a black background, and it is just as creepy as it sounds, but he wears it anyway because they gave it to him. "Go home. Do not take any paperwork with you. Relax. Do laundry. Catch a game."

We continue to blink at him.

"You do have fairly regular days off," he reminds us with a sigh. "You know how to survive them."

Sterling tilts her head to one side.

"No," he says sternly. "No sleepovers, no pub crawls. You each go to your own home, and you don't come to mine, because Jenny and I have the house to ourselves in what must be the first time in thirty years."

"Where's Marlene going to be?"

"My sister picked her up yesterday, and they're spending the weekend at the beach with the kids for the Fourth."

That's actually a little hard to imagine. Marlene is so active and healthy, but she always wears slacks and sweater sets with a single strand of pearls and her hair perfectly done. It just doesn't seem to fit with the beach.

"Now, all three of you, go home."

"We still haven't figured out lunch," Sterling notes as Vic walks away.

His voice floats back over his shoulder. "That's because you're all going home separately."

It's a weirdly normal afternoon. I go home and change out of my suit, clean the fridge of anything that's spoiled in the week and a half since I was last home to do it, hit the grocery store, pick up a box of cute cupcakes for Jason as thanks for the yard work because he loves the damn things but can't bring himself to order them on his own, and still have more day ahead of me than I'm used to. So I do laundry, and dust, and clean the bathroom, and when I put the second load of laundry in, I seriously consider following Sterling's example of sorting through my closet to pull things that don't fit or that I don't wear anymore.

I end up on the couch with a beer and a book of logic puzzles instead. I mostly enjoy shopping for clothes, but I loathe purposefully looking for things that don't fit.

It's evening, though still light outside, when my stomach reminds me that I never bothered to eat lunch. I head to the kitchen to poke around my groceries. I got eight million kinds of fresh vegetables because even I know our eating habits are atrocious (one of the many reasons Marlene and Jenny are so eager to feed us, I think), and cooking them up with teriyaki and chicken sounds downright delightful. Squash, zucchini, mushrooms, onion, broccoli, three colors of pepper, throw it all together with a little bit of oil, sesame, salt, and pepper on the small hibachi grill Eddison teased me for installing in the counter.

He teases still, but he will also eat anything and everything we make on it, so I think I win.

The chicken is more or less cubed and soaking in a bowl of marinade, and I'm just about through chopping the veggies, when there's a knock on the door. Before I fully register the sound, the knife spins in my hand to a position better suited for fights than food. It's an uncomfortable reflex to have in my own home. One by one, I force my fingers to open so I can put the knife down on the board. "One second," I call, reaching for the sink.

It's full daylight still; no one is going to drop off anything nefarious in broad daylight.

Drying my hands on the sides of my jeans, I head to the door and peer through the peephole, which is mostly obscured by vibrant red curls. "Siobhan?" I quickly unlock the door and open it. "You have keys."

She gives me a hesitant smile. "You throw the chain when you're home. And I wasn't sure . . ."

"Come in."

She looks uncertain in my home, in a way she hasn't done in a while. Not since the rocky bit last year, after I didn't want to move in together. "You're in the middle of something."

"Just making dinner. Have you eaten? I was planning on leftovers for the weekend, so I'm making a ton." I head back to the kitchen and the cutting board, letting her decide how comfortable she wants to get. She looks around like maybe it's changed since she was last inside (it hasn't) or maybe like she's looking for some visible sign that I've changed (I haven't).

The mothers told me a while ago that I needed to stop pretending. I'm starting to regret that I didn't listen to them sooner.

"The peppers are big, so you'll be able to pick them out," I tell her, ignoring the fact that she didn't actually answer me.

"Thanks." She puts her purse on the spindly table by the door and dithers a minute or two before perching on a padded stool on the other side of the counter. "No new children at your door?"

"Pretty sure Heather would have been wiggling with excitement at your desk if there had been."

"Probably, but you would have told me, right?"

"No. I told you first contact would be yours." I check the temperature of the grill and throw everything on, savoring the hiss and billow of rising steam.

"And you wouldn't break that to tell me that another child had been delivered to you."

"Well, the deliveries don't require signature confirmation, you see."

She sighs and folds her arms on the counter, a safe distance from the grill and anything that might spit out. "Are there any leads?"

"No."

"So they could just keep showing up."

"Yes."

"Mercedes."

"I don't know what you want me to say." I shrug, poking at the veggies with the metal spatula. "There aren't any leads, they could keep showing up, what else do you want me to say?"

"Can't they, I don't know, stake out your house or something?"

"It has to cross a threshold before the department can justify the expense."

"Since when has Vic been unwilling—"

"It's not an FBI case," I remind her.

"The police, then."

"The street is too quiet and open for a discreet stakeout, and they can't afford to take officers away from normal tasks for something with no routine or predictability."

"There's such a thing as simple answers, you know."

"You literally just scolded me for giving simple answers."

She drops her chin to her arms and doesn't respond.

I add some seasoning to the chicken and veggies, then open the fridge. "Something to drink?"

"Wine?"

"Sure." I pour us each a glass and go back to poking. I add the sauce to the veggies at almost the last minute, giving them enough time to cook through without getting soggy, and serve it up in equal parts between two plates and three plastic containers. Handing her a fork, I pull out one of my sets of chopsticks, the nice lacquered ones that Inara and Victoria-Bliss gave me for Christmas, and put them with my plate to one side so I can clean the grill while it's still hot.

We eat in silence, me leaning against the kitchen side of the counter, her seated opposite, and it might just be the loneliest meal of my adult life. When we're done, I rinse the plates and fork and put them in the dishwasher, then handwash the chopsticks and leave them on a small towel to dry. For some reason that makes me think of Sterling's coordinated kitchen, even though my dish towels are thin and ratty and pulled at random from the dollar bin at Target.

"I miss you," Siobhan whispers to my back.

"Is that why you're here?"

"Why do you think I'm here?"

The sound I make should be a laugh, but it really isn't. "Hand to God, Siobhan, I have no earthly idea. I'd love to think you're here because you want us to figure this out, but if I assume that, you'll tell me you still need space, so I'm not going to assume anything." I still have most of my glass of wine, but hers is empty, so I pour her another. "Have you decided what you want?"

She's silent for a long time. I don't try to prompt. I lean against the counter, sipping my wine, and let the silence settle between us. It's familiar, that silence, has always been there just under her steady stream of chatter. It's where substance is supposed to be. Finally she responds, her voice small and scared. "No."

"Then why are you here?"

"Because I miss you!" she cries.

"And we what, have a grand reunion and fall into bed, and everything's magically fixed? Because I thought we agreed, Hollywood is full of shit."

"How can someone so romantic be so utterly unromantic?"

"Situational response."

She flips me off, then looks at her middle finger and sighs. "I learn bad habits from watching you and Eddison together."

"That's okay, Sterling does, too."

"I don't know what you want me to say."

"That does seem to be our life right now." As long as we're not having a conversation, I go ahead and finish wiping down the kitchen, washing the cutting board and knife and setting them next to the chopsticks to dry.

"For one night, just . . . just one night, can we please keep . . ."

"Pretending?" I shake my head. "You don't really think that will help, do you?"

"But what could it hurt?"

So much. It could hurt so very, very much, but when she comes into the kitchen and kisses me urgently, the edge of the counter biting into my hip, I don't push her away. I've made worse mistakes before.

12

I'm pulled out of a half doze by the feeling of Siobhan's fingers tracing the words on my ribs, T. S. Eliot floating against a brightly colored nebula, *do i dare disturb the universe?* It hurt like a bitch to work over the bone like that, but when I got it, I didn't ever want to have to worry about it showing in the field. I love Eliot, in that slightly embarrassed and embarrassing high school kind of way, not for whole poems but for solitary lines and images, the way one line will jump out and cling to your thoughts even as stanzas and movements continue on. This line is more personal than that, the reminder that disturbing the universe can be a good thing; it's my skin, my blood that mixed with the ink to form the only scar I chose.

Her lips brush over the question mark, and I open my eyes to find the clock nestled between the teddy bear's legs on my nightstand. Eleven forty-five p.m. It's better than I've slept in a while.

"Your nose is twitching," Siobhan murmurs sleepily.

"My face itches."

She gives a soft laugh and pushes at my back. "Then go wash it."

I use the toilet and scrub my face clean of the makeup I left on longer than intended, pulling my hair back into a ponytail because sex hair doesn't do curls any favors. It's like hundreds of other nights; when I get back into the bedroom, Siobhan will be starfished across the bed, with only about a fifteen percent chance of her head being anywhere near the headboard, probably already asleep because she can drift off at will. But tonight isn't the same as all those other nights. I'm not good enough at pretending to convince myself that it is.

Groaning, I grab leggings and a camisole from the dresser, then head out into the living room to grab my phones. A few text messages have come in—Eddison, Sterling, Priya, and Inara—but nothing that needed an urgent response.

"Are you coming back?"

"Yes, just getting my phones."

She makes an indistinct sound at that, and when I head back into the bedroom to plug the phones into their chargers, she props herself up on her elbows to scowl. She's got one leg over the sheet, so it wraps over her other leg and half her ass and leaves the rest of her bare, her hair falling wild over pale skin. In better light, I'd be able to see the freckles that track over almost all of her. I love those freckles, love tracing constellations onto her skin with my mouth. "I think you're glued to those things," she mutters, and it takes me a second to realize she's talking about the phones.

My mind was definitely engaged with the freckles.

"Why are you dressed?"

"Because I went out into the living room."

"Why did you get dressed to move around your own house?"

"Because I always do?"

"Really?"

"Yes." Continuing the bedtime ritual, I kneel down to check that the gun safe under the bed is secure. I pull out all three guns—two personal, one Bureau issued—and make sure they're unloaded. My service weapon is still in hand when there's a knock on the door. Well, not a knock so much as pounding.

"Hello! Please be there! Help!"

"Get dressed but stay here," I snap at Siobhan, loading the gun and yanking my phones back off the cords.

"Mercedes!"

"Just do it!" Closing the bedroom door behind me, I head to the front door, with its locks and chain and peephole. There's a girl out there, face bloodied and panicked, but I can't see any sign of a car or another person. "My name is Mercedes," I call through the door, and I can hear the girl take in a shuddering gasp. "I'm going to open the door, okay? But I need you to stay where you are. Can you do that?"

"I can . . . I can do that. I can do that."

"Okay. You'll hear the locks disengage, okay? I'm not leaving." I shove the phones into the band of my leggings and throw the locks one-handed. When the door opens, she lurches forward, then restrains herself, wringing her hands in front of her.

She's early teens, not much older than Sarah, I think, with glasses sitting crookedly on her nose. There's blood on her face and both arms, and running down the front of her long tank top, which is the only thing she has on over underwear. She's got bruises, too, down her arms and across the visible parts of her chest. There's what looks to be a fresh cigarette burn on her collarbone.

There are no cars besides mine and Siobhan's in the drive or parked at the curb, no sign of one idling or driving away, no trace of another person around the house. "Sweetheart, how did you get here?"

"A lady," she says with a gulp.

"Is she still here?"

"N-n-no. We turned around and she told me to get out and walk back here from down the street. I heard her drive away."

Cógeme. Wait. The camera on the mailbox should have gotten something. Please let it have gotten something. "Okay, sweetheart. That's okay." I engage the safety and gingerly tuck the gun into the back of my leggings, and I will never understand people who think that's a great place to keep a firearm. Reaching out slowly, making sure she can see the movement, I touch her hand. "Why don't you sit down, *mija*? What's your name?"

"Emilia," she sniffles. "Emilia Anders."

"Emilia, are you hurt?"

She nods slowly. "My head."

"Can I look?"

Her nod comes even more reluctantly this time, but it comes. I help her onto the porch swing, where the light is best, and carefully, so gently, follow the blood trail up her face to her temple. Just past her hairline, a gash bleeds sluggishly over a swelling, purpling goose egg. "How old are you, Emilia?" I ask to keep her talking.

"Almost fourteen."

"Almost? When is your birthday?"

"Not until September," she admits, her hands curling into fists on her thighs. "But it sounds better than thirteen."

"I remember those days. I'm going to straighten your glasses, okay? And bring them down your nose a little so I can see your eyes better."

"Okay."

The earpieces are still a little crooked after I do my best—probably the screws need adjusting by a professional—but it's a little better, and clear enough to see her pupils are wide but not blown. Hit hard enough to daze and partially subdue, but probably not hard enough to cause a concussion. "Emilia, what happened, sweetheart?"

She tells a story that's already achingly familiar, but unlike the others—Ronnie, broken and submissive, and Sarah, protecting her siblings—Emilia fought the woman who woke her up and dragged her to her parents' room. "She called me ungrateful," she whispers, watching me text the information to Holmes and Eddison. I angle the phone so she can see the screen. Holmes responds while I'm typing Eddison, telling me she's on her way with an ambulance, and to keep talking to Emilia rather than call 911.

I can do that.

"Why did she think that?"

"She said . . . she said she was helping me. She was going to make me safe. She told me to stop fighting but I didn't. She hit me. She killed my parents, and I had to watch." Her breaths are coming faster, short and choppy, her shoulders quivering. I scoot to one side and press gently against her back to have her bend forward.

"Head between your knees, *mija*, or as close as you can get. Just breathe." I keep a hand on her back, just there, not rubbing, because I can see more bruises disappearing under the edge of her shirt and don't want to hurt her any more. "Just keep breathing." I can feel her muscles quivering under my hand, dry heaves she swallows back with whimpers. "You're safe here, Emilia, I promise."

I text Siobhan to tell her to stay inside. If she comes out, it will be to head straight to her car and leave, and ignoring whatever that will cost me personally, I really don't want Holmes to have to track her down to interview her. That will be traumatic on a number of fronts.

"I was safe at home," Emilia retorts, voice still thready and thin.

My pinky presses into the green-tinged edge of the bruise over her shoulder blade, and she winces.

"Parents are allowed to discipline their child," she recites in a mumble.

"They're not allowed to hurt them."

"So we just kill them? That's okay?"

"No. Emilia, no, that is not okay. We are going to catch this person."

"My mom . . ." She takes in a great, shuddering breath, and immediately loses half of it to an aching keen. "Mom told me not to fight, to do whatever I had to do to stay safe," she weeps, and I wrap my arms around her in a secure hold to keep her from pitching off the swing. "The lady moved on to my dad, and I was just standing there, like an *idiot*, holding my mom's hand as she died. My mom. I didn't do anything."

"You *couldn't* do anything," I tell her softly. "Emilia, that woman had a gun, and she'd already hit you. If you'd fought any harder, she probably would have killed you."

"But she said she was saving me."

I bite my lip, trying to sort through what I could tell a shocked, grieving child. "Emilia, when someone has a mission like hers, something they *need* to do, someone disrupting that can be in grave danger. She needs to save you, but if you fight too hard, if you make her think she *can't* save you . . . Sweetheart, we've seen that kind of thing before. She would have killed you, or at the very least hurt you very badly. You listened to your mom, and that probably saved your life. She must have loved you so much."

"She's my mom. She's my mom. She's my mom." Her words trail off into incoherent sobs and I just hold her, letting the motion of the swing rock her gently.

It's telling, though, even in her shock, that she hasn't really mentioned her father.

Eddison pulls up with Sterling in the passenger seat, followed by Holmes and the ambulance and the other police car. A few minutes later, Vic drives up as well, and the cul-de-sac is once again full of cars. As I introduce Emilia to Detective Holmes, I can feel Eddison's hands at my hips.

"Easy, *hermana*," he murmurs, and pulls the gun from my waistband, *gracias a Dios*. He slides a hand along for my other phone, as well, as Sterling picks up the work cell from the board by my knee.

"Siobhan is in the bedroom," I tell Vic, and from the corner of my eye I can see Eddison's eyebrows lift in surprise. I shake my head. Vic nods and heads into the house. He's absolutely the best choice for it; there's something about him that Siobhan's a little in awe of, and if there's any chance of her not going through the fucking roof, it's with Vic breaking the news.

As soon as Emilia settles into Holmes's questions and the attention of the paramedic, I ease away from her to the other end of the porch, perching on the railing. Eddison and Sterling follow.

"We'll make sure Siobhan gets home okay," Sterling says, hopping up beside me.

"Thanks."

We sit in silence as Holmes finishes with this round of questions and Emilia gets walked to the ambulance, wrapped in a shiny silver blanket.

"No teddy bear," Sterling notes.

"She dropped it in the grass a few houses down," Holmes says, joining our little knot. "Markey's getting it bagged."

I twist around on the rail, and sure enough, one of the uniforms is picking up a familiar-looking white bear. I sigh and turn back. "Was she able to add anything?"

"A little. She said when she was fighting, the killer got upset and started sounding more Southern."

We digest that for a minute before Sterling clears her throat. "Any particular kind of Southern?"

"No. But she said it was only when the woman got upset. Other than that she sounded like she didn't come from anywhere." Putting away her notebook, Holmes looks up and does a full double take. "Jesus, Ramirez, who'd you piss off?"

I lift one hand to trace the scars down my cheek, bare of makeup. "It was a long time ago."

"Looks too wide for a knife."

"Broken bottle."

"Jesus," she says again. She rubs at her eyes, bits of dried blood from when she'd touched Emilia's hands flaking off. "Mignone just got to the house. He says even at a glance, her story holds up. Signs of struggle in the hallways, and in both rooms."

"There've been complaints about her dad?"

"Did she say that?"

"Not in so many words."

"You said Agent Ryan is inside?"

"Yes. We heard the knock on the door and Emilia's cry for help, and I told her to stay put while I came out here."

"All right, I'll go talk to her inside then, if that's okay. Figure she'll be calmer there?"

"Where she can't see the blood streaks? Yes."

"Does the sleepover mean you two worked it out?" Eddison asks after Holmes enters the house.

"No. And given what came after . . ."

Sterling bumps our knees together.

It doesn't feel like a grand fight rearing up, the desperate stand to save a relationship. She's going to leave and I think . . . I think I'm okay with that. Three years and this is how a relationship dies, but can anyone really fault that? She can't handle this and I can't keep pretending, and we'll probably both be better off.

The hurt will come later, the cuts too sharp for the pain to register straight off.

Siobhan exits the house between Vic and Holmes, her face red and patchy from crying; a plastic grocery bag hangs from two fingers, carrying anything she'd left here. She glances at me once, flinches, and looks resolutely at her car. Sterling slides off the rail and takes the keys from Siobhan's other hand, gently urging her down the steps and toward her car. Vic nods at us and aims for his own car. He'll follow them to Fairfax and give Sterling a ride back, just to make sure Siobhan arrives safely. I hope, when the shock wears off, that she's grateful for it.

Happy Independence Day.

"We're not any closer," admits Holmes, leaning against the wall and looking exhausted. "Six people dead, and we really don't have a clue."

"Maybe we'll get lucky and find a link in the third CPS file."

"Do you think we'd be able to partner with the FBI on this going forward?"

"Probably, given that there's really no reason to expect she'll stop," Eddison answers. "It'll have to be with a different team."

"Conflict of interest."

He nods.

The silence resumes, and I find myself looking at the splotches of rusty brown where blood has dried on the porch. By the end of this I'll probably have to repaint, and what a stupid thing to be thinking of, but we just washed it Sunday.

Sunday. "Less time between kills, this round," I note. "Nine days between the first two, only five between the next."

"How do we know if that's significant?"

"If there's less time before the next," Eddison replies, not intending to be a dick but kind of coming off that way.

Holmes's face pinches, but she doesn't retort. Instead, she pulls her notebook back out and flips to a fresh page. "All right, Ramirez. Start with the morning. Was today a normal day?"

With Eddison leaning into my side, a warm press of support, I start. We used to have to role-play this stuff at the academy, practicing interview techniques on other trainees, and I think almost all of us hated it. You have to be detailed without being irrelevant, you have to be approachable without being cold or sentimental, you have to, you have to, you have to.

I fire up my laptop so we can sift through the security-camera footage leading up to Emilia knocking on my door. I recognize the car of one of the quiet college students sharing a house on the curve of the cul-de-sac, then the young parents three doors down, followed by the departure of their regular babysitter. Just a few minutes before the knock, an unfamiliar car drives slowly by, pausing near the end of my driveway, and continues on. A minute later, it's heading out.

Not long after that, the porch camera picks up Emilia stumbling across the lawn.

"Midsize SUV," Holmes mutters.

Even with the streetlights, it's impossible to discern the color beyond "dark." Black, maybe, or navy or forest, maybe a dark grey. Burgundy has a kind of gleam even in poor light, so that's discounted, and purple does the same thing, as rare as that is in cars.

"No plates," sighs Eddison. "She must have taken them off. There's not enough for an APB."

In the first frames, I can see Emilia slumped in a daze against the back passenger window. The driver is harder to make out, beyond the light hitting white clothing in a way that makes it seem to glow. In the opposite direction, there's a decent shot of the disturbing, featureless white mask, spattered with blood, surrounded by . . . huh. I zoom in to be sure.

"She's either got multiple wigs or one really good wig," I point out. "It's curled. Sarah said the angel's hair was straight."

"What about Ronnie?"

"Braid. Synthetic wigs usually don't restyle all that well. Human hair wigs can be pretty pricy."

"Are you sure it's a wig, then? Could it just be her hair?"

"See how the bangs start below that bulge of hair?" I point to the screen, sweeping my finger under the spot in question. "These masks are usually made of porcelain, sometimes plaster. They're thick. The bulge is from pulling the front of the wig over the edge of the mask. It's definitely a wig."

"Email me that footage," Holmes says. "I'll get the techs started on identifying the make and model of the car. We'll keep the shot of her to pass around."

"Or him," Eddison points out. "We haven't actually ruled that out."

Holmes glares at him, but nods. It makes sense—behind the wig and the mask, it could be a man—but no detective relishes having the suspect pool expanded. "You two are free to go."

I pack a fresh bag while Eddison loads the leftovers and most of my brand new groceries into a cooler, because there's no sense in leaving them to rot, and we head out in his car. Holmes and one of the uniformed officers remain there to tape off my house yet again. I'm so fucking tired, and my home feels less like home every time I'm in it, and I just . . .

What happened to this woman? Where did our paths cross, and why is she so fixated on me?

Once upon a time, there was a little girl who was scared of the color red.

There was just so much of it.

She remembered the blood on her mama's car windows, how dark it looked in the moonlight but how brilliant a red it was in the officers' flashlights. Her mama escaped that night, got away from Daddy forever, and didn't even try to take her little girl with her.

She knew the red on her body, blood from bites, and the pink from slaps, and the darker red of places that would become bruises. She knew the red of torn skin. It hurt for days after to pee.

Then there was a new red there, thicker, heavier, and Daddy laughed and laughed when he saw it. You're a woman now, baby girl. My beautiful woman.

One of his friends was a doctor, the special lady kind, Daddy said, and took her to his office for an exam. The doctor nearly cried when he got to touch her there for the first time. Daddy never let his friends touch her. After that, there was a pill every day. One of Daddy's friends laughed at the hair that started growing between her legs, said all the hungriest bitches should be redheads.

Daddy looked thoughtful at that.

She hated when Daddy looked thoughtful.

It wasn't long before he came home with two boxes of hair dye. They weren't even the same color; one was a fire engine kind of red, the other more orange, and he didn't mix them together right and he missed spots, but he laughed and called her beautiful anyway, and he took away the hair between her legs and under her arms.

That night, when his friends came to the basement for their party, Daddy showed off the dye job. Gentlemen, *he said,* if the price is right . . .

Amidst all the clamor, one of them had nearly $300 in his wallet, and he gave it all to her Daddy. Daddy readied his favorite camera.

They'd never been allowed to even touch her before.

They did love a redhead.

13

We're over hours for the pay cycle and that, as Vic likes to remind us, is a thing the Bureau cares about when you're working a desk. None of us are allowed to go in on Monday, which we spend sprawled over each other on Eddison's couch in front of the TV. I don't hear from Siobhan at all, and when I get into the office Tuesday morning, there's a box on my desk with the handful of things I kept at her apartment. Eddison peers over my shoulder and winces.

"I guess that's that."

"Guess so."

"*Olvídate de las hermanastras, la próxima vez encontraremos a la Cenicienta,*" he says, and there are so many things wrong with that I can't even try to list them out.

We're still standing there, just looking at the box, when Vic walks up. He identifies it right away and grimaces in sympathy. "I'm about to make your morning worse," he admits. "Agent Dern needs to see you. Then Simpkins's team needs to talk to you."

"They're paired with Holmes and Manassas PD?"

"Yes. They have all of Holmes's notes, but—"

"But they want to conduct their own interviews where possible," I finish for him, and he nods. Grabbing the box, I drop it to the floor and kick it under the desk, out of sight and hopefully, at least for a little while, out of mind. "Is Simpkins going to be okay for this?"

"What do you mean?"

"Last time Eddison and I worked with her, she was pissy as hell, and Cass said something happened on their case last week in Idaho."

"I don't know about Idaho, but she's a good agent, good enough not to let her disapproval of how I ran the team interfere with the case."

Eddison snorts, but doesn't offer further comment. Simpkins has never tried to pretend she approves of Vic's style, but the last time we were loaned to her, she rode our asses like we were baby agents who'd slept through the academy. It was distinctly unpleasant, and uncalled for.

Vic walks me to Internal Affairs and Agent Dern's office, which isn't at all surprising, and then follows me inside, which kind of is. He just shrugs when I give him a sideways glance. "Now what kind of friend would I be if I left you to face the Dragonmother alone?"

Agent Dern looks up from her computer with a wry smile. "I thought it was generally agreed not to use that name to my face. Agent Ramirez, please, have a seat."

The Dragonmother of Internal Affairs, Agent Samantha Dern has been in the Bureau for almost fifty years. Her face is creased and lined, and her light makeup makes no effort to hide it, just as the silver-white hair cropped in a flattering, kind of fluffy bob has no dye to mask it. A pair of plastic-framed reading glasses, the frames almost the same rose color of her silk blouse, perch on her nose, connected to a thin chain draped around her neck. She looks soft and kindly, like someone's favorite grandmother, but she's been known to make grown men cry in under ten minutes.

"Agent Ramirez, where would you like to begin? With Emilia Anders, or with Agent Ryan's call to HR?"

"What, already?" I blurt, and clap a hand over my mouth. Hopefully the makeup covers just how badly my face is burning at the moment.

Agent Dern pulls off her reading glasses, slowly spinning one of the earpieces between her fingers. "Well," she says eventually, her face caught somewhere between sympathy and amusement. "At least that's not how you found out things were over, I suppose."

"Sorry. I was just . . . surprised, I guess. It took me four months to convince her we really had to tell HR we were dating, and even after we did, she was jumpy about letting colleagues find out about us."

"Understanding that in this instance, you have every right to tell me to butt the hell out: Are you doing all right?"

"I am, actually." I smile at her, feeling the week's exhaustion tugging at the muscles. "It sucks, but I can't say I didn't see it coming."

"Secret admirers can be difficult to deal with, and they're rarely as charming as movies make them out to be."

"Emilia is the first kid the killer has injured. Now that she's done it, though, I worry about whether or not she'll think it's easier to subdue the kids with violence first."

"Agent Simpkins will want to hear that concern; we've got some different details to go over at the moment. Have you worked with Dru Simpkins before?"

"Yes, ma'am. Eddison and I were last assigned to her on the child-swapping-ring case ten months ago."

"That's right. That's when this idiot was in the hospital."

"I was doing my job, Sam," Vic says mildly.

Agent Dern simply shrugs. "You stepped in front of a bullet meant for someone who raped and murdered eight children."

"And whether or not he merits execution is for the court to decide, not the grieving father of a victim. We don't get to uphold just the laws we like."

It has the sound of a conversation that's happened many times, the details changing and the tone remaining the same. Agent Dern waves off the distinction with a careless hand. "Back to the first point: Agent Ryan. You don't work in the same department, so there won't be any need to shuffle things around, but we would ask that you be . . . discreet . . . when people ask what happened."

"I'm not interested in dragging her through the mud, ma'am," I say respectfully. "Things didn't work out. That's sad, but it's not anything like a reason to sully her name through the Bureau."

"I appreciate that, and I'd expect no less from one of Vic's protégées, but HR asked me to mention it. Now for the part you're not going to like."

Vic shifts uneasily in his chair.

"We have to take you off active duty," says Agent Dern, straightforward in a way I'll probably be grateful for later.

"Sam!"

"It's not my call, Vic, not really." She regards me frankly, not making apology or excuses. "You know how lawyers can be. Any of the cases currently in the works—any case you touch while this is happening—could blow up at court. It's stupid, I know. If anything, you're being targeted by the killer because you excel at your job, not for any nefarious purpose, but the Bureau can't afford any perception that a clever lawyer could exploit to imply complicity."

"So I'm . . ." I shake my head, trying to process this. "So I'm suspended?"

"No. But it does mean you need to be hands off on cases. Your team has been on desk rotation anyway, and I suspect Agents Eddison and Sterling will revolt if anyone tries to send them off without you, so you'll all be kept to Quantico until this is resolved. They'll be able to work on consults."

"But I can't even do that."

"No. You're going to have two distinct assignments, Agent Ramirez." She points to the corner of her desk nearest me, where three enormous binders stuffed with paper rest. "First assignment: your section chief feels, and I agree, that there needs to be training in place for new agents when they're assigned to Crimes Against Children. Something specific to your division, intended to help agents adjust to one of the most difficult sections in the Bureau. Suggestions for content have been solicited from section and unit chiefs, Bureau psychologists, and agents. You might remember the questionnaire that went out a few months ago."

I remember Sterling walking up behind Eddison and startling him so badly he spilled his coffee all over our questionnaires. I don't remember them being replaced and turned in.

"We want you to write it."

"Me?"

"You've been in the CAC division for ten years," she reminds me. "And then there's this." She holds up a much smaller binder with Sharpie calligraphy across the front: *A NAT's Guide to Life.*

"Oh, Mother of God." I can feel the blush burning down my neck and ears.

Vic laughs and reaches out to nudge my shoulder. "What, didn't know it was still floating around?"

"Why would anyone still have that after ten years?"

"Because they reproduce it and pass it around to all the new agent trainees in their first week," Agent Dern informs me dryly. "It's informative, personable, and humorous, and it helps settle the NATs wonderfully. Realistically, Agent Ramirez, there is very little the Bureau will ever be able to do to prevent the burnout that happens so quickly in CAC. What we can do, however, is increase our efforts to make sure those who start working there are better prepared for what they'll face. And if that means, after reading such a guide, that they don't feel themselves suited for the division, we can transfer them out early."

"I wrote that very drunk," I inform her bluntly. "A good third of us spent the weekend before graduation getting roaring drunk together, and that was the result. That entire thing was born in truly terrible tequila."

"Written drunk, but edited sober," she points out. "And ten years of trainee agents have been using it as their bible. This isn't just a throwaway assignment; we've had you in mind from the beginning.

We weren't planning on asking you until later in the year, but there's no reason not to go ahead and ask it now."

"You said there were two assignments."

"Go back through all the cases you've worked where you've had direct contact with the children. Not the consults, not cases where you were primarily at the precinct or working with adults. Look through your notes, anything you wrote about the children. Not just the victims. Any child. Somewhere in there may be the key to finding this murderer. This is personal for her; *you* are personal. If we're very lucky, somewhere in the past ten years, one of your kids is going to ring a bell. Don't look at the case details, don't look at the things that seem similar at a stretch. Look at the children, Agent Ramirez. That's your second assignment."

"That's . . . actually already in progress, ma'am."

Vic gives me a startled look that quickly shifts to a proud smile. I am thirty-two years old but damned if I don't get all warm and fuzzy every time he shows he's proud of me.

"Agent Alceste is getting the files together on a drive so I can see everyone's notes, not just mine. I should receive them soon."

"You braved Alceste?" he asks, the smile turning impish.

"I've always wondered why no one refers to her as the Dragonmother of the Archives," Agent Dern agrees.

Because dragons sometimes interact enough for a game of riddles and she is the least motherly human I've ever met, but I'm not about to say that out loud. Instead, I look at the beginnings of my other assignment, all the notes and suggestions from agents and leadership on what should be included in a survival guide. Training manual. The binders on the corner of the desk are a mess. Tabs and Post-its stick out in haphazard places, and there are pages that are just shoved in, either because there wasn't any more room in the rings or because people were just being lazy. Even odds, really. It's a hell of a lot of work, and I don't know that it'll do even half of what the bosses are hoping. No matter how prepared you are intellectually, working in CAC is an anvil chorus; the hammers always hit hard.

"Eddison is going to chafe at being chained to his desk for even longer," I observe eventually.

"Probably," agrees Vic. "But even if we gave him the option of fieldwork, he isn't going to leave you behind."

"Sterling is a blue-eyed ball of mischief. If there aren't enough consults and she gets bored . . ."

"Personally, I'm hoping she'll provoke Agent Eddison into finally trying to bell her," Agent Dern replies placidly. "It should be quite entertaining to watch."

"You know," I say before I can think better of it, "for someone called the Dragonmother, there's been remarkably little flaming."

She smiles deeply, soft lines creasing around her eyes and mouth. "I joined the Bureau at a time when females were largely considered second-class agents," she explains. "Then, of course, I was put into Internal Affairs, which meant I was supposed to be the nagging, critical, never-lets-you-have-any-fun wife. I was the enemy. It was necessary to become a bit of a dragon, simply to ensure that no one looked at me and assumed they could get away with something. It became something of a habit, even after the reputation meant I didn't have to roar as much. Good agents, Ramirez, never have to fear Internal Affairs. We're here to maintain accountability and a degree of transparency, yes, but we're also here to support our agents. You're not here because you've done something wrong. I don't need to bite or roar or flame or any such thing."

It makes sense, now, that she and Vic are old friends. I don't think they came through the academy together—she's probably got a decade on him, at least—but they likely came through some of the same people. It's the way they believe in people, the way they work toward not just what the Bureau is, but what it should be, and insist on holding others to a higher standard, not to see us fail but to see us improve and achieve.

"Do you accept the assignments, Agent Ramirez?" she asks gently.

Aware of Vic's eyes on me, I nod. "Yes, ma'am. Thank you."

"Excellent. I'll have someone deliver the binders to your desk along with an official memo about what's desired. Vic, you'll take her on to Simpkins?"

"Of course." He stands and offers me a hand up, and it's a little silly to make someone else trek all the way over when I can just carry the binders myself, but he slaps my hand away. "Along with a memo, Mercedes. It's not in there yet."

A memo can be emailed.

"Stop that," he chides, and it takes a second to figure out if I said that bit out loud or if ten years have taught him to read my face entirely too well. From Agent Dern's cocked eyebrow, I'm going to guess the latter.

I murmur a goodbye to Agent Dern, get a highly amused farewell in turn, and follow Vic out the door.

"Doing okay?" he asks quietly.

"I get it," I sigh. "I don't like it, but I get it, even if I think the handbook is a bad idea. I just . . ."

He drapes an arm around my shoulders and pulls me into a sideways hug, then keeps it there as we walk. It draws a few looks from people as we pass. He ignores them. "A lot has landed on your doorstep, literally, and there's no one way to feel about it. This woman has invaded your home. I know you, Mercedes. I know what that means to you."

I was assigned to Vic and Eddison straight out of the academy, but Vic has known me a lot longer. Sometimes, inexplicably, I forget that. And then, like now, I remember.

"How do I sleep there, knowing another child might be walking up the steps?" I whisper. "How do I stay anywhere else, knowing another child might have to sit there in blood and fear, and wait?"

"I don't have an answer for you."

"I'd call bullshit if you did."

He smiles and squeezes my shoulder, using the motion to give me a small shove into the open elevator. "You're going to get through this, Mercedes, and we're going to be right beside you to make sure of that."

"What happens . . ."

Giving me a curious look, he waits for the doors to close, for that sinking feeling that says the car is in motion, then hits the emergency stop. "What happens when?"

I pace the small space from wall to wall, gathering the worries into words I hope make sense. "What happens when she checks on the kids?"

"What do you mean?"

"We're operating under the theory that she's going after these parents because they're hurting the kids. She brings the kids to me to keep them safe."

"Right . . ."

"So what happens when she checks on Sarah, Ashley, and Sammy and finds out that they're having trouble finding a home that will take all three of them? Ronnie's doing fairly well at his grandmother's, but Emilia's only family seems to be either in prison or living out of the country. What kind of home is she going to get put in? My first few foster homes . . . not all of them were terrible, but some of them were. What happens to Emilia if she's put in a bad home? And at what point does this killer decide that she isn't bringing me kids to protect just for me to put them back into a flawed system?"

"You think she could come after you."

"I think we have to acknowledge it as a possibility. We're not going to understand her framework or compulsions until we find her, not really. So what happens when she gets more pissed at the system than at the parents?"

"She hasn't given any indication of that," he says after a moment. "If it was the system as a whole she was worried about, wouldn't we see foster parents in the mix?"

"We might yet. There's only been three. Realistically, she's just getting started."

"But she didn't start with them. What do you think the difference is?"

He's not asking Agent Ramirez; he's asking Mercedes.

"Fosters are strangers; you never know what you're going to get. Your parents are the two people in the whole world who aren't supposed to hurt you. The wounds are deeper, in a way."

He thinks his way through that, his weathered face mobile with the emotions that latch onto shreds of ideas or theories. Eventually he leans against the side wall and opens his arms, and I accept the hug gratefully, conscious of the still-tender scar over his heart. "I don't know how to rescue you from this," he admits softly.

I shake my head. "We do our jobs. We trust Holmes and Simpkins to do theirs. I'm not sure there is a rescue."

We stand like that until someone from the next floor yells to let the fucking elevator move already, and he leans over to flick the car back into motion. Because he's Vic, and he's sometimes a little petty, he overrides the stop to skip the next floor.

It makes me smile, even if it probably shouldn't.

14

Vic insists on all of us joining the family for dinner, and I both get it and am grateful for it, and with all three of his daughters home for the evening for once, the house is full of noise and laughter. No one mentions the case, or how no one can decide if I should go home or not. Holly and Brittany, the older two girls, are full of stories from college, their classes and campus life and competitions. Both are on athletics scholarships, Holly for cross-country and Brittany for swimming. Janey is still in high school, but she regales us with tales from rehearsals for her summer shows, and Vic is so proud of all three of them he can hardly see straight.

As agents, we're trained to recognize the elephant in the room, to approach it somehow, but tonight it is merrily ignored.

I'm back at Eddison's for the nights, though Sterling mentioned kidnapping me next week in some sort of bizarre joint-custody arrangement. While I get changed into T-shirt and boxers—and it's even my "Female Body Inspector" running shirt, just to make him laugh—Eddison fiddles with his laptop and the cables until he's got Skype up on his massive television, Inara and Priya sprawled across the screen.

"Victoria-Bliss is at work," Inara offers instead of hello.

"Looks like you two are, as well," I reply, accepting the bottle of beer Eddison hands me and sinking down onto the couch.

They both shrug, but they also both look a little proud. "The literary agent I'm interning with has me reading queries and submissions," Inara says. "She makes all the decisions, of course, but she wants to know my opinion on them, and then shares her process. It's interesting."

Priya fans a stack of photos in such a way that we can only see corners, nothing of the subjects of the pictures. "Looking at layouts."

"School project or your personal project?" Eddison asks.

"Personal."

"That we still don't get to see?"

"You'll see it eventually." Priya grins at him, sharp and familiar, and I can actually see Eddison debating whether or not he really wants to know. Inara sees it, too, and buries her face in the quilt to stifle her laughter. "So what's up? There's not a good game on, and just about anything else could be done through text or phone call. You guys okay?"

"Wanted to update you guys on what's happening down here," Eddison says, and both girls nod, blink, and focus on me.

Our team doesn't adopt many kids the way we did these two and Victoria-Bliss, but I'm always glad we've got them. *Almost* always glad we've got them—being the sole focus of their considerable attention and powers of observation is a little like settling into the confessional at church.

Despite it being mostly my story, Eddison is the one who tells them about the newest deliveries—that they happened, anyway, without sharing details—and about Siobhan. Inara nods along absently, but Priya's eyes narrow when Eddison gets to the breakup. Then again, Priya never actually liked Siobhan. Didn't care about her one way or the other as a human being, just didn't like that we were dating. Once, and only once, she told me why: she didn't like that I seemed only half myself with Siobhan. And in the beauty of hindsight, she was absolutely right.

But she's also the first one to ask, "Are you okay?"

"For now," I tell her. "I guess I'm still waiting for it all to weigh in."

"But you're going to be okay?"

"Yes."

She starts to say something, then shakes her head. "It's okay if you're not, you know. For a while."

Inara snorts along with Eddison, and it's been a long time since either of them have looked horrified to agree with each other. How many times have we told Priya—and Inara, for that matter—that it's okay not to be okay?

"Speaking of not okay," Inara starts with a frown, "have you heard from Ravenna since she visited you? She still isn't answering her phone, and hasn't responded to the email."

"She hasn't called, no. Is there a specific reason you're more worried than usual?"

Inara blushes, honest-to-God blushes, and looks down at the quilt. Somehow, despite everything, she didn't lose the ability to care for people, but she can still get embarrassed by someone pointing it out. Much like Eddison, in fact. "If you were going to rank the surviving Butterflies by most likely to snap and murder someone, Victoria-Bliss is, no contest, number one, and I'm a close second."

Eddison and Priya both nod.

"Ravenna is an easy third."

I set my beer on the coffee table with a thunk. "Really? She said she's been doing better, at least until that last fight."

"Yes and no. Separating Ravenna and Patrice-the-senator's-daughter, or just figuring out how they exist together, isn't going to happen around her mother or the constant publicity."

"Mum offered her the guest room," Priya adds. "Paris might give her enough distance to start truly working through it, and she'd have a safe place to stay with people who care about her, and a steady link to Inara."

Inara's blush, which had been fading, returns full force, as it always does when someone reminds her that she's basically the Butterfly housemother, even still.

"I'll let you know if she contacts me," I promise.

We catch up for a bit, telling the stories that don't translate well across texts. A little after midnight, my personal phone rings.

I don't recognize the number.

At almost any other time, I'd let it go to voice mail, but this month has seen a rather spectacular set of circumstances, hasn't it? Eddison goes very still beside me, and the girls follow suit, their faces blurred a bit by the crappy webcam and the giant screen.

On the third ring, I accept the call. "Ramirez."

"Ramirez, this is Dru Simpkins."

Shit.

I thumb it over to speakerphone. "Simpkins, I've got Eddison here with me. What's up?"

There's no comment on Eddison and I being together at midnight. Half the Bureau thinks we're fucking, the other half thinks we haven't realized yet how much we should be fucking.

"Just got a call from Detective Holmes," the woman answers. "A seven-year-old boy named Mason Jeffers was dropped off outside the emergency room entrance of Prince William Hospital. He was covered in blood, none of it seems to be his. He hasn't spoken, but he's got a note safety pinned to his teddy bear that gives his name, age, and address, and says to ask for you."

"And his parents?"

"Holmes wants you out at the boy's house. I'll allow it this time."

This time. Simpkins is already on a roll. "What's the address?"

Eddison scrambles for a pen, finds a Sharpie, and writes the address out on his forearm for lack of accessible paper. "We'll be there in twenty," he promises, and Simpkins acknowledges before hanging up.

Inara and Priya watch us gravely as we lever up from the leather couch. "Be safe," Priya charges us. "Let us know what you can."

"Do we need to cancel our trip down this weekend?" asks Inara.

"Don't cancel the trip," Eddison says. "Marlene stocked the freezers. You are not allowed to leave us with that many pastries."

"Well . . . we board the train at six o'clock Thursday afternoon, so if things change, that's the point of no return."

Eddison shakes his head, reaching for the laptop to shut it down. "Only you think six o'clock is afternoon."

"You think six o'clock is morning," she retorts.

"It *is* morning."

"Not if you haven't gone to bed yet."

"Good night, girls."

"Good night, Charlie," they chorus, and grin at his pained look. Just before the screen goes dark, I can see the worried looks they flash to me.

"I'll call Sterling while I'm changing," I tell Eddison. "You'll call Vic?"

"*Sí.* Not that either of them can do anything, but we'll keep them updated."

Sterling takes the news calmly, telling me to keep her informed through the morning, and she'll take care of the first couple of coffee runs. Sterling is an angel. I come back out in jeans and a windbreaker, with a different T-shirt on underneath, because I just cannot make myself put on a suit after midnight. I have better clothes at the office if we don't get to come back, and besides, I'm desk bound anyway. If I can't use that excuse to bend the dress code, what's the point?

The Jeffers house is all the way on the west side of town, what should be a thirty-minute drive with cooperating traffic lights. The lights are not cooperating, but neither is Eddison: we get there in eighteen minutes. After signing in with the uniform at the door, we head inside and nearly run into Agent Simpkins.

Dru Simpkins is a well-respected agent in her midforties, with a mane of coarse, dark blonde hair that never looks quite tame. She guest lectures at the academy about the impact of psychology on children's writing, specifically looking at how to pick up cues and subtext in diaries or writing assignments, and leads that portion of the CAC-specific training. The BAU wanted her pretty badly for one of their profiling teams, but she's resolutely remained in Crimes Against Children. She was the one to correctly identify that I wrote the NAT's survival guide. Apparently I have "a voice."

"Other three cases, it's always been the father who got the worst of it, right?"

She also doesn't believe in small talk.

"Yes," I reply. "Father was subdued with gunshots, mother was killed, father was finished off. Not the case here?"

"Doesn't seem like it. Come take a look."

We grab booties in the hallway and slip them on over our sneakers before following her down the hall to the master bedroom. The medical examiner gives us a two-fingered wave as she keeps the thermometer steady in Mr. Jeffers's liver. He has several stab wounds across his torso, but not nearly to the extent of the other male victims.

Mrs. Jeffers, however, *Jesucristo*. Her face is destroyed, and the carnage continues downward. Her groin is a solid cluster of wounds, and the other stab wounds littering her stomach stretch up into slices at and around her breasts. Her husband's death was pretty straightforward, but this woman suffered. And, judging from the negative space on her side of the bed, her son was forced to stand there and watch.

"You said Mason wasn't speaking?" I ask.

Detective Mignone, standing by the father's side of the bed, looks up and nods. "Neighbor says she doesn't think he's spoken in years."

"So it's not trauma based."

"Or it's not based on this trauma," Simpkins notes. She pulls one of the framed pictures off the wall and holds it out to me, then realizes I don't have gloves and keeps it steady so I can see it. There's blood spattered on the glass. Not a lot, not at this distance, but some. It's not enough to obscure the way the family is posed in the portrait, Mrs.

Jeffers's hand wrapped around her son's arm as he tries to pull away toward his father.

"Sexual abuse by the female parent," Eddison murmurs over my shoulder. "That's uncommon."

"Why do you assume the abuse was sexual?" asks Simpkins, who clearly already knows the answer but is asking it anyway.

That would be the teacher part of her personality.

"The way the wounds are clustered," Eddison answers automatically, because we are both used to Vic, after all. "Groin, breasts, mouth. That's very specific grouping."

"Social Services?" I ask.

"We have a call in. Their social worker on call is already at Prince William on a different case, so she was going to put a call out for backup."

"Seems like Mason might do better with a male social worker."

"She's going to do her best to get one in. They're understaffed, at the moment."

All the public services in this county are.

"The teddy bear? Was it the same?"

Simpkins carefully replaces the frame on the wall. "White, gold wings and halo."

"And the note was pinned on the bear?"

"Handwritten or typed?" adds Eddison.

"Typed," Simpkins answers. "We had a look at the computers, but the killer brought the note with them. The Jefferses don't even have a printer."

"So the killer knew in advance that Mason probably couldn't be coached to say anything. She came prepared."

"Why are you saying she?"

Eddison and I trade a look, and Mignone drifts closer to join the conversation. "The description the children gave," Eddison says finally. "They all called her a lady."

"But we don't actually know that it is. Saying 'she' could blind us to avenues. I'm not implying the children lied or even that they were mistaken, but just because someone in a costume seems to present as female . . ."

"It doesn't mean they are," Mignone finishes. "Could be a tactic to throw suspicion the wrong way."

"Precisely."

It's perfectly reasonable and actually better practice to not block off avenues of investigation, but my gut says we're looking for a woman. A man might dress as a female, given the appropriate impulses, but the phrasing would be different. This killer says the children are going to be safe now; a man would say he was rescuing them, or making them safe. Men are more likely to announce actions, women states of being.

And judging from the way Simpkins is watching us, she's already come to the same conclusion, she's just putting us through the paces. Exhibit A as to why I always learn a hell of a lot from Simpkins, but I don't actually like working with her.

"Holmes is at the hospital with the boy," Mignone says. "She wasn't in the room during the examination, but he had a panic attack when the doctor needed to check beneath his underwear. They actually had to sedate him."

"Did they finish the examination?" Eddison asks with a frown.

But Mignone shakes his head. "He didn't seem obviously injured, and they want to try to build a measure of trust with him. They did some scans to assess for internal damage, to make sure they could wait, but otherwise they want him to be awake and allowing them."

Eddison's shoulders relax.

"Do you mind if I go to Mason's room?" I ask. "I won't touch anything, I promise."

For an answer, Simpkins offers us pairs of gloves.

Okay, so maybe I will touch things.

Eddison trails after me, along with Mignone.

Mason's room belongs in a magazine. Being officially on the case, the detective can be our crime scene chaperone, as it were, able to swear, if a problem comes up later, that no evidence was planted, taken, or altered. The walls are painted in halves, the top a dusky blue, the bottom a deeper, royal blue, separated by a white-paper border covered with colorful figures in a number of different professions. I can see cowboys represented, astronauts and doctors, different branches of the military among others. His bed is plastic and low to the ground, shaped like a cartoon rocket, and except for the indentations where he lay and one corner folded back from when he got up, the blue sheets and comforter are perfectly made. Everything in the room is picture-perfect, designed for appearance rather than function.

Nothing in here actually says *little boy*.

Eddison opens the drawers of the dresser, his gloved hands easing between layers of perfectly folded and color-coordinated clothing. The closet is as pristine as the room, clear storage bins on the top shelf eliminating any chance of Mason using them to hide anything.

Children like the idea of secrets; they don't actually like keeping them, usually. Children *want* to tell people things.

The action figures in the toy box look barely touched, but the stuffed animals show a troubling bit of personality: they all have pants stapled onto them. Some of the pants are heavy construction paper, some look like doll clothes, but they're stapled into the fabric of the animals in a very worrying, very telling way. Eddison grimaces when I show him, but nods.

"That can't really be all," he says.

"Maybe not." Heading back to the bed, I ease my hand behind the head of the bed and feel the glove slip over something with a different texture. "Mignone?"

The detective lifts his camera and snaps photos of the bed, before and after we pull it from the corner. A plastic sheet protector, like a report cover, is taped to the back, filled with sheets of extrathick cardstock.

Mignone slowly lowers his camera. "Are those paper dolls?"

"Yes." I pull the pages out of the protector and spread them across the floor. They were probably torn out of a book at some point. A family of paper dolls, but the father and both children have pants attached front and back, not with the folded tabs but with more staples.

The doll for the mother is colored over with black marker, drawn so firmly the marker soaked through and tore the thick paper in places.

"Shit," mutters Eddison, and Mignone nods even as he lifts the camera again to snap pictures.

"I'm not top of the game for child psych, but that's a pretty distinctive sign of sexual abuse, right?" asks the detective.

"Yes. Yes, it is."

Eddison lightly kicks my ankle. "You think there's a CPS file, don't you?"

"It fits the pattern, and these markers—the pants on the toys and paper dolls, the mother being crossed out so vehemently—are so clear, someone had to have noticed and reported it."

"What's your theory, Ramirez?"

To give myself time to finish sorting the thought into words, I stack the paper dolls back together and slide them into the sheet protector, giving the whole thing to Mignone. "I think there was some sort of accident somewhere. Maybe at Sunday school, or a friend's birthday party. Something. Maybe a bathroom accident, maybe just something spilling, but enough to need to change pants, and an adult offered to help."

"A little boy freaks out to that degree about someone helping him change pants, questions are going to get asked," Eddison agrees.

"Maybe it was even at school. Someone asked his parents—"

"Probably his mother," adds Mignone. "Mrs. Jeffers isn't employed."

"—and of course his mother says he's just body shy, and he'll grow out of it."

"But whoever asked the questions is still bothered by it, and eventually makes a report."

"But how do you get from a report that vague to murder?"

"Until we hear back from Social Services, we don't know if it was vague," I remind Mignone. "They may have followed up, maybe even done an exam. If there isn't penetration or bruising, the abuse isn't going to be as obvious."

"You know, I sort of assumed getting a new team member would break you and Eddison of that habit," Simpkins drawls from the door. "Instead you're indoctrinating others."

"Groupthink is a useful tool, if it's not overused," I say mildly.

Simpkins doesn't encourage that degree of interdependence among her agents. She and Vic used to argue about it sometimes, especially after she got stuck with us for a month while Vic was in the hospital.

"That isn't your entire theory," she says after a minute.

"I think you need to look at the social workers," I admit. "When a parent is sexually abusing a child, the father is usually the safe assumption, but this person knew to go after the mother. This is someone with access to the accusations, at least, maybe even the files themselves. This is someone in the system."

"Or someone attached to someone in the system."

Eddison shifts uncomfortably. "That would be a pretty big indiscretion, Agent Simpkins. Someone who spills secrets like that would be fired pretty quickly."

"Perhaps. Or perhaps they only spill secrets to one individual."

"Even if that's the case, they're still complicit," I point out. "These murders have been hitting the news; the details may not be out there, but the names are. Even if the one in the system isn't doing the killing, they have to realize that it isn't a coincidence. If they're actively part of it, if they're just trying to protect a partner, they're still helping a murderer."

"We'll see," she says noncommittally. "Thank you for your assistance, agents. You can leave now." She takes the paper dolls from Mignone's hand and disappears back into the hallway.

Mignone stares after her, looking conflicted. "Is she always . . ."

"Yes," we answer in unison. Eddison gives me a ghost of a grin and continues, "Whatever word you were reaching for, yes, the answer is always yes."

"She plays things very close to the chest," I add. "She doesn't like assumptions, she doesn't like what she perceives to be sloppy language, and she thinks verbal free-for-alls are undisciplined. For all that, she's a very good agent with a solid track record."

"Uh-huh."

"After she meets Holmes and forms an opinion, she'll assign one of her agents to be the main point of contact with MPD. She's got good people under her."

Mignone's salt-and-pepper moustache twitches; it's bushy enough that his exact expression is a little hard to read. "When honesty and loyalty collide, which wins?"

"Honesty." At the repeated unison—unintentional this time—Eddison and I turn and stick our tongues out at each other, and Mignone barks a laugh.

"It's a shame you two can't work this. I get it," he continues quickly, holding up one hand, though I'm not sure either of us was about to protest. "Just a shame."

My skin crawls with the need to be working this case, to push everything else to the side and find out who's doing this, who is this person who cares so much in such a twisted way.

That's probably exactly why I'm not allowed to.

Once upon a time, there was a girl who was scared of angels.

Some of Daddy's friends called her that, pretty angel *or just* Angel. *Mama used to call her that, but she'd stopped even before she died. One of the men even had a little pewter pin of an angel he always wore on his shirts, between his collar and his shoulder. She stared at it whenever Daddy took his money. He said it was his guardian angel.*

She tried to think of other things, like the fort back in the woods. It seemed so far away, and she'd dreamed of taking a blanket and a bag of clothes and running away to live there forever. The other kids in the neighborhood played there, but she'd never been welcome. Or maybe she could just walk, and walk and walk and walk, and end up someplace new every day, and Daddy couldn't follow. But she couldn't escape. No matter how hard she tried to think of other things.

One night, while she stared at that angel pin, there was a knock on the door upstairs. You could always hear everything in that house; it had no secrets. All the men froze. There was never a knock at night. Everyone was already there. There was a voice calling something, loud but indistinct over the music. The little girl kept her eyes on the angel.

But the noise continued, and before Daddy and his friends got to their feet, the basement door was kicked in with a blaze of light, forging halos behind the people who stood there. The man with the pin pulled away from her, and in the panic and babble, one of Daddy's friends lifted a gun.

The little girl didn't pay much attention to the gun; that was never the thing to hurt her.

Instead, she watched one of the new people approach her, dark curls limned in light. The woman crouched over her, covering the little girl's body as much as she could, but her gun stayed in her hands and trained on Daddy's friend until he dropped his gun to the carpet and put his hands in the air.

Then the woman grabbed a blanket and wrapped the little girl in it, hugging her close but oh so gently. Her eyes were kind and sad, and she stroked the girl's hair and whispered that she was going to be okay, she was going to be okay. She was safe now. She gave the girl a teddy bear to hug and cry into, and stayed with her even as others crowded into the basement to take away Daddy and all his friends. Daddy was furious, yelling terrible things, but the woman just hugged the girl, and covered her ears so she didn't have to hear what her daddy said. The lady stayed with her in the ambulance, and in the hospital, and told her she was going to be okay.

Once upon a time, there was a little girl who was scared of angels.

Then she met one, and she wasn't afraid anymore.

15

Late the next morning, when the caffeine from the many coffee runs has stripped a hole in my gut, I take the elevator down to the cafeteria to pick up some bagels or whatever else strikes my fancy. On the way back up, another agent skips into the otherwise empty car just before the doors close.

"Have you eaten lunch yet?"

"Hello to you, too, Cass."

Cassondra Kearney is on Simpkins's team, but she's also a friend. We came up through the academy together and now that I think on it, she's probably the biggest reason the survival guide has, well . . . survived. She's wearing her glasses, which means she's at least halfway to exhausted. "Lunch?"

I look down at the bundle of plastic-wrapped sandwiches in my arms, then at the slightly manic glint in her eye. That glint never spells good things for me. "Let me give these to Eddison and Sterling, and I'll grab my bag."

"Great. I'll wait for you here."

"In the elevator?"

She glances at the opening doors, then positions herself in the corner with the control panel, where she can't be seen from the hall. Cass attempting subterfuge is invariably frightening. As bad as she is at it, though, she always has a good reason for it, so rather than argue, I'll go along with it.

Eddison isn't at his desk, but Sterling is at hers, reading through a consult request I'm not allowed to touch. I pyramid the sandwiches on the corner of her desk. "Tell him I'm off to lunch with a friend from the academy?"

"He'll know who it is?"

"Probably." Most of my friends from those days aren't based in Quantico, so it limits the pool of possibilities. The fact that I didn't mention the name should be the real tip-off. "I'll be back."

"Roger that."

When Cass said she'd wait there, she really meant *right there*. She's got a foot stuck in the track to keep the doors from closing. Anderson tries to get past her into the elevator, and she actually snarls at him. I wait just inside the bullpen until he gives up and uses the stairs, then join Cass.

We don't talk on the way down, or on our way to the garage. "Are we avoiding being seen together?" I mutter.

"Please."

"Then I'm on level two; pick me up on the way down."

She nods, not looking at me. Her keys bounce against her thigh. She jogs off to the garage elevator, and I walk up the ramp to my car on the second level. I don't think anyone's watching, but just in case—and because it will probably make her feel better, as worked up as she is—I rummage through my trunk like I'm looking for something. When I hear her car pull up, I close the trunk, lock the car, and slide into her passenger seat.

"Now are you going to explain?"

"We're going to make a quick stop before we eat," she says.

"Where?"

"Manassas CPS."

"Oh shit, Cass." I close my eyes and let my head thunk back against the headrest. "You wouldn't be pulling this cloak-and-dagger fuckery if you hadn't explicitly been told not to involve me."

Her pained silence is answer enough.

"Cass, *¿Qué mierda?*"

"Simpkins says we're not allowed to update your team at all." The farther we get from the Bureau building, the more she relaxes into her seat. "It's not like we took a case over from you; this is your life."

"Cass."

"They were able to finish the exam on Mason Jeffers," she says all in a rush. "There were signs of intermittent penetrative abuse, but here's the kicker: he's got herpes."

"Herpes."

"Type one, so basically cold sores, but he's got it on his genitals."

"Let me guess, his mother has a history of cold sores."

"Right."

I sigh. "A seven-year-old with an STI."

"Holmes wants you to talk to the earlier victims. Mason still won't speak at all, and the psychologist doesn't think we should push it with having women around him, but Holmes wants you to check in with the others. Simpkins says no contact."

"What does Holmes think checking in will do?"

"Show the killer that you're still on this."

So Holmes had the same thought I did, that the killer's rage might turn on me if it looks like I abandoned these kids.

"Unless Holmes withdraws the request for Bureau assistance, Simpkins is agent in charge. She gets to make that call."

Cass sneezes. Our entire academy cohort called her Kitten, because she sneezes every time she laughs. "You're not really going to try to convince me you like it."

"No, I fucking hate it, but it's not my call. And I don't get to go behind her back."

"Actually, I was thinking of telling Holmes to go to Hanoverian."

I thump my head against the seat several times, hoping it will knock something useful loose. "You want to tell the local detective to go over your boss's head to the unit chief so a targeted agent can talk to previous victims."

"When you put it like that, it sounds bad."

"I wonder why."

She sneezes again.

"If you're trying to sneak me to the kids, why are you kidnapping me to CPS instead of the hospital?"

"Because I need to stop at CPS. I was on my way and figured the car ride was the best chance to talk to you." She chances a glance over at me as she merges onto the highway. "You know how Dru is about your team; she doesn't think it's healthy for a team to stay the same for so long. She's even talking of trading out the Smiths, and they've been on her team for six years."

"But we're not the same anymore. Vic got promoted. We stole Sterling from Denver."

"She put her name in for unit chief ten months ago."

"Shit."

"No one ever thought Hanoverian would do it. He's turned it down so many times before."

"But then he got shot in the chest, and it was his only way to stay in the Bureau. She must have been pissed."

"She doesn't like the way he does things, never has. You know that."

Most of the case ten months ago had involved Simpkins trying to retrain me and Eddison. I've been in the Bureau ten years, Eddison's been here . . . sixteen? We're not NATs. It made the case hell because she insisted on treating us like we've never learned anything useful under Vic. Eddison's promotion and Sterling's transfer came as welcome news, because it meant we were staying a separate team rather than getting folded permanently into Simpkins's.

"So what are you going to be doing at CPS?" I ask, not even pretending to reach for a graceful segue.

"She's got a theory that the killer may be a social worker."

I snort in spite of myself.

"Let me guess: Your theory?"

"That she seemed disinclined to pursue."

"She's been a field agent for over twenty years; she wants to move up the ladder while she's still young enough to make a good run of it."

"I hate politics," I groan. "I just want to do my job. I do not want to keep track of who wanted what promotion or who doesn't like who."

"Well, you'll be able to put warnings in the welcome guide."

"Speaking of which—"

"Hey, what do you want for lunch when we're done?" she chirps.

"Nice try. Why did you give them the NAT guide?"

Her sheepish smile is the only admission of guilt I really need. "We need something, Mercedes. It's the beginning of July and we've already had twenty agents either transfer out of CAC or leave the Bureau entirely, just this year."

"So why don't you write it?"

"How many times did you have to talk me out of quitting the academy?"

"Every time we had to fire a gun. That just means you don't like guns. You were fine at everything else."

"But a field agent who can't stand guns isn't much use as a field agent, is she? You got me past that. Be as pissed as you want that we didn't tell you the guide was still getting passed around, that's fair, but you're the right choice, because no matter how many times you had to talk one of us down, or talk one of us up, you never lied. You never said one single thing that was untrue. *That* is what we need for the new hires. They don't need to be babied, they need to be honestly warned. Who's going to do that better than you?"

"The only reason I don't hate you entirely is because this stupid handbook is the only thing between me and suspension."

"I accept gratitude in the form of Marlene Hanoverian's iced cinnamon-raisin rolls."

"Don't push it."

My phone buzzes with a text from Sterling. *Simpkins is here. Eddison needs to talk to you when you get back from lunch.*

"Problem?" Cass asks, passing a car going fifteen below with its hazards on for no apparent reason.

"If you and Holmes want me checking on the other kids, we need to do it while we're here. Once we get back, Eddison has to tell me we're hands off."

"And him telling you that now doesn't apply?"

"He didn't tell me that. He had Sterling tell me something around that."

"Okay, *maybe* I'm starting to question the wisdom of having you teach the noobs."

"Too late now."

"Well then." She hits the gas, pushing us to ten, fifteen, twenty over the limit. "Let's make the most out of lunch."

16

Manassas Child Protective Services is quiet over the lunch hour, most of the staff either out for the meal or eating at their desks so they can keep working on paperwork. The social workers, nurses, and administrators have their own offices, but the center of the largest room is a cluster of half-wall cubicles that stand guard in front of the physical file room. Every digital file has a physical counterpart, just in case, and the clerks are also in charge of putting together duplicate files for law enforcement or the court. There are small, restrained personal touches on the desks, an awareness that for all that this is their working space, it's also a public space, such as it is.

"Can I help you?" asks the woman at the closest cubby. She's probably early twenties, with a bright smile and a lanyard covered with the FSU logo. There's a row of fuzzy pastel pencil toppers stuck to the top of her monitor, a cheerful lineup of cats, foxes, puppies, and rubber ducks, with a teddy bear in the middle, and a small, neatly framed cross-stitch that reads *Life sucks and then you die: some days it's hard to tell the difference* in a charming block font with a border of hearts and flowers. She looks familiar in the same way so many of the new agent trainees look familiar: a twenty-something's wonder at the world beyond college and the struggle with the lingering freshman fifteen. It makes me feel old, and I'm still too young for that, damn it.

Cass steps forward, given that I'm not really supposed to be here. "I'm Agent Cassondra Kearney, with the FBI. What is your name, please?"

"Caroline," the clerk replies, a dimple deepening in her cheek. "Caroline Tillerman. How can I help you today, Agent?"

"If I give you a list of case numbers, are you able to give me a list of everyone who's worked on those files?"

Caroline's smile dims, her head tilting to one side. "I can take down your information and give it to one of the admins," she says after a moment, "but I'm pretty sure they'll need a warrant. I mean, I know it's not as sensitive as the files themselves, but I don't think I'm allowed to give that out. Sometimes families can get a little angry, you know?"

Oh, I know.

"Which admin would you be passing that to?" Cass asks. "Because we have a warrant in the works, and if I can get their information, I can just send the warrant along once the judge signs it. Get a jump start on both sides of it."

"Our direct supervisor here in Records is Derrick Lee, and he's in his office. I can introduce you?"

"That would be excellent, Caroline, thank you."

Caroline stands and adjusts the heart-shaped locket at her throat with a gesture that looks ingrained, and leads Cass back into the hallway. She throws a curious look at me over her shoulder, but I'm probably going to cause enough trouble just by being here. I don't really need to give a supervisor reason to remember I was here.

Instead, I stroll down the aisle that splits the sections of cubbies, taking in the personalizations. Either someone in the office cross-stitches or they bought them together, because all six desks have a similar frame to Caroline's, all of them just a little subversive until the last, tucked away in a corner where visitors are least likely to see it, raises the bar with its flower-bordered *Bless this fucking office*. It's both charming and disheartening.

"What are you doing back there?"

I turn to the front, keeping to the middle of the aisle with my hands cupped loosely around my elbows to be nonthreatening and show that I'm not holding anything. The woman is probably mid- to late forties, with a severe expression and an ugly corduroy patchwork blazer. Her lanyard is plain black, no buttons or pins. "Admiring the cross-stitch," I answer simply. "Which one is yours?"

Her eyes flick to the last desk, the one with the most subversive saying. "No one is allowed behind the walls."

"My apologies." I walk past her, back to my spot near the door. "I'm an FBI agent; Agent Kearney is back with the administrator and Caroline."

She leans against the sturdy divider between Caroline's desk and the one behind it. "And you're not back there why?"

"Not my case; Kearney needed to stop in before we got lunch."

The woman pulls the blazer closer, tucking her hands deeper into the sleeves. The air-conditioning is limping, working not well enough, but she looks genuinely cold in the warm office. She gags suddenly, coughing harshly into one sleeve. Her other hand braces against the divider to keep her upright. I sway closer, but her ferocious glare pins me in place through the rest of her fit. When it's done, she carefully gulps in deep breaths, the blotchy flush slowly receding. Then the color flares back in full force when she lifts a hand to her hair and realizes she coughed hard enough to set her blonde wig askew.

I look away, watching from the corner of my eye as she straightens it with shaking hands. She has the look of someone losing weight, an underlying pallor and skin sagging slightly in unexpected places. It could explain her feeling cold even in this heat. "Can I get you some water?" I ask neutrally.

"Like water's going to help," she wheezes, but she does move back to her desk to pick up a tumbler. The name tag on the divider says she's Gloria Hess.

My phone buzzes with another text from Sterling. *Simpkins is sending a pair of agents to the hospital after lunch. Eddison and I are eating with them, so we can tell them what we observed about the kids.*

Okay, come on, Cass. We've got to go.

After a few minutes of silence and Miss Gloria glaring at me from across the room, Caroline and Cass return. Cass comes to my side, and I hold the phone out so she can see the message. This one doesn't take a great deal of familiarity to decode, and she nods quickly.

Crossing to her desk, Caroline smiles at her coworker. "Gloria, this is Agent Kearney. She's working on the case with those poor kids."

Gloria arches a carefully drawn eyebrow. "Can you think of a case in this office that doesn't include 'those poor kids'?" At Caroline's blush and stammer, she turns to Cass. "Are you able to tell us which case?"

Cass glances at me, and I shrug. The incidents have hit the news, even if the details and their connections have been withheld, and confidentiality aside, an office is an office; people gossip. "The Wilkins, Carter-Wong, Anders, and Jeffers murders."

Both women look startled at the length of the list, and Caroline pales. Gloria moves up to pat her shoulder. "There was another one?" the older woman asks. At Cass's nod, Gloria looks at me with narrowed eyes. "You're Agent Ramirez, aren't you? The one the children are taken to."

Damn. "Yes," I acknowledge, "but please don't mention I was here. I'm not actually allowed to work the case, not when it involves me to such an extent. I'm just worried about the kids, so Agent Kearney allowed me to tag along." I rummage up a sheepish smile. "Honestly, I was kind of hoping to run into Nancy, maybe get an update."

"She's doing visits all day today," Caroline informs me. "But I can leave a message?"

"Oh, no, I don't want to get her in trouble," I say quickly. "I'm supposed to be hands off, but these kids . . ."

To my surprise, Gloria seems to thaw a bit at that. "We'll let her know you called, unofficially. If there's been a change, I'm sure she can find a way to let you know."

"I'd appreciate that, thank you."

She nods slowly, thoughtfully, like I've given her something new to consider.

"Agent Kearney!" A man hurries out from the admin hallway, holding a neon green Post-it in his hand. It nearly matches the polish on his fingernails. He's a slender man of average height, with a soft voice. "When you get that warrant signed, this is my direct line," he tells her in a faded Charleston accent. It's the only city I know where rushed and clipped Southern is a thing that happens. "Give me a call and we'll get right to work on that list for you."

Cass murmurs a thank-you and tucks the note into her credentials. "Mr. Lee, this is Agent Mercedes Ramirez. Mercedes, this is Derrick Lee, the file administrator."

He takes one of my hands in both of his. "Isn't this all just awful? How are you holding up?"

At the moment, I'm a little distracted by his eyeliner game being fiercer than mine. How does he get the wings so even? "I'm okay for now, Mr. Lee, thank you. Just trying to find out how the kids are doing."

"Nancy says they're all being terribly brave." He squeezes my hand and lets it go. "If you two need anything, and I mean just anything, please let us know. We all want those little angels safe, don't we?"

"Thank you, Mr. Lee."

Cass repeats her own thanks and a goodbye, and we head out to the car. "What's on your brain, Mercedes?" she murmurs as we're buckling in.

"When the warrant clears, see if the filing clerks are listed on the files they work the way the nurses and social workers are."

"Which name should I look for?"

"Gloria Hess."

"Any particular reason? If charming personalities were conclusive factors, after all, Eddison would have been jailed years ago."

"Blonde wig and a port in her chest; she's got cancer. You spend your life face-to-face with the best and worst the system has to offer, what's a thing you want to do once you have nothing left to lose?"

Cass blinks.

"Also Derrick Lee," I add. "We haven't definitely ruled out that the killer could be male. Put a wig and loose clothes on Lee, he could easily be mistaken for a woman. So we should check him out as well."

Cass stares at me for a moment, then lowers her forehead to the steering wheel and swears emphatically.

17

We speed to the hospital, because there's really no telling how long Sterling and Eddison can stall Cass's teammates. I mean, I have a healthy respect for their ability to bullshit and inconvenience—Sterling once managed to make a person of interest not only miss his flight, but willingly leave the airport to give her a ride back to the precinct, it was gorgeous—but Dru Simpkins keeps a pretty tight rein on her team. If she tells them to leave NOW, it won't matter if they don't have all the information.

Cass has only been on Dru's team about a year and a half, and I give it another few months or one more bad case before she goes to Vic and asks to be moved to a different team. She approaches life and investigations more like we do.

Oh, God, Cass on our team.

Poor Eddison.

Mason, Emilia, and Sarah are all in the hospital for treatment, but they allowed Ashley and Sammy to stay with their sister rather than move them to a group home or foster family. We stop in with the Carter and Wong trio first. Sammy is fast asleep in Sarah's lap, a stuffed tiger fisted in his hands. The teddy bears the killer gave the children have all been taken into evidence, but they gave them different plushies for comfort. I don't see Ashley in the room.

Sarah flinches at first, when the door opens, but she smiles when she recognizes me. "Agent Ramirez."

"You can call me Mercedes, Sarah. How are you doing?"

"We're . . ." She hesitates, running her fingers through her brother's dark hair. He squirms at the touch, then relaxes into it, drooling a little onto the tiger's bright fabric. "We're okay," she finishes. "Okay for now."

"Can I introduce you to someone?"

She looks curiously at Cass and nods. She's met an endless succession of new people in the past nine days (God, has it really only been nine days?) so getting asked for permission must be a switch.

"This is Agent Cassondra Kearney—"

"Cass," my friend interjects, with a cheery wave.

"—and she's on the FBI team that's officially partnered with the Manassas Police to find the woman who killed your mother and stepfather. She's also an old friend of mine, and someone I trust."

Cass blushes a little. We've been friends for ten years, and there's a lot that's implied by that level of friendship, but I don't think I've ever stated it so explicitly. I'm not sure there's ever been a reason to.

Sarah gives her a shy smile, but it quickly drops into a frown. "So . . . you're not on our case anymore?"

"Technically, I never was. I can't be."

"Because it's your house?"

"Right in one. Cass is part of a team, and I think you're going to meet a couple other members of the team this afternoon, but I wanted to check on you. After this, I might not be allowed."

Sarah looks between me and Cass. "Those are strange rules."

"They are," I agree, "but they're meant to protect you. Speaking of which, where's Ashley?"

"A volunteer took her down to the cafeteria. They're getting ice cream. I think they're just getting her out of the room." Her lip wobbles a bit, but she takes a sharp breath and squares her shoulders. "She really liked Samuel. He gave her things she wanted."

"She's angry."

"Really angry. She keeps saying it's my fault." Her eyes are bright as she looks down at her brother. "Mercedes . . ."

"I'm right here, Sarah." I sit next to her on the bed, one hand on her shoulder.

"Nancy doesn't think we're going to find a place for all three of us. I don't . . . I don't want them to split us up, but Ashley is so angry . . ."

I change the hand to a sideways hug, rocking her gently. "Sounds like Nancy is keeping you in the loop."

She nods against my shoulder. "She says it'll help me. Maybe I don't get a say in what's going on, but I at least know about it."

"Have you talked to your grandparents?"

"Once. They're . . . they're really . . ."

"Racist?"

"Yeah."

Settling into a chair near the bed, Cass's eyebrows climb toward her hairline, but she doesn't say anything.

"And like I said, Ashley really liked Samuel. If she had to listen to our grandparents bad-mouthing him, I think she'd run away. And, well, Sammy." She sniffs back tears, and it breaks my heart to see her working so hard to look strong. I already know she's strong; I know what she's survived. "What did you do?"

Cass shifts in her chair. She knows I've got a personal reason for being in CAC, it's the kind of thing that gets around, but I've never told her what that personal thing is.

"I was the only one taken away," I tell Sarah softly, "and my extended family was never really an option. It's different for you."

"The doctors said I'm clean," Sarah says abruptly. "That's like health-class stuff, right? Like diseases?"

"Diseases, and making sure you weren't pregnant."

"What if I had been? Pregnant, I mean."

"It would depend a lot on how far along you were, if it was posing risks to your health, who got custody of you. There's not really one straight path there. Did they say how you're healing?"

"I have an infection, but they said it's a really common one. An, um . . . a *youtee*?"

"UTI. It means *urinary tract infection*, and yes, it's really common for women for all sorts of reasons. Fortunately those don't have long-lasting effects and they're pretty easy to treat."

"They won't let me put sugar in the cranberry juice."

"Yeah, that is pretty gross, isn't it?"

We stay for a little bit longer, but I don't think she's lying when she says she's okay for now. Ashley isn't back yet when we leave; that may be for the best. If she's as angry as Sarah says, she's probably pissed at me too. It's not entirely logical, but anger and grief and trauma so rarely are.

"I always forget," says Cass as we head to Emilia's room.

"Forget what?"

"How honest you are with victims."

"Kids," I correct. "I'm honest with kids, and I think everybody should be."

"No Santa Claus for you?"

"That's different. Santa Claus isn't asking them to trust him."

We announce ourselves at Emilia's room, and she calls out for us to enter. She's pacing in front of the long window, one arm up in a sling. I introduce her to Cass, just like I did for Sarah, and ask her how she's doing.

She snorts and looks down at the sling. "I don't want to wear this, but they said I have to."

"What's wrong?"

"They said my shoulder's dislocated and, um, my collarbone is cracked. Said they have been for a while, so they want me to wear this for a few weeks. Let everything 'heal properly.'"

"Why does the sling bother you?"

"It . . . it . . ."

"Emilia, there's no wrong answer here as long as it's an honest one."

"It looks like I'm begging for attention," she admits, slumping down on the end of the bed. "Or showing people the easiest place to hurt me."

"They found somewhere for you to go, didn't they?"

Both she and Cass look startled. "How did you know? Oh," she continues quickly. "Of course they told you."

"They haven't, but you wouldn't worry about looking injured as long as you're in a hospital. It's kind of what it's for."

"She used to do this in the academy, too," Cass fake-whispers to Emilia, who actually giggles.

Running her fingers along the sling's strap, Emilia adjusts it away from the small square bandage that covers the cigarette burn. "My dad has a cousin in Chantilly."

"Were your dad and his cousin close?"

"Yeah, it's like twenty minutes away, they said."

Cass grins. "I meant were they friends?"

"Oh. They'd get together to watch games, sometimes, but not really. I've met him, though. Before, too, and he came yesterday to ask me if I'd be okay with living with him. He seems nice."

"Well, that's a plus, isn't it?"

"I'll have to change schools. But . . ." Emilia looks between us and takes a deep breath. "Maybe that's not a bad thing? I mean, no one in Chantilly would know about my parents being murdered, right? They won't know I was bad?"

"You were not bad," Cass and I say in unison, that startled look jumping back into Emilia's eyes.

I reach out and touch her knee with the back of my hand. "Emilia, I promise you, none of this happened because you were bad. Your dad lied to you for a very long time, and maybe he lied to himself. Maybe he convinced himself you were bad so he wouldn't feel guilty for hurting you. But you weren't. I promise you, you weren't."

"Lincoln, Dad's cousin, wants me to go to therapy."

"I think that could be a big help."

"Dad always said therapy was for sickos and wimps."

"Your dad was wrong about a lot of things."

She looks like she needs to chew on that thought for a bit, so we say goodbye, and remind her she can call Cass for anything she needs, even if it's just to talk. Closing the door, we hear a sharp "There you are!" and flinch.

It's not Simpkins, though. It's Nancy, the social worker.

"Sorry," she huffs, jogging down the hall. "Didn't mean to sound pissed off, I just didn't want you to walk away. One of the nurses said you were here."

"Just checking up on the kids," I tell her.

"What would you think about meeting Mason?"

Um. "Is he going to be okay with that? Us being female and all?"

"Keep a good distance from him and he seems to listen calmly enough. And he's started communicating with us, a little."

"He's talking?"

"Writing, but to be honest, I consider that amazing."

"Nancy, have you met Cass Kearney? She's on Agent Simpkins's team."

Nancy holds out her hand, and she and Cass shake briskly, exchanging good-to-meet-yous. "Mason read the note last night, and I think he wants to know who you are, Mercedes. I don't know if meeting you will help him or not, but I don't think it'll hurt him. Tate agrees."

"Tate is another social worker?"

"He is; he's been in with Mason all day." Nancy leads us down the hall to another room, knocking on the door with a "Tate, it's Nancy. I've got a couple of agents with me."

"Come on in," calls a warm male voice.

"Rule of the room," whispers Nancy as she turns the handle. "No women past the track of the privacy curtain. He seems to do okay with that amount of space."

Seven-year-old Mason Jeffers sits on a beanbag on the floor in the far corner of the room. A few feet away, a very tall, lean black man sits on the floor as well, long legs stretched out in front of him. Mason's socked feet rest on Tate's legs, just below the knee. Mason's shoulders hunch when he sees us, fear jumping into his eyes, but otherwise he doesn't move, just watches us with his hands around what I'd guess is Tate's iPad.

He's too thin, almost to the point of sickly, but otherwise he looks physically unharmed. I know that's not the case, especially not with what Cass told me in the car, but even with that visible fear, he's unnervingly calm.

"Mason, these are the agents Nancy and I were telling you about," Tate informs the little boy. "That's Mercedes Ramirez"—I give Mason a nod and a little wave—"and this is . . ."

"Cass Kearney," she says, echoing my gestures.

"This is Mason Jeffers."

Eyeing the curtain tracking in the ceiling, I sit down on the floor against the same wall as Tate, making sure not even a hair is over the line. It puts me about ten feet away, with Tate in between us. "You've had a pretty bad morning, huh?"

He nods solemnly.

"This might be a pretty difficult question to answer, but are you doing okay right now?"

He seems to think about that, then shrugs.

"Okay, let's try something easier: As long as we stay over here, are you okay with us being in here with you?"

He frowns a little, then shrugs again.

"Okay. If that changes, Mason, if you want or need us to leave, just let Tate know, okay? And we'll go. This is your space, and we don't want to make you uncomfortable."

He doesn't look like he knows what to make of that, which isn't as surprising as I'd like it to be. He's never really been allowed to have any idea of what "his space" should be.

"Do you mind if I ask you some questions? They'll be yes or no, and if you don't know the answer or don't remember, that's perfectly okay."

There are times in this job when I say okay so many times it no longer feels like a real word in my mouth. But Mason nods, after an uncertain look at Tate, so I settle more comfortably against the wall, crossing my legs tailor-fashion and keeping my hands on my knees, palms up and fingers loose, to be as nonthreatening as possible.

"Did the person who brought you to the hospital talk to you?"

He nods slowly.

"Was it a lady?"

Another nod.

"Was she wearing a mask over her face?"

His nod is more confident this time.

"This one is important, Mason: Did she hurt you?"

He shakes his head.

"Did she mention any other kids or families?"

He shakes his head again.

"When you were in the car, did she bring you straight to the hospital?"

He nods.

That's . . . odd.

"Was she as short as Agent Cass?"

She's only five-foot-one, so it's a fair question, however much the discreet kick to my thigh tells me she's unhappy about it. Mason looks her up and down, his eyes sliding over to Nancy before he finally shakes his head.

"How about Miss Nancy, then: Was she as tall as Miss Nancy?"

He pulls one hand away from the tablet to wobble it in midair.

"How about a thumbs-up for taller, or a thumbs-down for shorter. Can you do that for me, Mason?"

He studies Miss Nancy again, who gives him a soft smile and stays precisely where she is. Slowly, uncertainly, he gives a thumbs-up.

"This is going to be a little bit harder: thumbs-up if she's closer to Miss Nancy's height, thumbs-down if she's closer to my height."

He looks between us for several moments, then puts his hand back to the iPad and shrugs, his shoulders staying up near his ears. Why the hell did I ask that sitting down?

"That's okay, Mason. It's okay if you're not sure. I know there was a lot going on all at once."

He doesn't smile, but his shoulders drop a bit and his lips twitch in something that's probably as close to a smile as he gets.

I want to keep that almost smile. I ask him more open questions, ones that turn it into a silly guessing game, like what's his favorite color, or who's his favorite superhero, and gradually, as my guesses get more and more off the wall, he starts leaning forward in the beanbag, eager to nod or shake his head to each one, and Tate gives me a broad smile. When Mason starts yawning, we say our goodbyes, leaving him with Tate, and follow Nancy out the door.

"Does he have family who can safely take him in?" asks Cass.

Nancy nods and walks with us to the elevators. "His uncles are making arrangements to get here; they're hoping to arrive tonight or tomorrow if they can get things squared away with their bosses. His father's brother and his husband, I believe."

"If he's comfortable with the iPad, can you ask Tate to show him different kinds of cars? If we can narrow down the make and model of the car, that would be a big help."

"I'll pass that along."

I press the call button for the elevator. "One of your filing clerks, Gloria," I say casually, aware of Cass stiffening beside me. "Is she always that grumpy?"

But far from suspecting anything, Nancy gives a soft, sad laugh. "Oh, dear. Gloria. She's . . . well, she's having a time of it, I'm afraid."

"She's ill."

"Yes. Breast cancer, but it's spread into her lungs and down into her abdomen. She insists on working, though, any day she feels strong enough. I think having something to do helps her a bit emotionally. And, well . . . this may be something that makes the CPS gossip rounds more than the national news, but did you hear anything about the CPS office in Gwinnett County? Down in Georgia?"

Cass and I both shake our heads.

"She grew up just outside of Atlanta, and her sister and brother-in-law both work in that office. She's a nurse, and he's a social worker. There was a big scandal there recently, and an investigation uncovered that several of the employees were purposefully concealing some abuse cases, or declining to investigate fully, and they were all cases involving employee kids or the kids of friends."

"Her sister and brother-in-law?"

Nancy nods reluctantly. "So they're off to prison, but the court wouldn't let Gloria take her nieces and nephews because of the cancer. They said she's not healthy enough to take care of five kids. And, truthfully, she's not, but the kids got split up between different family members, and then with her husband's sudden death, she's just really had a bad few months. If she offended you—"

"Oh, no, nothing like that. She was snippy, but clearly she has reason to be. I was just wondering if we'd caught her on a bad day, or if she was just generally a grump. Every office has one, you know."

"Lord, yes. Tell you what, though, give her a name and she can find the file in under ten minutes without even having to look it up. She knows the name of every kid who comes through our office, and last year she got the entire records room reorganized so it actually makes sense now, and got all the digital files tagged and cross-indexed."

"How's her prognosis?"

"Not very good, I'm afraid. She found it late."

"We'll pray for her," I say, and Nancy beams. "Just . . . maybe don't tell her that."

"God bless you both. Off to see Ronnie next?"

"He's with his grandmother, right?"

"Yes, she's up in Reston. Let me get her number for you."

We wait to call until we're out of the hospital. Cass's phone has been buzzing intermittently for the last hour, and every voice mail and almost every text is from Simpkins. Those that aren't are from her teammates. Warning her, I assume. I can't make out the words of the second voice mail, but the tone is pissed.

"Try not to get written up for my sake," I tell her, tapping in the number for Ronnie's grandmother.

"What if I get written up for the kids' sakes?" she asks. "It did them good to see you."

"Voice mail. Do I leave a message?"

"Sure. You haven't been told otherwise yet."

It drove our instructors nuts at the academy. As much as I'm willing to split hairs to achieve something, Cass takes it to the subatomic levels.

I clear my throat just before the beep. "This message is for Mrs. Flory Taylor. Ma'am, this is Agent Mercedes Ramirez, with the FBI, and I was hoping to check in on Ronnie, see how he's doing with everything that's happened. I'd be grateful if you could please call me back when it's convenient for you." I leave my number, then Cass's name and number for good measure, and hang up. "All right. Anything else we need to do in Manassas before we face the music?"

"Holmes and Mignone won't be on duty yet, will they?"

"Not for several hours yet."

"Then I can't think of anything else. Lunch?"

"I'll bet twenty Simpkins complains to Vic that his team is a bad influence on her agents."

"I'll take that bet. No way she bitches at the unit chief like that, not out-and-out."

18

You won twenty bucks yesterday, you're buying the coffee today, Eddison informs me via text while I'm brushing my teeth at his kitchen sink.

The fact that he felt the need to send that text from the bathroom is . . . disturbing? He could have just yelled it.

It's also a harbinger of how entirely shitty the rest of the day is going to be, because Simpkins spends a good two hours raking us over the coals for "interfering in her investigation." Vic eventually has to step in, and that's when it gets nasty. Vic rarely yells—he doesn't like giving anyone the satisfaction—but it's been a long time since I've seen him that close to it. Whatever Simpkins's ambitions, though, Vic quite simply outranks her, both in actual position and in tenure; he's been an agent with the Bureau for thirty-eight years.

He started in the Bureau two months before Eddison was born.

Weirdly enough, it's Eddison who's the more bothered by that particular fact.

Once we're out of Dodge, I get to spend the rest of the morning digging into the hard drive freshly delivered from Archives. It's dropped off by one of the baby agents, and before she even gets to my desk, I know where she works; the baby agents assigned to the archives are all immune to the Eddison catnip because they're all so terrified of Agent Alceste at first. By the time they realize they don't have to be afraid of

Alceste as long as they leave her alone, they've outgrown the catnip vulnerability, for the most part.

I hate this, digging through old cases to see which child might have grown up to be a murderer. Not just the kids we rescued but their friends and family, the friends and family of the ones we couldn't save, even—in some cases—the children of the ones causing them harm. In a few terrible cases, the kids causing the harm. Reading through the files to assess perceived connections, plugging them into our system to find where they are now . . . it's horrific.

Kids who face monsters can grow up to become monsters, I know that, and some grow up to chase monsters. I just don't want to think that a child I held and comforted could grow up to do this.

It's slow, tedious, heartbreaking work, and far too vivid a reminder that a rescue is a moment, not a state of being. Whatever we saved them from, we were powerless to influence what came next. I know that better than most.

This, I think, is exactly why we're trained to let go of cases once they're done. How could we do this job if we're constantly aware that even our successes can lead to terrible things?

By the end of the day, everyone is either short-tempered or walking on eggshells in the bullpen. Sterling and I are sitting atop Eddison's freakishly organized desk, our feet on his thighs to keep him seated, passing around menus to decide on dinner, when Vic walks up. We all watch him warily.

Because there's this thing that Vic sometimes does, where he will absolutely have your back in public, but in private he will break down in excruciating detail exactly what you did wrong and why you need to never do it again. It's not cruel or hateful, it's not even mean, it's just . . .

He gets so disappointed when he has to do it. Disappointing Vic makes you feel lower than dirt.

"Stop that," he chides. "You're not in trouble."

"Are you sure?" Sterling asks doubtfully.

"Simpkins was out of line. Yes, you probably shouldn't have wiggled around the lines as much as you did, but we got a call from the lead social worker telling us how much it helped the kids to see Mercedes, so clearly you did what was needed. Now. None of you are coming in tomorrow."

"We're not?"

"No. We've been over this. When you're on desk rotation, there's this thing called overtime that the Bureau doesn't want to pay you. You're done for the week. Go home. Better yet, go to the train station and pick up the girls, because I have to sit down with the section chief and explain the ruckus today."

Gathering up the handful of menus, Eddison stacks them neatly and tucks them into the top drawer, gently moving Sterling's legs out of the way to do so. "All right, we'll take them out."

"We were just going to do pizza at the house," Vic tells him.

Eddison just shrugs. "I'm not letting them see that apartment until you're there to show it to them, and you know Jenny will automatically lead them to it."

Vic gives him a long look, but surrenders without another word. "I'll let you know when I'm leaving the office, then."

Launching herself off the desk, Sterling nearly skips over to her bag, pulling a slim something in a garbage bag out from behind her filing cabinet. "I was hoping we'd get to pick them up."

"Are you going to show us what that is?" Eddison asks, eyeing the bag.

"Not yet."

We take Vic's car to the station, leaving Eddison's keys with him, as Vic's is the only one capable of legally seating at least six people. When we get there, Sterling excuses herself to the restroom while Eddison and I figure out where we need to be. It's a bit of a zoo, with the commuters hitting the road home. Amtrak is the way Inara and Victoria-Bliss prefer to come down. Inara, who never really seems afraid of anything, absolutely hates flying, and has done it all of once. Not once round-trip.

Once. She actually cancelled the return flight and caught the train, she hated it so much. Priya has never seemed to care one way or the other, but she's not going to fly down separately from them for a couple hundred dollars more.

"Has Ronnie's grandmother called back yet?" Eddison asks when we get vaguely where we need to go.

"Yes. She told Cass that Simpkins had told her not to answer or return my calls, and she was very confused. I didn't envy Cass having to explain that."

"You were allowed to speak to Cass?"

"When Anderson went to lunch, I borrowed his computer for the interoffice chat, so if Simpkins gets twitchy, it looks like Anderson did it."

"She'll eat him alive."

"I'm okay with that."

"It's not just you, right? All the women in the office hate him?"

"Hate who?" Sterling asks suddenly, popping up behind the violently flinching Eddison.

"Bells," he mutters. "I swear to God, bells."

"Anderson," I tell Sterling.

"Oh. Yes, most of us hate him."

"And the others?" he asks, one hand still over his heart.

"Don't have to interact with him. Ooh, that's them!" She hands the garbage bag to Eddison, tears open the knot, and pulls out a folded posterboard sign with huge, glittering green letters that say, **BITCHES BE HERE**.

"Christ," sighs Eddison, staring at the ceiling for inspiration or patience.

We can tell the exact instant the girls coming down the steps see it, because Victoria-Bliss doubles over cackling, losing her balance, and both Inara and Priya have to grab the back of her shirt to keep her from cracking her head on the stairs. "I LOVE IT," she yells across the terminal, either not noticing or not caring about the glares sent her way from other passengers and families.

As soon as they're close enough, it's a tackle of hugs, and even Victoria-Bliss punches Eddison on the arm. It's basically her version of a hug if you're male.

"Where's Vic?" asks Priya, looping her arm around Eddison's waist and pinching him when he tries to take one of her bags.

"Office politics."

She rolls her eyes, and pinches Eddison again when he makes another try for the bags. "Is he regretting the promotion yet?"

"Not as much as he would be regretting retiring if he hadn't taken it." Giving up on Priya's duffel, Eddison manages to get both Inara's and Victoria-Bliss's overnight bags.

At which point Inara reaches out for Priya's duffel, which the other girl willingly surrenders.

Eddison *wilts*. There's really no other word for it. He looks like a puppy who doesn't know what it did to get yelled at.

"Stop pouting," Priya tells him calmly. "I made a promise to Keely about some of the pictures in there."

"Have I ever gone through something of yours without explicit permission?"

"You have not, but this was about making a fifteen-year-old more comfortable with letting me take the pictures, so I promised her that Inara and Victoria-Bliss are the only ones other than me who'll touch the bag, much less the pictures."

He considers that for a moment, then adjusts his grip on the other two bags. "Fine."

It's a cheerful ride to the restaurant, a Mongolian grill at which Priya insists we eat at least once per visit. They tell us about shows they've seen and some of the weirder patrons at the restaurant where Inara and Victoria-Bliss have worked for years. Priya shows us a picture of the giant colorful sticker chart on the back of the door where they mark off different ethnic foods they're trying this summer, and for some reason none of them can explain, the stickers are all of professional wrestlers.

Once Vic sends us word he's on his way home, we finish up and herd everyone back into the car, still laughing and talking over each other. It's later than I realized, the sky edging into night. Inara is the first to spot the house. "Oh, he finished repairing the garage," she notes.

I catch Sterling's grin in the rearview mirror, but she doesn't turn around to share it with the girls.

Eddison pulls the car into Vic's usual spot on the driveway and we spill out, grabbing bags at random to carry in, with the exception of Priya's duffel, which she grabs herself. Vic meets us outside, twirling three key rings on one finger. All three girls pile against him for a hug, and he's laughing as much as any of them.

Sterling snaps a picture on her phone.

"All right, these are for you," Vic announces, handing each of them a ring with a key. Each key is different, the fun decorated ones you can cut at the hardware store rather than the boring silver or brass ones that come standard with a lock. The girls look at the keys, at each other, and then back at him. "This way." He leads them onto the new mini-sidewalk that curves off from the driveway to the outside of the garage, ending near the back of it at a sturdy door. "Try it."

"Vic . . . ," Inara says slowly.

"Try it."

Her key is bright blue with ladybugs on it, and it slides easily into the lock. She's immediately met with a narrow, fairly long flight of stairs, and the other two follow after her when none of us show signs of moving. Then we race up after them.

As we round the corner, there's a bright flash from a camera, which has to mean Jenny and Marlene were already waiting. Over the spring and early summer, the hired crew has been hard at work adding a second story to the garage, the top level fully insulated and wired for electricity. There's a small kitchen, mostly built for snack purposes, a full bathroom, a bedroom with a set of three staggered beds, a cross between triple bunk beds and a stepladder, and the biggest part, a living room with comfortable couches and beanbags and with a TV in one corner.

"Welcome home," Vic says simply, as the girls stare around in wonder.

They drop their bags and tackle him in another hug that sends him toppling back onto a couch. Just before he lands, Priya grabs one of the throw pillows and tucks it behind Vic's back to soften the landing. She grins, bouncing on the seat beside him, and Victoria-Bliss laughs and chatters, but Inara, eyes bright, turns her face into his shoulder and holds tight.

Slipping between me and Eddison in a move that only startles Eddison a little, Sterling puts her arms around our waists. "Today's a good day," she says quietly.

In spite of everything that happened earlier, I have to agree.

Eddison doesn't say anything, but he's got the small, soft smile that only comes out for family, and that's better than a cheer.

The next day, Vic drops the girls off at Eddison's on his way to work with a stern warning to spend the day relaxing, and Sterling joins us shortly thereafter with breakfast. None of the three girls are especially morning oriented, and I'm sure they stayed up far too late with the giddiness over the apartment. When they're a little more awake, we cycle through turns in the bedroom to change into swimsuits and head down to the pool. Inara and Victoria-Bliss in high-backed one-pieces don't surprise me. However comfortable they've grown with the enormous butterfly wing tattoos that were forced on them, they don't generally choose to have them show in mixed company.

Priya walks out in a royal blue bikini and an open baseball shirt. I glance over to Eddison, who sighs and bites the inside of his cheek to keep from begging her to put on something more concealing, because, while Eddison is wonderful at respecting bodily autonomy, Priya is his little sister. I don't know how many brothers are ever comfortable with their little sisters (or sisters in general, I guess) in bikinis. Then Sterling walks out in a bubblegum-pink two-piece with a flirty ruffle along the hips, and Eddison's cheeks turn a shade close to matching.

As the rest of us settle into deck chairs for some sun, Eddison immediately dives into the pool to start laps. He isn't going to say it unless I press, but I suspect he's a little uncomfortable at how his being part of the company could be perceived by people who don't know us. It does look a little like a harem. I don't press, though. He's a genuinely good man, and he's uncomfortable for our sake more than his. There's not really a way to talk him out of that one.

"Does your mother know about that?" Sterling asks, pointing to the tattoo that stretches along Priya's entire left side.

"Helped me pick the parlor and went with me to every session," the girl answers with a laugh. At the beginning of summer, she kept slipping into French whenever she wasn't directly addressing one of us, her brain hardwired from three years of living in Paris. She hasn't done it in a couple of weeks, though.

I lean over in the chair so I can see it better. I knew she was working on it over the spring months, but she didn't tell us what she was getting. Last time she was down here, at the beginning of summer, the final session was still healing, so she didn't show us. If the size of it is somewhat surprising, the images are absolutely Priya. A large chess queen, made of colorful stained glass, stands in a base of flowers. Jonquils, calla lilies, freesia, all the flowers left by the serial killer who murdered her sister and then hunted Priya. Chavi's flowers, sunshine yellow chrysanthemums, ring the queen's crown. Above the chrysanthemums float two butterflies, large enough to make out their specific coloring.

I don't have to look them up to know what they are: a Western Pine Elfin and a Mexican Bluewing, which can be found in more detail on Inara's and Victoria-Bliss's backs respectively.

"I felt like I could finally leave it behind," Priya says quietly.

"It?"

"The sense of being a victim. Like somehow it was all finally mine, and under my skin where it belonged rather than shredding me."

Without conscious thought, my fingers trace the scars on my cheek, covered with waterproof makeup. Priya's seen them bare, but I don't think Inara and Victoria-Bliss ever have.

But then, even outside of the tattoos, they have their own scars. Inara's hands will forever show the trials of the night the Garden exploded, burns and bits of glass leaving their marks when she fought to keep the other Butterflies safe in impossible circumstances. Priya's hands have thin, pale scars across her palms and fingers where she fought for possession of a knife, and a worse line across her neck, a blade held to her pulse.

Scars mean we survived something, even when the wounds still hurt.

The day offers a much-needed sense of relaxation, even after the heat chases us inside to the air-conditioning. As night falls and the temperature starts dipping a little, we return to the patio with arms overflowing with s'mores fixings, because Sterling learned that Inara has never had a s'more. There isn't a fire pit in the complex, but shortening the legs on one of the grills places the flames at a comfortable height, and Priya has her camera out to capture Inara's first bite. She closes her eyes like she's tasting heaven, a bit of melting chocolate clinging to the corner of her mouth, a blob of marshmallow sticking to her nose, and I can't wait to show that picture to Vic.

Then my work phone goes off.

We all freeze, staring at it where it sits innocently on top of my shoes. None of us have mentioned the case today. Somehow there was just this sense of agreement to leave it alone for another day, maybe two. Just . . . later.

Sterling leans over to read the screen. "It's Holmes," she says quietly. I grab it and accept the call. "Ramirez."

"I don't care what Simpkins says," the detective says by way of hello, "these kids are hysterical and they need you here."

"Which kids?"

"The three who wandered into the fire station half an hour ago with teddy bears and your name. Get to Prince William."

Once upon a time, there was a little girl who was scared of crying.

It seemed she'd spent her whole life crying. Those few days in the hospital, after Daddy was arrested, whenever she cried, a nurse or social worker would hurry into the room if the angel wasn't already there. They'd comfort her with soft voices and gentle hugs, things she'd never known before, and she would feel stronger until the fear got the better of her again. Then it was off to that first foster home, where only tears given to God had any meaning. She didn't know how to give her tears to God.

She didn't know how to give anything to God.

But that home didn't have children anymore, not since one of the boys passed out in class and a doctor discovered they were all being starved. They all got sent to different homes, and the little girl liked the second home. The woman was funny and kind, and the man had sad eyes and a gentle smile and always seemed to know which of the girls were the most broken because he would speak softly to them, hands by his sides. He never touched them, never cornered them, was so careful to give them space and never called them pet names.

He never called her angel, *or* baby, *never called her* beautiful.

But then there was a car accident, and unlike Mama's, this one really was an accident, and another group of kids was scattered. The next house was all right, everyone fairly content to ignore each other outside of meals, but then the man's sister and children came to live with them, and the sister was sick, too sick for the man and woman to take care of children who weren't theirs.

That's when the little girl was sent here, to a woman who passed her days in a haze of pills and her nights with alcohol and sedatives, and never knew what her husband did to the children in their care.

Daddy would have liked the husband.

She cried, because this wasn't supposed to happen, she was never supposed to have to suffer through this again (ever, the angel had said; she wasn't supposed to have gone through this ever) but the man came to her room and told her that she liked it, she knew she did, she knew she'd missed this, being taken care of properly.

But she couldn't stop crying; she never could.

19

"Sterling, get the girls back to Vic's. Come on, Ramirez, we need to change." Eddison dumps the emergency bucket of sand over the grill, extinguishing the flames, and grabs up whatever packaging he can. After a moment, the rest of us pitch in, then jog up to his apartment. The girls grab bags and give me hugs or kisses as they follow Sterling out.

It seems stupid to take time to change clothes, especially when we're not the ones working the case, but I can't well show up in shorts and a halter top. We yank on jeans, and Eddison tosses me a long-sleeved University of Miami tee to throw on over the halter top. We're out the door less than two minutes after the girls, and actually pull out of the parking lot before they do.

"They wandered into a fire station," I tell him, hanging on to the oh-shit handle for dear life. Eddison doesn't dick around when he's driving to a scene. "Three kids, they're being taken to Prince William."

"Got it." He curses at a red light, then, seeing no one coming down the cross street, runs it. "Three days. The time between kills is getting shorter and shorter."

The car screams into the hospital's parking lot just behind the ambulances, and then we're running to the ER entrance to follow the kids who are way too small for the gurneys they're on. The boys look like twins, so thin it's impossible to guess their age, and the girl doesn't look any better. Holmes is waiting at the nurses' station. She draws herself up to greet the children, but upon actually *seeing* them, her giant coffee slips from nerveless fingers to splash all over the floor.

"Are they *high?*" she hisses.

One of the boys is shaking, not a seizure so much as a full-body tremor, grinding his teeth as his head sways back and forth. He plucks and tears at the skin around his fingernails, leaving great bloody streaks behind, and he can't seem to stop talking, the words spilling out fast and half-formed. His twin is silent, but his pupils are blown so wide he can't possibly see anything, and his skin is bright with sweat. He keeps trying to swallow, but each time, his dry throat clicks and catches, and he tries again. Their sister . . .

Their sister is screaming, stopping only long enough to draw another ragged breath, and her arms are belted to the gurney, I assume to keep her from adding to the scratches all down her arms. She's absolutely hysterical, pupils blown and eyes unfocused.

"They've been exposed to meth," I say breathlessly. "A *lot* of meth to have this kind of effect."

The nurses jump into action, the charge nurse snapping instructions and sending one of them running for doctors.

"How much do you think, to get that?" Holmes asks.

"Their parents have to be cooking it." Jesus, my hands are shaking. I've seen kids under the influence before, but never to that extent. Usually when someone's drugging a child, it's to subdue them, not hop them up. "Has anyone made it out to the parents yet?"

"The closer fire station," she answers grimly.

"The house is *on fire?*"

Eddison curses under his breath. "Meth kitchens explode pretty frequently, but I'm going to guess this one had help. If the parents were inside . . ."

"Explains why the only blood on the children is what they've drawn themselves."

"Mignone is out at the scene; we called Simpkins, she and some of her agents are heading out, but the girl, Zoe, she kept chanting your name. Can you—"

"Yes." Leaving Eddison and Holmes mopping up spilled coffee, I head behind the girl's curtain. Zoe, Holmes said. She's fighting the nurses as they unstrap her, her bony arms flailing as she continues to scream. "Zoe? Zoe, can you hear me?"

If she does, she's too worked up to answer.

"Zoe, my name is Mercedes, Mercedes Ramirez."

The screams stop, at least, and she stares at me, or tries to, her shoulders heaving with labored, gasping breaths. "Mer-mer-mercedes. Mercedes. Safe Mercedes, she said that."

The charge nurse frees a hand to point at a spot on the bed. Obediently, I sit there, pulling on the gloves she tosses me, and when they transfer Zoe to the bed, I'm at the perfect position to take her hands in mine, gently but too firmly for her to pull free and scratch. Around the long, frenzied scratches, bright rashes bloom up and down her arms.

"That's right, Zoe," I say softly, "you're safe now. You're at the hospital, your brothers are here. We're going to help you. You're safe here."

The shuddering gasps turn into sobs, and she collapses forward, letting me cradle her against my chest. I carefully prop my shoulder under her cheek, keeping her face away from the exposed skin at my neck. I don't want to get an accidental contact high from the meth on her skin and clothes. "We've got you," I murmur, holding her steady for the nurses.

They work quickly, getting her vitals settled and an IV started for fluids. With a bit of coaching, Zoe turns her arm to let them draw blood. Meth is a given, but they'll need to check to make sure that's all it is.

"My brothers," she chokes out.

"They're here, Zoe, it's okay. They're getting help, too. They're just on the other side of those curtains."

She's starting to wheeze, and I rub a gloved hand in circles against her back to try to settle her a bit. "The lady. She kept. She grabbed. The lady." She flaps her hand, hard enough to almost dislodge the second draw needle at her elbow. There are red impressions around her wrist, darker than the rash. Fingers? The beginnings of bruises?

"She grabbed your arm, didn't she, Zoe? Kept hold of you so your brothers wouldn't fight?"

Nodding, she draws in a deeper breath. It's still shaky, but it's stronger, and followed by another good breath. "An angel, Mercy. She didn't have wings."

"Zoe, were you and your brothers sleeping when she came in?"

"Sleeping? Trying. Trying, but our skin was alive." She looks down at her arms and tries to pull her hands away to scratch. One of the nurses holds her IV arm still, and I keep the other one against Zoe's thigh.

"When did your skin come alive? Zoe? When did it start?"

"We wanted dinner. The beds were out of food. Mommy and Daddy made us dinner. We never eat in the kitchen. We ate in the kitchen, though, with Mommy and Daddy."

"*Cagaste y saltaste en la caca. Jesucristo.*" Those idiots weren't cooking meth in a shed or garage; they were using their own fucking kitchen. The beds were out of food? Did the kids hide food in their rooms so they wouldn't have to go to the kitchen? *Santa madre de Dios.*

"You had dinner, you were trying to sleep. Zoe, what happened then? Zoe?"

"An angel came." Her words are softer, her voice cracked and raw from screaming. "Angels have wings. Didn't have wings."

"What did the angel do, Zoe?"

"She . . . she . . ." With a sudden gasp, she starts seizing. The nurses grab her out of my arms to lower her to the bed, supporting her head and neck against the spasms. One of them eyes his watch, timing the fit.

"How long?" snaps a young doctor, pushing through the curtain.

"Forty-two seconds," answers the one with the watch.

They push an injection into her IV, close to her hand, but it still takes a couple of minutes for the seizure to ease. Once she falls limp, they loop an oxygen mask over her face.

"I'm sorry, Agent, I need you out of here," the doctor says, and to her credit, she does actually look sorry.

"Of course. Her brothers?"

"Not seizing. You can try."

I peel off the gloves and get a fresh pair, just in case, and head to the next set of curtains. The quiet one is there, his hands shaking finely as he gulps down water under the watchful eye of a nurse. When the cup's empty, he tries to hand it back to her, but can only hold it out vaguely in her direction. She pours in a little more from a pitcher and gives it back to him. He's already got a self-adhering bandage looped around his elbow from a blood draw, the IV taped to the back of his hand. Because they didn't have to struggle with him the way they did with Zoe, he's also got heart monitor pads on his chest, and an oxygen mask is sitting on the bed by his hip.

"Dry mouth," the nurse informs me quietly. "There's only so much the water can help right now, but we'll get the mask on him in a couple of minutes."

I give her a quick smile and look back at the boy. "My name is Mercedes," I tell him, and he nods, seeming to recognize it. "Can you tell me your name?"

"Brayden," he rasps.

"Okay, Brayden. How old are you?"

"Nine. Caleb, too. Zoe's eight." He blinks rapidly, but his eyes won't focus. "Is Zoe okay?"

"None of you are okay right now," I answer honestly, my hands curling around the foot of the bed. "You're getting help, though, and right now that's what's important."

"They sounded scared."

"She had a seizure." The nurse looks startled, and opens her mouth like she's about to cut me off, but subsides. "They gave her something to calm the seizure, and they're going to run tests so they know how else to help her."

"But she's gonna be okay?"

"I don't know, Brayden, but the doctors are doing their absolute best, I promise."

"Mom and Dad didn't get out of the house," he tells me. "They were still sleeping. She had Zoe, and she pushed us out of the house, and it exploded. She said it was the way it needed to be."

"Did she say why?"

"She said you were going to keep us safe."

"Brayden, do you remember anything about the lady?"

"She was an angel." He frowns, draining the rest of his cup. "She looked like an angel, maybe. Maybe? I don't see too good. But she looked all white. Like the moon."

"Did she give you anything?" I ask, already knowing the answer but curious how he'll answer it.

"Bears," he replies promptly. "White bears, and parts of them were noisy."

"Noisy like what?"

"Like . . . like . . . like Bubble Wrap blankets," he decides after some thought. "Like a tissue paper present."

"Were you in a car, Brayden?"

With the nurse watching his vitals and giving him just a little bit of water each time he empties the cup, I ask Brayden all the questions I can think of until a doctor comes in, and then I move down to the next curtain. I don't swap out the gloves this time, because I didn't touch Brayden. Caleb, however, is in no condition to be answering questions. He doesn't seem to hear what the nurses and doctor are asking him. Beneath the oxygen mask, he keeps up a steady stream of half-formed words, and occasionally cocks his swaying head as if he's listening to something, but what he's saying doesn't seem to have anything to do with what the rest of us can hear.

So I peek back behind Zoe's curtain. They've got her hooked up to a heart monitor now, and it's going a little crazy, so I don't try to go in. Instead, I walk back to the nurses' station. Eddison is there, but Holmes isn't.

"She went outside to meet Simpkins," he answers before I can ask the question.

"*Mierda.*"

"She specifically wanted you here, and it calmed the girl."

"Yeah, calmed her right into a seizure."

He flicks the center of my forehead, more irritating than painful. "One has nothing to do with the other. Stop."

"Extrapolating from what Brayden said"—I sigh, peeling off the UM tee so I can lean against the counter without worrying about castoff meth from Zoe—"our killer prepared the explosion before she woke up the kids. She woke up Zoe first, and kept hands on her so the boys wouldn't risk fighting, if they were even in any condition to do so. Parents were still sleeping in their room, she pushed the boys outside, did *something*, then carried Zoe out and got all three kids a safe distance away before the explosion. Brayden said he felt the heat, but they weren't in danger of burning. She got them in the car—a big car, he said—keeping Zoe in the front seat, and gave them the bears. Brayden tried to open the door, but the child lock must have been engaged. He doesn't know how long they drove for. She stopped in sight of the fire station to let them out, and gave them the instructions and my name. He looked back when they were at the station door, but he couldn't see well enough to know if she was still there. One of the firefighters ran out and looked but didn't see any cars out of place, so she must have gone."

Being in the halter top has me anxious, especially knowing Simpkins is right outside, but I'd really prefer *not* to wear the meth-rubbed shirt any longer than I absolutely have to.

"He's seizing!" calls a voice from Caleb's curtain. A moment later a similar cry rises from Zoe's partition.

Eddison grabs my arm before I can race back to Brayden's bed. "Doctor is in with him," he says softly. "I know you want to comfort him, but right now you'll be in the way, especially with the other two in such unstable condition."

"Why do you think he isn't as bad as them?"

"We don't know that he isn't, just that he isn't seizing yet."

"Ramirez, what the hell are you wearing?" snaps Simpkins, stalking inside with Holmes at her heels. The two Smiths, who have been on her team about as long as she's willing to keep anyone, follow, giving us small nods of acknowledgment.

I stand up straight and point to the bundle of fabric on the counter. "It has meth castoff from calming the girl," I answer calmly. "It wasn't safe to wear, and we didn't have time to change before we came."

"You shouldn't have come here at all."

"It was my call," Holmes reminds her in an aggrieved tone.

"Clearly the children don't need you now," Simpkins continues, ignoring the interruption. "Leave."

"No," retorts Holmes. "I called her in."

"You chose to partner with the FBI—"

"Partnered, yes, I did not give up the case to you, and I need her checking in on these kids."

The two women stare each other down, and honestly I'm very glad I get to stand off to one side for this particular pissing match. Surprisingly, Simpkins is the one to look away. "Who can give me a status report?" she yells, stomping toward the curtains, and two nurses and a doctor glare at her.

The taller Smith shrugs out of his windbreaker and holds it out to me, while the stouter Smith pulls a plastic sack from the bag at his side. I drop the shirt into the sack, following it with the gloves, and then gratefully accept the jacket. It's cold, true—hospitals are nearly always cold—but I feel more exposed than I'd like, in a way that doesn't really have anything to do with clothing or skin. The jacket helps anyway.

"We'll be in the waiting room," Eddison tells Holmes and the Smiths. "They don't need more people in those cubbies right now."

"We'll send someone," the taller Smith promises. They've been partnered up for thirteen years, six of them on Simpkins's team, but I have never heard the Smiths referred to as anything but a cohesive unit. I honestly do not even know their first names, because they are always, *always* the Smiths.

The waiting room is nearly empty. In one corner, a sobbing woman rocks back and forth in an uncomfortable chair, her fingers moving along her rosary. In her other hand, she clutches a passport and a work visa. Eddison drops into the chair beside me, taking my hand to lace our fingers together, and I lean against his shoulder.

"Have you updated Vic and Sterling?" I mumble.

"Yeah. I'll send another in a minute."

My eyes are burning, and I want to say it's just from castoff somehow, but it's exhaustion and rage and fear, and the twisting claw in my gut from wondering if we're actually going to catch this person, and what kind of reaction the community will have if it happens. In the same breath that people abhor those who break the law, they also love vigilantes with an appealing cause.

Rescuing children from abuse? The public will eat that up when it all comes out. So far the papers have been quiet about the details. The murders have happened in different parts of town or even outside of it but still in-county, so no one's drawn big blinking lights around them to connect them. And, too, the editor down at the main paper is usually good about squashing stories that exploit kids as victims.

I want to go home.

I'm not sure home *is* home anymore.

20

Zoe Jones dies at 2:13 in the morning, when a series of hyperthermic seizures causes a massive stroke.

Caleb Jones dies three hours later of rapid organ failure, including his heart.

Brayden's doctor tells us the boy is physically stable for now, though they'll be monitoring him closely as he starts into withdrawal symptoms. Emotionally? Brayden isn't talking to anyone. Not to me, not to Simpkins or Holmes, not to any of the doctors or nurses. He cries when they tell him about Zoe, but when they have to come back and tell him about his twin, he just shuts down.

Tate, the social worker who'd been with Mason on Wednesday, shows up around six, and listens gravely as we fill him in. "It took me longer to get here because I stopped to get their case file," he explains, holding up the folder. "A home inspection was done four months ago based on an anonymous complaint, likely from one of their previous neighbors, but they had just moved into the house. Everything was still clean. When we interviewed the children, Zoe and Caleb said they played outside most of the time. Brayden stayed inside the house more. Presumably, he was the one who would go into the kitchen to get supplies if they ran out of food. They had a mini-fridge in the boys' room, tubs of food under the bed they said were snacks. I think if they ran out, Brayden was the only one to go into the kitchen."

"He built up a slight tolerance, so he didn't overdose as badly last night," I translate, and he nods. "But yesterday their parents broke pattern. They made dinner for their kids and sat down together to eat in the kitchen. The other two were exposed in greater quantity than they're used to, and even Brayden was probably in there longer than usual."

"We requested a drug test on the children following the inspection, but it was rejected because the house was clean."

"What about a drug test on the parents?" Eddison asks.

"House was clean," Tate repeats. "We don't think the Joneses were purposeful users; our theory was that they rode the contact high from cooking it, and sold it for income. They didn't demonstrate the more overt symptoms of tweakers. Their prior residence had already sold, so we were refused permission to test there."

"And so the kids fell through the cracks because of technicalities." I scrub at my face, which is itching like crazy from the combination of old makeup, chlorine, and hospital. "Do you happen to know if the warrant for who had access to each CPS file has been finalized?"

"I believe so. I know Lee has been working on things. He and Gloria had their heads together."

That . . . does not fill me with confidence.

Vic and Sterling come in not much later, laden down with coffees and tinfoil-wrapped plates of baked goods, courtesy of Marlene staying up all night worrying about us. Sterling pads up behind Eddison, but rather than trying to spook him like she normally does, she lays a hand against the back of his neck and holds up a large travel mug of coffee. He still flinches at the unexpected touch, but it's smaller, more contained, and he leans into her side, mumbling a thank-you.

Vic carefully lowers himself into a chair across from us, leaning forward so he can keep his volume low. "Simpkins called Section Chief Gordon to bitch about your being here," he tells us. "He checked in with Detective Holmes before calling me, and we're going to pretend I'm not sharing this, but you should have the heads up."

"Así que esto va bien entonces," Eddison mutters.

"Her team will still be working the case, but she won't be. He's pulling her up on administrative review."

We both blink at him, then look at Sterling, who settles in next to Vic and shrugs. We look back at Vic.

"Did Cass tell you anything about their case a couple weeks ago in Idaho?"

I shake my head. "She said it was a clusterfuck, but we didn't get the chance to get drinks for the stitch-n-bitch before this came up. At lunch on Wednesday we were talking about this case."

"Simpkins rode the local law enforcement officials so hard they withdrew their request for aid before the case had been solved."

"In Idaho?" Sterling squeaks. "It's hard enough to get invited in there."

"It should have gone to me as unit chief, but Simpkins took it over my head to the section chief. IA was reviewing the situation when the request from Holmes came in, but they hadn't reached a conclusion and Gordon wanted the lead agent to have at least twenty years. It brings a weight to it that can go far in protecting the targeted agent."

"I've heard rumors that she put herself forward for your job," Eddison notes.

I look down at my hands. I'm not going to throw Cass under the bus by confirming it.

Vic grimaces. "We don't know yet if that's connected," he cautions. "She hasn't been notified, so mouths shut. It'll be later today, once Gordon can get everything together."

"The Smiths have the most seniority," I note, "but neither of them is suited to leading a team. Cass is a great agent but she doesn't have the leadership experience, not for a case like this, and Johnson is still transitioning back from medical leave, so he's desk bound. That leaves . . . who—Watts and Burnside?"

"He's asking Watts. Burnside is the best on the team at tracking through digital trails, so they want him focused on the CPS office."

"Watts is good," Eddison says, more to me than to the others. "She's steady."

"Simpkins was, too."

Sterling brings her legs up onto the chair, sitting cross-legged with a napkin across her lap to catch the crumbs from the croissant she's picking apart. She's frowning a little; this is her deep-in-thought frown, one of the distinctive ones, marked by her mouth twisting into a sideways moue. I watch her for several minutes, the frown shifting minutely as she works her way through the set of thoughts.

Then Eddison throws a blueberry at her from his muffin, and she looks up with wide, startled eyes. "Share with the class, Thumper," he says.

"What if it isn't anything nice?" she retorts automatically.

"Two kids died this morning, and a family of five became a family of one very broken little boy," I say softly. "I don't think there's any nice right now."

She takes a deep breath and lets Vic pull the mangled pastry from her hands. "The killer was too late to save the kids," she says in a rush. "It's even possible that the stress of the so-called rescue exacerbated the effects of the drugs on their systems. So. She didn't save the kids. Add that to the fact that she's already accelerating the kills, and what happens next?"

"She *needs* to save these kids." Eddison scowls down at what's left of his muffin. "Whatever's driving her, whatever personal trauma is nipping her heels, doing this is a need. Failure will either drive that violence inward, or—"

"Or outward, exploding in a frenzy," I finish.

"She's not even trying your house anymore," Vic notes. "Sterling checked your cameras. Only two cars came through that didn't belong to residents, and they went to homes and stayed there all night. Are still there, in fact."

"But she's still giving them my name. Why?"

"How far did you get into your cases yesterday?"

"Thursday? Not far. Assessing and running every name takes time."

"Can you make a rubric to narrow them down, so we can help you sort through? You can dismiss the cases where the victims were boys—"

"We can't, actually," Sterling interrupts with a wince. "He could have had a sister, a cousin, a neighbor, a friend, some girl who was influenced by Mercedes helping with the rescue. We give bears to all the kids, not just the immediate victims."

"And we haven't eliminated the possibility of the killer being male," adds Eddison. "Plenty of men have higher-pitched voices, or can fake it. Given popular depictions of angels, the wig may not even be out of place. We don't know gender. It's just easier to say 'she' because that's what the kids assume."

Despite our instincts screaming otherwise, he's right. "And we can't rely on cases where I felt a particular connection with someone, because they're not always mutual. I could have had a drastic impact on someone's life and have absolutely no idea."

"Shit," sighs Vic, and we all flinch. He so rarely swears; I think we've all grown to think of him cursing as a sign that things are really fucked.

Cass clears her throat from the hallway, getting our attention before she joins us. "I thought you'd want to know, CPS contacted both sets of Brayden's grandparents. Paternals live in Alabama, maternals in Washington State, and both have indicated they want custody. They also really don't like each other. It could get nasty."

I sigh. "Cass, one of these days, you're going to remember the difference between *want* to know and *need* to know."

She gives me a tired smile. "The warrant went through. Mr. Lee should be getting me the list of file access by end of business Monday. Burnside got approved for access to their system to examine digital footprints."

"Word to the wise, Gloria Hess is helping Lee put the list together."

"Fuck." She glances at Vic and turns bright red, but doesn't apologize.

His lips twitch in a reluctant smile.

"Brayden isn't talking to Tate," Cass continues after a moment. "He isn't talking to anyone. But he doesn't seem to mind Tate staying with him."

"Tate seems like very good people."

"I got that impression too." She straightens out a wrinkle in her shirt, then frowns down at it. "I can't tell if this is inside out or backward."

"Backward," Sterling answers. "I can see the lines of the tag."

"Huh. Anyway, Brayden probably isn't going to communicate for a while. Tate said, and Holmes agrees, you should probably head on home and get some rest. You know, if you want."

I eye the last splashes of my coffee and wonder if I can fall asleep before the caffeine kicks in.

"Thank you, Cass," Vic says for all of us. "You'll keep us updated?"

"Yes, sir."

Eddison and I both snort, followed by Cass's blush deepening. Sterling just gives her a commiserating look.

"Cass? Killer left bruises on Zoe's left wrist; I don't know if you'll be able to get fingerprints, but it can probably tell you her general size. Talk to Holmes and her medical examiner."

We end up following Vic home and sacking out in his living room rather than separating. Sterling curls up in the armchair, face buried in her knees. Eddison and I each take a couch, and it says a lot that despite the adrenaline, the caffeine, the light pouring in through the sheer drapes, we're out cold pretty damn fast.

Several hours later, the ringing of my personal phone snaps me awake in nothing flat, my heart thumping painfully against my ribs. Sterling wakes just as abruptly, flailing off the chair and landing on the floor with a squeak that has Eddison attempting to prop himself up on an elbow, and sort-of managing it three attempts later.

The screen says *Esperanza*. "It's not another kid," I announce, and Eddison drops back into the couch and blanket.

"You're not answering it," mumbles Sterling, hauling herself up the chair.

"I'm not sure if it's my cousin or my aunt."

"Are either of them bad options?"

"One of them is."

"Oh."

Eddison cracks open one eye. "Why is it still ringing?"

"Because I don't want to pick up if it's Soledad." I wait for it to go to voice mail, and listen to the message. It's Esperanza, *afortunadamente*, but her message doesn't really tell me much. *There's something big, call me back so I can be the one to tell you, rather than my mother.*

Big or little, I really don't want to know. Don't need to know.

Before I can decide whether or not to call her back, the phone starts vibrating and ringing again, her name lighting up the screen. Damn it. With a bone-deep sigh, I accept the call. "Hello?"

Sterling winces at how rough my voice is.

"Mercedes? It's afternoon where you are; why do you sound like you just woke up?" My cousin's voice is frazzled, which is uncommon for Esperanza. The biggest reason I allowed the reconnection was her calm and common sense.

"We were up all night for a case. What's wrong?"

"Family meeting this morning."

"Oh, God, I do not need to know this."

"Yes, you do. *Tío* is sick."

"Which *tío*?"

There's a heavy silence, and after far too long, it clicks. "Oh."

My father.

"Pancreatic cancer," she continues once it's clear I won't.

"Painful."

"The family wants to get him out of prison for treatment."

"Probably not happening, but not any of my business regardless."

Eddison is almost sitting up now, slumped against the arm of the couch and desperately blinking to keep his eyes from staying closed.

"Mercedes . . ." Esperanza huffs into the microphone, and it distorts like a hurricane through my speaker. "You really think the rest of the family isn't going to bother you about this?"

"That's exactly what I think, because I'll be turning off my personal phone until I can switch the number."

"Most of the grandkids have never even met him."

"Lucky them."

"Mercedes."

"No."

"Pancreatic cancer isn't all that treatable. You know he's probably dying."

"Mucha carne pal gato."

"Mercedes!"

"Is that her?" I hear her mother in the background. "Let me speak to her, that ungrateful, malicious—"

I end the call and turn the phone off, which is how it will stay for a while. The kids in the hospital have my work number, as do Priya, Inara, and Victoria-Bliss. Anyone else can email me. Have to admit, I'm disappointed in Esperanza. She was supposed to be the one person in the extended Ramirez *familia* who understood that that wasn't my life anymore.

"Throw it against the wall?" mumbles Eddison.

"I have some pictures and shit to get off it first. Then we can destroy it."

"Okay. You okay?"

"No. Go back to sleep, though. This problem isn't going anywhere."

He immediately burrows back into his blanket so only his shaggy dark curls are visible.

Sterling regards me solemnly, and it's amazing how young she looks when her hair is down and messy around her face. "Need to talk about it?" she offers quietly.

Sterling doesn't know the story the way Vic and Eddison do, like her old boss Finney does, for that matter. It took me years and half a bottle of tequila to finally tell Eddison. But Sterling is . . . she's important, and I've finally settled into trusting that sense in a way I hadn't when I told Eddison. She's my team, and she's my friend. She's my family.

"Not yet," I say eventually. "When the world isn't on fire."

"Sounds like a date." She curls back into a tight ball, a little pill bug twisted into a tag-edged fleece blanket with Care Bears all over it. It is Brittany's favorite blanket in the world, and she very rarely lets it come downstairs for anyone else to use.

As tired as I am, as drained, it still takes a long time to sleep again. My arms ache for the comfort of the black-velvet teddy bear on my nightstand, but this case . . . I don't know if that bear will ever be what it was. It saved my life in important ways, or reminded me my life was worth living, however that distinction can be drawn.

I stare at the ceiling for I don't even know how long before Vic's face swims into blurry focus. His warm brown eyes look somewhere between sad and amused, and his callused hand is gentle as he strokes my hair back from my face, thumb lingering over the scars. "Sleep, Mercedes. You're not alone."

The laugh comes out more like a sob, but I close my eyes, and he lightly pets my hair until I fall asleep.

Once upon a time, there was a little girl who was scared of change.

But—

Some fears, she'd finally learned, were good things. Some fears weren't the terror and pain, they were just . . . thrills. Sparks of nerve.

Despite the uncertainty of all of her foster homes, where impermanence was the only permanent thing, the little girl had worked hard at school, learning all the things her lackadaisical homeschooling had never taught her. She worked hard to catch up, and then she worked harder to get ahead. When it came time to apply for colleges, she had stellar grades and a fistful of personal essays that struck a carefully crafted balance between the horrific experiences of her past and a heartwarming determination for her future.

Her guidance counselor, perhaps the only person the little girl tentatively labeled On Her Side, had laughed herself silly when she read them, promised her she'd strike gold with them.

She had.

She got acceptances and scholarships, and when combined with the money the court forced her father to give her nearly four years before, it meant she could even go out of state, start over somewhere entirely new. Somewhere no one knew what had happened to her (unless they worked in Admissions). She even changed her name, legally and officially. It made the school paperwork a nightmare, but it was worth it. Her old name belonged to that other girl, that girl who'd been hurt by so many people and could never do anything to stop it.

She was someone new, someone without the baggage and the accent, someone from nowhere and anywhere. There was nothing to tie her to where she'd come from.

She loved college. It was scary and overwhelming and wonderful, with freedoms she'd never dared dream of. She even made friends. Slowly, cautiously, not entirely honestly, but friends enough to make her genuinely happy for the first time she could remember. She didn't date—she wasn't brave enough for that, wasn't sure she wanted to be—but her friends protected her when people didn't want to take no for an answer, when her old instincts fought against her new courage, and she was grateful.

She found a job that didn't require her to interact with people much, and let her face some of her old fears in small ways, and she was surprised by how restful it was. She enjoyed her friends and classes, liked getting together with other people, but working gave her time alone to recover, to re-center. She liked the balance, and was proud of herself for discovering and maintaining it.

Once upon a time, there was a little girl who was afraid of change.

She went out bravely into the world anyway.

21

The events at the hospital and the Joneses' home happen too late to get into the Saturday paper, but they start spinning around on social media that afternoon, and half the front page on Sunday is dedicated to "A Tweaker Tragedy" and I really want to stake whatever asshole came up with that headline. The only blessing to the relentlessly slipshod reporting is that none of the other murders are brought up. The article doesn't even classify the Joneses' deaths as suspicious; it makes it sound like the kids wandered away from home to get help and their home exploded while they were gone. It lists the wrong fire station, totally misses the detectives who were present, and misidentifies the FBI agents as DEA agents.

It's some form of protection for Brayden, at least, and all the other kids.

Priya pokes my shoulder at breakfast, which is eaten sprawled out in the living room because there's too many of us even for the seldom-used dining room. "What time is Mass?"

"What?"

"Mass," she repeats patiently. "What time?"

I blink at her, too tired to fully comprehend what she's asking.

"You feel better when you go to Mass, Mercedes. It's a Sunday. So what time?"

"She likes the nine-thirty best," Eddison tells her around a mouthful of half-chewed apple tart.

"Hmm." Priya checks her watch and pushes to her feet. "We should get dressed then."

Priya rarely chooses to take charge of things, but when she wants to, she's a lot like her mother: impossible to resist. Before I'm fully aware of moving, my clothes are changed and I'm sitting in the backseat with my makeup bag and Priya holding a mirror steady, Sterling in the front passenger seat as Eddison drives us to church.

It's a bizarre mix. Priya isn't a practicing Hindu, if that's the right description, but she does wear a bindi on a daily basis, and Sterling is Jewish, despite her deep and abiding love for bacon. Eddison was raised Catholic, but his faith didn't survive his sister's kidnapping and so-far permanent disappearance. He occasionally sits with me, usually at Christmas or when I'm having a rough time, but the memories, so engrained in him through his childhood, make him uncomfortable in churches.

But there we all are, stretched out in a pew near the back, Priya and Sterling subtly watching others for their cues and Eddison blushing every time he's standing or sitting or kneeling by rote. When everyone else starts moving, pew by pew, for Communion, Priya gives me a questioning look.

I shake my head. "You can't take Communion without confession."

"And you can't do confession because of your job?"

"Job isn't really a factor, as long as I don't share confidential information," I whisper. "It's more that I can't receive absolution for sins I don't genuinely repent." She still looks confused, and despite everything, it makes me smile. "I don't think God hates queers, but the Church isn't fond of us. What I am, how I feel, is a sin, and I can't repent."

"Oh." She chews on that the rest of the service. Priya wasn't raised in any religion, and she has an outsider's fascination for them, not just the stories and imagery, but the rules and rituals, all the ways we try to structure what people are allowed to believe.

When the sanctuary is mostly clear after the service, Eddison nods toward the priest. "Go on. We'll wait."

Priya's head tilts to one side. "I thought she couldn't—"

"Confession isn't the same as counsel," he tells her.

Leaving him to explain the distinctions to Priya and Sterling, I ease out of the pew and up to the altar. Father Brendon is only a couple of years older than me, and he's a good sort. Half the preteen and teen girls have crushes on him, because he's safe, and because he's respectful of their feelings without encouraging them. He's a vast improvement over Father Michael, who used to scowl at me during homilies.

"Ah, Mercedes," he greets me, smiling as he hands the last of his regalia to a waiting altar boy. "You've been busy these last few weeks."

Which is a very nice way of pointing out that I haven't been to Mass in almost a month.

"There's been . . ." How the hell do I even put it?

Nodding, he sits down on the edge of the dais, clasping his hands between his knees. "Work? Or personal?"

"Yes," I answer decisively, sitting beside him.

He laughs, warm and soft, and I need to remember to thank Eddison and Priya later for this. "Is everything okay with Siobhan?"

"She dumped me."

"I'm sorry to hear that."

"I'm not sure I am. Sorry, I mean."

He listens gravely as I carefully fill him in on what's been happening, with the children and Siobhan, even with my father. I never told Father Michael, because being a priest doesn't preclude the possibility of being an asshole, but Father Brendon is easy to confide in, and this is far from the first time a case has scraped up against the scars.

"That's a lot," he says eventually, and it makes me snicker. "Maybe it feels like you're besieged on all sides? Lost in the woods?"

I flinch, but then, there's a reason he used that phrase. "These kids . . . they're being rescued from horrendous situations. It's impossible not to acknowledge that, even as we have to and should abhor the methods."

"And you wonder what you'd be feeling if someone had made you one of these children, way back when."

"When we catch this person, the media coverage is going to be a zoo. A vigilante rescuing kids? The public will eat that up. It makes our job a lot harder to do. And it . . ." I swallow, trying to work my way through that. "She's clearly pissed at a system that isn't protecting these kids, but how is dumping them deeper into that same flawed system going to keep them safe?"

"Those who turn to violence don't usually have solutions to offer. Or they tried, and lost, and think this is their only way forward."

"Something's driving them."

"Something drives you," he reminds me. "It's probably not all that different."

"That's what I'm afraid of."

He nods and hums, waiting for me to continue. I do.

"Someone who chooses to do this can choose to stop. Someone who needs to do this . . ."

"Someone who can't stop must be stopped. It must be hard to do that, if you can see where your lives diverged." He pauses thoughtfully. "The agent who carried you out of that cabin: Did he do more harm than good?"

"No," I answer reflexively. "He saved me."

"And you save others. What comes after that isn't your fault, Mercedes. Your job demands a great deal of you, but not this. Don't take on more than is yours to bear."

That feels like the end of the conversation, something to mull rather than easily accept. I thank him and stand, dusting off the seat of my pants.

"Mercedes?" He gives me a sad smile when I turn to see him better. He hasn't moved to stand. "About your father?"

I brace myself.

"Give it to God," he says simply. "How you feel about it is yours and yours alone. Whether or not you should be judged; that's for God."

It's a lot to think about, and I'm quiet as I rejoin the others and we head back to Vic's house. We take a detour by my home so I can pick up some more clothing, check the mail, and talk to Jason. He's kept up with the lawn, and he also shows me the cameras he's installed on his porch and mailbox, just like mine.

"I haven't seen anyone," he tells me regretfully. "I've looked."

"Thanks, Jason. Listen, my normal phone died, so I'm going to give you my work cell, just in case."

"Gotta say, I miss having you around, kid."

"Hopefully this will all resolve quickly, and I can come home to stay."

After dinner, Sterling takes me home with her. Whatever time-share she and Eddison planned out, it's fully intact. Rather than making up the couch-bed, though, she gives me a gentle push into the bedroom. "Do you really want to be alone right now?" she asks at my token protest.

No.

Knowing what the rest of her apartment looks like, her bedroom is utterly unsurprising, all black and white and blush pink in elegant coordination. A large, light brown teddy bear in an FBI windbreaker sits on the mound of pillows at the head of the bed. I pick it up, touching the black thread nose.

"Priya gave that to me when I got the transfer request."

Of course she did.

We plug in phones and situate guns, checking emails and messages one last time before setting the alarms. When we're changed and settled under the fluffy comforter, she doesn't even blink at me cuddling the teddy bear, even though its jacket is whispering with every movement, like the real ones. She just flicks off the light. Noises drift through the walls: her neighbors walking and talking, playing music or games or watching TV. It's not obtrusive, just sort of there, comforting in its own way, like Sterling's steady breathing beside me.

Then my phone goes off.

"It's only been two days," Sterling whispers over the ringtone.

I roll over to grab the phone off the nightstand. "It's Holmes," I tell her, and answer the call. "What's happened now?"

"Eleven-year-old Noah Hakken just walked into my police station," she reports grimly.

"Is he injured?"

"Bruised to hell and back but he swears he's not abused. We're taking him to the hospital now."

"I'll be there."

The call drops, but the glow of the screen takes longer to dim.

"Hospital?" Sterling asks, throwing back the blanket to reach for the light.

"Yeah. Sorry."

The smack upside the head, gentle as it is, still takes me by surprise. "Mercedes Ramirez, don't you dare apologize for any of this," she says severely. "It is not your fault."

I know that, I do, but I still don't really have a response for that right now. "We should grab our bags for work. I doubt we'll be getting back before the office."

The ER isn't anywhere near as frantic as two days ago. *Jesucristo. Dos días.* A nurse at the station recognizes me and points me to one of the closed curtains. Sterling stays at the counter to talk to the nurse as I walk over, stepping a little too hard on purpose so the sound can announce my approach. "It's Ramirez," I say.

Holmes pulls the curtain back, revealing a pair of calm nurses and a boy sitting on the bed, tear-stained and confused and splashed with blood. He's in an undershirt and boxers, showing a lean, muscled body that's unusual for a boy his age. Holmes was right, though, he's got a lot of bruising, and one of the nurses is bent over a red, swollen ankle.

"My name is Mercedes Ramirez," I tell him, and he jerks his head up to look at me. "Someone gave you my name?"

He nods slowly. "She killed my mom," he says. His voice sounds slurred, not mushy so much as drugged, maybe?

"She hit him pretty good on the back of the head when he fought her," Holmes explains, "and he's been having problems with allergies the past few days, so his mother gave him some Benadryl to help him sleep. They'll do a scan for concussion but they don't want to give him anything for the headache until the Benadryl wears off a bit more."

It's a little scary that Holmes and I have now spent enough time with each other for her to interpret my expressions that well. I lean against the foot of the bed, curling my hands around the plastic frame so he can see them. "Noah? Can you tell us what happened?"

"I was sleeping." He shakes his head, his eyes going momentarily out of focus. "Mom sent me to bed early because it's an early morning. We're driving to Williamsburg tomorrow, to Busch Gardens. For my birthday."

¡Por amor de Dios, tenga compasión!

"What woke you up?" Holmes asks. She must have already questioned him a bit, before she called and on the way over, but you'd never know it from her face or body language.

"I thought it was a nightmare. One of those creepy mannequins. A hand shook my shoulder, I opened my eyes, and there it was. The hand covered my mouth when I tried to scream." He mumbles the last bit, a blush creeping up his neck, and there's something perversely reassuring about the self-conscious pride of preteen boys. "She said I had to be quiet."

"She?"

"Sounded like a she. I mean, I guess it didn't have to be, like a drag queen or something, maybe, but um . . ." He blushes a scalding pink. "I wasn't walking too straight. She put an arm around me, like to steer me? And she was, uh, soft. You know? Like . . ." Blushing even more fiercely, he cups a hand against his chest and squeezes.

One of the nurses ducks his head to his shoulder to hide his smile.

The story is heart-achingly familiar. She took him to his mother's room and forced him to stand beside the bed while she stabbed his mother to death. He fought her, but she pistol-whipped the back of his skull hard enough to make him groggy, and she finished the job, took him to the van—or an SUV, he isn't sure, but it was bigger than his mom's sedan—gave him the bear, and dropped him off one street over from the police station.

After, of course, giving him my name.

"She kept saying she was saving me," he says, his voice small and pained. "Saving me from what, though? She said my mom had to pay. That she couldn't keep doing this to me. Doing what?"

Holmes and I trade a look, and she nods for me to take it. "Noah, this person has been going after parents who hurt or endanger their children."

"My mom never hurt me!" he retorts, straightening so fast he visibly fights off a bout of nausea. "She *never* hurt me."

"Noah—"

"No. We watch those crime shows, I know a lot of kids say that even though they're being abused, but I'm not!"

"When you were at a friend's house a couple of weeks ago, someone called Child Protective Services to lodge a concern," Holmes tells him. "They said you were badly bruised and limping when you arrived."

"My dad was an Olympic gymnast." His eyes are bright but determined, so rather than derail what seems to be a non sequitur, we stay silent. "He won bronze medals for the Netherlands. When he and Mom got married, they moved here and he started training gymnasts. He died when I was little. All I've ever wanted is to go to the Olympics like my dad, but our gym closed two years ago. I wasn't good enough yet to get into one of the competitive gyms. Last year, I was on the wait list. No spots opened up. They said if I kept practicing, I could audition again next month."

"You practice at home."

"Mom converted the basement for me. We're not rich, though. That's why I was wait-listed, because I have to have a scholarship slot. Our mats are old, and the padding isn't great, so I get bruised. I twisted my ankle trying a new beam dismount. And . . ." He blushes again. "I've been trying to get it down for the audition, so I haven't let it heal. You have to believe me, my mom has *never* hurt me. All my friends know how hard I practice."

"Noah, do you know if someone from CPS came to your home?"

"Yes, a lady named Martha. We showed her the gym in the basement, and she watched a couple of my practice routines and some of the videos. She said she believed us, and she'd get it taken care of." He blinks rapidly, trying to keep back tears. "Is that why this lady killed my mom? Because she didn't believe us?"

"Noah . . ." Moving around the end of the bed, I sit near enough to offer a hand. He takes it immediately, squeezing punishingly hard. I don't tell him to ease up. "This person, whoever's doing this . . . she's so caught up in the need to do it that she's rushing, and she isn't getting all the information. I know that can't be easy to hear, and I'm sorry. I am so sorry for what happened to you and your mom."

"Why you?"

For the first time, I finally feel like I have an answer that's almost good enough. "Because whoever she is, she knows I care. She feels like other people aren't paying enough attention to kids being hurt and my whole job is to find and arrest people who hurt kids. She gave you my name because she knew I would drop everything to be here for you."

The tears trickle down his face, smearing the dried blood that hasn't been wiped away. "My mom."

"Loved you. Beyond words, beyond reason, beyond death. She loved you, and loves you still. Don't ever forget that, Noah."

He nods gravely.

Holmes glances down at the notebook in her hand. "Noah, what was your dad's name?"

"Constantijn Hakken," he sniffs. "With a *j*."

Halfway through writing it, Holmes blinks. "Where does the *j* go?" she asks helplessly.

The smiling nurse chokes a little.

Turns out the *j* comes after the *i*, and there's an alphabet joke in there somewhere if I'm brave enough to make it (I'm not). His mother's name is Maartje, and when we ask about his grandparents, he shifts uncomfortably on the bed. His father's parents, he explains, didn't think gymnastics was good enough for their son, and they haven't had contact since his father was a teenager. His mother grew up as a ward of the state, and never knew her parents.

I have the feeling, though, that when the elite gyms he's auditioning with learn his story, he'll find a space and a host family to be his legal guardians. I hesitate to think of it as One Good Thing, but at least it'll be something.

One of the uniformed officers stays with Noah when a doctor comes to take him for a CT. Holmes and I wander out to the waiting room to join Sterling and the newly arrived Cass.

"Agent Watts is on her way," Cass immediately reports to Holmes. "She lives up in Norfolk."

"Hell of a commute. That's what, three hours each way to work?"

"Her husband is stationed on the base at Norfolk; she spends the weekends there, cases allowing, and stays with her brother-in-law and his wife on base at Quantico during the week."

Holmes shakes her head. "That sounds exhausting."

"She'll be here as soon as she can, but she asked me to come ahead."

"Let's fill you in, then."

22

"I'm just going to . . ." I hold up my phone, and Holmes nods, focused on the attentive Cass.

Sterling follows me to the waiting room, where I can actually make a call without getting scolded. "You believe him, then? That he wasn't abused?"

"I do, and that's going to be a problem."

"That you believe him?"

"That he wasn't abused."

"You want to run that one by me again? We're supposed to be happy when kids aren't abused."

"So far as we know, she hasn't killed any innocent people," I tell her quietly. The waiting room isn't frenzied, but there are a few people there, and our professional clothing is already getting some looks. I take her by the elbow and lead her outside, a safe distance from the doors so we don't get in anyone's way. "Mason's father, Paul Jeffers, *maybe*. We don't know if he was aware of what his wife was doing. Probably not, but we'll never know, and I don't think our killer is capable of drawing a line between ignorant and complicit."

"Okay . . ."

"Zoe and Caleb Jones died, and she's going to take that as not saving them soon enough. She's going to take that on herself, and it's going to make her rage burn even faster, and even messier. And when word gets out that Noah wasn't remotely abused, that she murdered a completely innocent woman who loved and supported her son?"

Sterling pales in the crappy outdoor lighting. "There have to be hundreds of at-risk kids in this county. We have no way to know who she'll go after. There's no way to warn anyone." She touches the thin gold Star of David at her throat. "Mercedes . . ."

"I know. Watts needs to start really digging into the CPS employees. We also need a list of kids who fit this killer's criteria. Anything that's gone through the Manassas office. I know it's probably a huge list, but we have to have something to work off of. We're running out of time."

I text Eddison and Vic to let them know, hoping they'll sleep through the alerts. There's nothing they can do right now anyway. Still, it's not entirely surprising that not long after we head back inside, Eddison walks in with a drink carrier.

"It was a gas station," he says gruffly, handing one to Sterling. "I didn't want to trust the tea. It's hot chocolate."

He is absolutely not awake enough to safely drive, how the hell did he get here?

Then he throws away the empty cup in the fourth spot of the carrier and picks up a second cup of jet fuel for himself, so there's that terrifying answer. He holds the last cup out to me, a mix of hot chocolate and coffee because they're both shitty at gas stations but mixed together, they're not half bad. Somehow.

"If we head to the office, we can keep working on your files," he says after listening to the full update. "Maybe we can find her."

"Check with Holmes. She might want me here for when Watts questions Noah."

But Noah, when he gets out of CT with the good news of no concussion, is fast asleep and hard to wake, the trauma adding to the Benadryl to knock him out. They wheel him to a room in Pediatrics, and he doesn't so much as stir when they shift him to a normal bed. At least they cleaned him up before the scan and changed his clothes. We stand in the doorway and look in.

Holmes smiles a little at the sight, something soft and maybe a little wistful. "How far is it to Quantico?"

"This time of day? About half an hour."

"Then go ahead. Watts can call you back if she wants you here for questions."

"All right. We'll be at the office for the foreseeable future."

"Mercedes."

I turn to look at her more fully. "I think I've been in the Bureau too long; hearing my first name from adults makes me start to worry."

"Mignone and I have been partners for five years; I'm still not convinced he knows my first name," she agrees. "What you said to Noah, earlier, about why? It was a good answer."

"I keep struggling toward a why," I murmur. "I think that's part of it. It's my part of it. I don't think it's all of it."

"We'll find out the rest, with any luck. But for now it was the right answer."

We let Cass know we're heading out, and once outside, Eddison starts rooting for his keys. Sterling slips her hand into his pocket, yanks out the ring, and shoves them deep in her purse. "Uh-uh," she tells him flatly. "You're not driving."

"I always drive."

"You're not driving."

"But I always drive."

"And yet, you're not driving."

I bite my lip against a laugh. It's like counting on the tides.

Spreading out in the bullpen's conference room, we gradually settle into a system. Eddison and I pore over all of our team's old cases, skimming over details and notes from the digital files, and whenever a reference to someone—a family member; a neighbor; a hospital worker; a lawyer; a victim, really anyone that makes us look twice—strikes us as interesting, we call out the name for Sterling to research, to find out where they are now.

It is very quickly a depressing venture.

Being a victim isn't something that disappears as soon as you're rescued. It doesn't vanish the moment the people who hurt you are taken into custody. That sense of it, that awareness of being not just victimized but a *victim*, it sticks to your bones for years, even decades. That sense of the thing can cause as much damage as the original trauma, as life goes on.

Being a victim has its own nasty form of recidivism.

In the days following the destruction of the Garden, as girls either succumbed to grievous wounds or began to improve, thirteen Butterflies survived, Inara, Victoria-Bliss, and Ravenna among them. Six months later, there were only nine. Now there are seven, though, to be fair, Marenka died in a car accident. All the rest were lost to suicide as they struggled to live in a world that was supposed to be better, where they should have been able to leave their trauma behind them. As calm as I tried to be, I understand Inara's worry about Ravenna.

Suicide, whether of the original victims or their friends and family, is a common thread through our research. So is drug and alcohol abuse. So is prison. So is continued victimization through domestic violence.

"Have you ever given out a bear with wings?" Eddison asks when we stop for a break.

By which I mean I slammed the laptop shut because I needed five fucking minutes without a depressing-as-shit statistic, and he decided that meant time for breakfast.

Which actually meant splitting a giant bag of Reese's Peanut Butter Cups.

"No," I sigh, forehead against the cool surface of the table. "I buy our bears by the gross. They come in a variety of colors but there are no accessories."

"So the angel means something to her specifically."

"The kids have mostly described her as looking like an angel," Sterling notes. "It could just be something that she took on for herself, especially if someone in her family or fosters were religious."

"Or a reflection of her name. Angel. Angelica. Angelique. Or if she had a brother named Angel. Angelo."

"I'd say this is a bad time for Yvonne to be on maternity leave but she'd only yell at us for being this vague," I mumble.

"Why the blonde wig, though?" he continues, ignoring me. "Even in classical art, angels had hair colors in the full range. They're not all blonde, whatever Precious Moments would have you believe."

Sterling shrugs and very kindly doesn't comment on his familiarity with Precious Moments. "Don't look at me; Jewish angels are properly terrifying. Have you ever read those descriptions? There is nothing blonde or pretty about them."

"And Jesus wasn't white, but who wants to admit that?"

With a deep groan, I open the laptop again. "Okay, try Heather Grant," I tell Sterling, along with the date of birth and social security number. "She went missing in Utah and was found a month later in a field; said angels had taken her."

"And those angels turned out to be?"

"An older couple who desperately wanted kids but hadn't been able to have or adopt any of their own. He had a heart attack, she left to get help, and Heather wandered away. She was only calm for interviews if she was in my lap where she could play with my crucifix."

"Let's see, she is now . . . fifteen. Doing okay, still lives on the family ranch. Her mother died a few years ago, but her grandmother came out to live on the ranch so she wouldn't be the only female. No red flags."

"Sara Murphy," Eddison reads off his screen. "She'd be twenty-four now. The man who kidnapped and kept her for his 'heaven wife' had dozens of sets of wings hanging from the ceiling of his cabin, made out of all kinds of found things. She wouldn't sleep unless Mercedes was in the room."

"In jail for assault," Sterling reports after a minute. "She escorted a friend to an appointment at an abortion clinic with protestors. One of the protestors tried to hit her friend with a sign, Sara grabbed the sign and beat him with the two-by-four it was stapled to. She's got another few months."

"Huh. You hear 'jail' and you don't expect to be proud by the end of it."

"Cara Ehret," I say. "She'd be twenty-three now, and really, what didn't happen to her at home."

"Moved around through a lot of foster homes, graduated high school at seventeen and falls off the grid. I . . . actually can't find her past that. We'll have to get one of the techs on it when they get in."

"Now you're allowed to say the maternity leave is badly timed," Eddison tells me.

I throw a peanut butter cup and hit him just under his eye. "Put her on the short list."

She's the fourth name on there, and we're only a year and a half in.

Vic comes in at seven with actual breakfast and drinks. "How's it going?" He regards us all with grave, worried eyes as he hands out bowls of western scramble, like omelets but lazier.

"We've got a few names for the analysts to dig into deeper," I tell him around a yawn.

Eddison pushes to his feet with a groan and walks around the table to Sterling, standing over her shoulder to pick all the mushrooms out of his bowl and put them into hers. "This is also going to take forever." He moves on to picking the red peppers out of Sterling's breakfast to put in his bowl.

She watches his progress with a bemused, slightly horrified expression.

Vic watches, too, but chooses not to comment. "Do you want to update the Dragonmother, or would you like me to do it?"

"I'll do it," I sigh. "I could stand to move around a bit."

"Eat first."

And then he parks himself in one of the chairs to make sure we do.

Once he's satisfied we're not trying to subsist purely on caffeine, he leaves us for his office. I take a moment to finish my coffee, trying to sort out words and reports so I don't look like an idiot in front of Agent Dern. Eventually, I'm as prepared as I'm going to get and head out into the bullpen.

I'm not quite to the elevators when a massive cheer goes out in Blakey's corner of the floor, which is a hell of a lot more crowded than it usually is. I can recognize a handful of agents from the cybercrimes division, and there's no division between CC and CAC as agents collapse into hugs on each other, some of them crying, a couple laughing giddily and jumping up and down.

"Ramirez!" Blakey calls. "We got Slightly!"

"Slightly," I repeat blankly. "Oh, holy shit! Slightly! One of your Lost Boys!"

She laughs and throws herself at me in a hug. "He's going to be okay. We got him, he's going to be okay, and the bastard who had him gave us leads on Nibs, Tootles, and Curly!"

I hug her back, holding on just as tightly. They've been tracking these boys and several others for months, trying to break through a ring of pedophiles who use pop-up forums to arrange trades. They found one boy a few weeks ago, but the man holding him panicked and killed him when they closed in on the house. Slightly safe, and solid leads on three others? This is a very good day for Blakey's team and their partners in cybercrimes.

But it makes me think of Noah, trying to understand why his mother is gone when she hadn't done anything wrong.

I hit the call button, waiting for the elevator, and it opens to frame Siobhan and two of the language experts from the Southeast Asia desks in Counterterrorism. After a minute or two, I might even remember their names. But they give each other wide-eyed looks that gradually transfer from me to Siobhan and back again, and step out of the elevator. "We'll just . . . hey, that looks like a party!" the younger one announces awkwardly, and drags her teammate out behind her.

"What kind of horror stories have you been spreading?" I ask dryly, stepping in and hitting the button for Internal Affairs.

"Don't have to," Siobhan retorts, voice as stiff as her posture. "You really think the whole building doesn't know you're getting deliveries?"

"None at the house anymore."

"Really?"

"Really." I study her discreetly in the wavering reflection on the doors. She looks exhausted, worn in a way that doesn't have anything to do with sleep. It's on the tip of my tongue to ask how she's been in the . . . *cógeme*, ten? Ten days, since I've seen her.

It feels so much longer than ten.

But I let the silence carry us down the floors. She walked away, and I let her. I'm not sure there's really anything else to say. We hit her floor first, and the doors slide open with a ding. She walks past me, shoulders squared, and hesitates over the tracks. She turns her head, just barely, like she's going to look back at me.

But she doesn't. Someone in the hall calls her name, and she flinches, then walks out without a word or a look. The doors slide shut and leave me alone in the car.

I don't have an appointment with the Dragonmother, so I spend several minutes sitting outside her office while she volubly reminds another agent just how she earned her nickname. Her assistant looks torn between being mortified and proud. I suppose if you're the guardian at the gates for a dragon, you can't help but be pleased when she roars.

"Inappropriate conduct with a witness," he murmurs, tossing me an unwrapped pink Starburst. "Probably a lawsuit coming. She's not happy."

No shit, and so not my business, Christ.

A red-faced agent stomps out, sans badge and gun, and after another few minutes, the assistant pokes his head into the lair to announce me.

"Would you like to feel sorry for Agent Simpkins?" Agent Dern says instead of hello when I walk in.

"If I say I already do?"

"She got served with divorce papers two weeks ago. Her ex-husband-to-be cited irreconcilable differences stemming from her consistently putting her job above their marriage and family."

"Why are you telling me this, ma'am?"

"Because I know you won't tell anyone outside your team, and you deserve to know that it wasn't you, your team, or your case that sent her round the bend," she says bluntly. "Sit, please."

I sit. She's wearing lilac today, in some kind of fabric that drapes and shimmers becomingly, and I think this is who Sterling should grow up to be, someone who can wear the pastels and the feminine things without it taking a millimeter of authority away from her. Sterling just has to wait until she doesn't look like jailbait.

"I'm told you haven't seen any of the counselors here."

"I've talked with my priest about everything. I felt like I could be more forthcoming."

"How goes your research through your old cases?"

I run her through the parameters we're using, not shying away from explaining the glacial pace. Because a lot of our search is based on instinct and impression, we can't just turn it over to the technical analysts as is. We have to narrow it down first.

She looks back over her page of notes, written in some ultraefficient shorthand possibly known only to her. "You're still staying with your teammates?"

"Yes, ma'am."

"If you would feel more comfortable at home—"

"All due respect, ma'am," I interrupt softly, "it's not about feeling unsafe at my house. I just feel better with Eddison and Sterling. Less exposed."

She nods thoughtfully, her dark eyes very aware in ways I'm not entirely comfortable with. "Are you going to sell the house?"

"I don't know. I'm honestly not planning to think about it until all this is done."

"That's understandable. Professional opinion, Agent Ramirez: When do you think this person is going to strike again?"

I take a minute to run back through all the factors and variables that have been hammering at my skull for hours, days maybe. In the end, though, there's really only one answer.

"Two days, if we're lucky. Very likely less."

Once upon a time, there was a little girl who was scared of breaking.

Or breaking more. She was honest enough with herself to acknowledge she'd been broken for a very long time. Some of that she'd fixed; some she was still working on. Some, she knew, could never heal. Even if her body someday gave up the scars, her soul would still carry the wounds.

It hurt, every time, to acknowledge that she'd never truly be whole.

But she did acknowledge it, because some pain was necessary, even healthy.

When she rammed against those broken places—when a nightmare was too vivid, when someone touched her in a way too rich with memory, when someone asked her why she hated being in photos—she reminded herself of all the ways she wasn't that little girl anymore.

She had a new name, one her daddy and his friends had never touched.

She'd gone to college and graduated with honors.

She had friends, though she'd left most of them behind when she graduated. But she kept some of them, even after she'd moved, and she was making new ones.

She'd moved back to Virginia. She almost hadn't, but it seemed silly to avoid an entire state just because she'd been so miserable for so many years. It was hardly the state's fault. And because returning to Virginia was brave, she didn't call herself cowardly for avoiding her old city. That much allowance she would give herself.

She had a job she loved, and was so proud of it. She was helping people, helping children. Children who were like the little girl she used to be. There were a lot of things she still wasn't strong enough to do or be, maybe never would be, but this she could do. She could help the children who so desperately needed it, and she didn't have to push herself past the breaking point.

And whenever she started to doubt, whenever she felt like she was more scar tissue than real person, she remembered her angel, and drew strength from the memory. The teddy bear still sat on her bed, a gift and a kindness. It had seen so many tears from her over the years, but eventually it saw joy as well, and the kind of tears that came of laughing too hard.

And she had the angel herself, in a way. She'd been shocked, at first, to see the angel while she was out running errands for her small apartment. She wasn't entirely sure why. After all, even angels had to live somewhere. But it was such a big world. It was a sign, she decided, that she was exactly where she needed to be. She was here, helping children, and her angel was still helping children. She was still an angel.

She was healing, and she wasn't as afraid.

23

I'm pretty sure the only thing that keeps Sterling from slipping me sleeping pills is the very real possibility of us getting called in. She is, however, clearly out of all fucks for my fidgets, because she eventually rolls over in bed and knees me right in the ass. Once it hits two o'clock, it's like all the tension floods out of me. None of the calls have been that late. Early?

Despite having set the alarm on my phone for six-thirty, I don't wake up till a little after ten. Sterling, already showered and dressed and sitting at her table with the crossword puzzle, just shrugs at my glower. "You needed the sleep. Vic said not to come in until you woke up on your own."

There's only so much I can mutter about that. I mean, I do, because it makes me feel perversely better to grumble about it like Muttley, but I'm well aware it doesn't accomplish anything.

It takes every trick I've ever learned with concealer to make the shadows under my eyes look vaguely human, and even then we'll call it a partial success. When I come out, Sterling hands me a bowl of oatmeal, a glass of orange juice, and the front page of the paper.

A picture of Noah's mother fills a third of the space above the fold. Constantijn Hakken (and it's spelled differently each of the three times it's written, which, *come on, paper*) is mentioned, with his Olympic history and his unexpected death from an aneurysm when Noah was three.

If he'd lived, his son probably would have been in intensive training from a young age rather than trying to play catch up from a hobby gym. Maartje Hakken managed a local credit union and volunteered at her son's school one day a week, as well as assisting with a number of PTA events. As a legacy, loving your son and working hard is pretty decent.

Below the fold, however, the article mentions the rash of similar murders. It doesn't connect the explosion at the Jones house—the methodology was too different—but it lists the Wilkinses, the Wongs, the Anderses, and the Jefferses, and asks in bold letters if Manassas has our own serial killer.

"Comerse el mundo," I sigh.

"I'm going to assume that whatever you said doesn't require an answer."

"It's not anything new enough to need one."

I check in with Watts, just in case she isn't at the office when we get there, and send her pictures of the more relevant paragraphs of the article. She texts back that the kids in the hospital have been moved to a corner block of rooms with a pair of guards at all times, and an agent has been dispatched to Ronnie Wilkins's grandmother to fill her in and make sure she isn't besieged by the curious or prurient.

As soon as we get to the office, Cass pounces and drags me into the conference room, which is still in our setup from yesterday. "We've got the list from CPS, file-by-file access. They're working on identifying the kids in similar circumstances, but it's going to take more time than we have, I think. They'll forward them in bunches to the Smiths."

Eddison grunts from the other side of the table and slides me a chipotle hot chocolate.

For the most part, the list is exactly what you'd expect it to be. The social workers and nurses are logged as they follow up on different aspects of each case, and the clerks are the ones who add in paperwork from external sources as it comes to their office. And it makes sense that the clerks occasionally log in to the files to make sure that all forms are accounted for.

"Is Gloria Hess a supervisor?" I ask, spreading the pages out in front of me. "She's the only name on every file until this week, when Nancy, Tate, and Derrick Lee went through."

"She's the senior clerk," answers Cass. "It's not technically a supervisory position, though."

"So she might train others, but she's not the one who should be going back through to make sure it's done correctly?"

"Right. Every file?"

"Every one, and it goes back weeks. A lot of log ins, come to think of it, especially for someone too ill to work full-time anymore."

Cass leans over the table to grab a folder from the stack at Eddison's elbow. He's too absorbed in what's on his tablet screen to even snap at her. "Our analysts dug into Gloria."

The picture on file, copied from the DMV, is precancer if the hair is any indication, ashy blonde and thick, bound into a long braid over one shoulder. Her face is fuller, her color better, and all in all she looks . . . happier. Less hollowed. "Her husband died a few weeks after her diagnosis," I announce, trailing my finger under the words. "Dropped dead of a massive heart attack, absolutely no warning signs or obvious risk."

"Who did she piss off upstairs?" Cass shakes her head, her chin digging into my shoulder so she can see rather than pull the file closer. "Advanced cancer, her husband dies, her sister and brother-in-law go to prison for abuse, she gets rejected for the care of their kids, her cancer isn't responding to treatment . . . It's like some wicked angel put their thumb down and started to squish."

"But would she be healthy enough to manhandle the kids this way? Ronnie Wilkins was carried to and from the car. She had to half-carry Emilia Anders. She carried Mason. She half-carried Noah."

"Not the others?"

"No. She used Sammy to keep Sarah and Ashley compliant, and Zoe for Caleb and Brayden. They weren't going to fight her when she could hurt the youngest."

"I feel like there's something really important no one's brought up yet, and I'm not sure there's a good way to do it."

"Why are the kids white?" Sterling offers, not looking away from her laptop.

"Okay, so it has been brought up."

"Not really. It's just the obvious question. All of the families, with the partial exception of the Wongs, have been white. Generally argues that the killer is white, as well."

"This type of mission as a whole argues a white killer," I remind her. "And you're forgetting the racism inherent in the system."

Sterling nods, but Cass looks between us in confusion. "Applying how?"

"Minority kids are significantly more likely to be taken from their families on less documented cause, and less likely to be given back to their families without more oversight on the parents. They take minority kids 'for the good of the kids,' but leave the white ones 'for the good of the family.' Minority kids are more likely to get treated poorly in foster homes but this killer is going after the parents, thus far, not the fosters, so they're going after the white parents who get their kids back against evidence." At the silence from my shoulder, I tilt my head to see Cass frowning. "What?"

"You didn't even have to think about that one."

"It's well documented. We get taken faster and it's harder to get us back."

"Were any of the kids' files accessed by Gloria the day of the murders?"

I lift Gloria's file to check the papers below. "All of them."

Cass pushes back from the table, phone already in her hand. "Burnside," she says on her way out the door. "This is Kearney; I need to know what files Gloria Hess has accessed most recently. Check Derrick Lee as well, just in case."

I wonder if there's a way to borrow an administrator from a CPS office in another county to oversee a more detailed audit. After all, if Lee is in charge of the clerks, he might know their log ins. As much as we're all thinking *she*, Lee hasn't been eliminated as a possible suspect.

My cell goes off, but it's a number on the Bureau exchange so the ringing doesn't cause the same frisson of fear it's come to impart recently. "Agent Ramirez."

"Agent, this is the front desk; you have a visitor down here."

"A visitor?"

Sterling and Eddison both look up, but I shrug.

"Her ID says Margarita Ramirez."

"Cógeme."

My phone buzzes with another call, and I pull away from the screen to see Holmes's name. "I've got a call about a case coming in; tell her I'll be down soon, have her sit tight." Without waiting for an answer, I switch over. "Ramirez."

"A pharmacist at Prince William took a smoke break and found twelve-year-old Ava Levine asleep on a bench. She had *two* angel bears."

"Blood?"

"No."

"I'll grab Watts and Kearney and come down." I really want to throw this fucking phone against the wall; it does not bring good things. Ending the call, I take a deep breath and consider my options. "I have to head to Manassas," I tell my partners. "Girl was found sleeping outside the hospital."

"Sleeping? Like she was drugged."

"I don't know. I'll tell Vic."

"What about your visitor?" Sterling asks.

"Also Vic." Before I can be tempted into explaining, which is not something I have time for even if I did have the inclination (I don't), I grab my purse and leave the conference room, hooking my elbow through Cass's and walking her backward. "We're off to Manassas. I have to give something to Vic to handle; grab Watts?"

"Why are we—but it's midmorning, how is there just now a victim? Someone would see something."

"I'll tell you both in the car." I twist her around to point her in the right direction and give her a swat on her ass to keep her moving.

And because we've been friends for ten years, she just shoots me the bird and flounces down the stairs to find Watts.

Vic is in his office. He gives me a distracted good morning, head down as he makes notes on a file, but the sound of the lock turning has his full attention on me. "Mercedes? What's wrong?"

"Two things." I tell him the very little I have regarding the newest child, and he nods gravely.

"What's the second thing?" he asks when I struggle to continue.

Deep breath, Mercedes. "My mother is downstairs."

That has him putting down his pen and leaning back in the well-padded chair. "Your mother."

"Probably. I guess it could be one of the cousins. It's a popular name in the family. But . . . yeah, it's probably my mother."

"When was the last time you saw her?"

"She tracked down my foster home when I was thirteen. That's when they transferred me out of their system to another city." Nineteen years.

"And you have an idea about why she's here."

"My father was recently diagnosed with cancer," I say and, at his raised eyebrow, add, "Pancreatic."

"I'll go speak with her. Do you want me to convince her to leave?"

My gut screams, *Yes*, but that part of me that will always, *always* feel guilty despite knowing my choices were mine and were right for me says, *Wait*.

And Vic reads that hesitation for what it is and comes around his desk to give me a long hug. "I'll see if she's got a hotel. If not, I'll get her set up in one."

"Not in Manassas, please."

"Not in Manassas. I promise."

I lean my head against his chest, feeling the ridges of the surgical scar even through his dress shirt and undershirt. That bullet changed his life, but it changed our lives too. Such a little thing to have so much weight. As he pulls back, he smooths the stray wisps of my hair that always fight the clips and ponytails, his hand warm on my scalp as he presses a kiss to my forehead.

"Go check on that little girl," he murmurs. "I'll get your mother settled somewhere, for when you're ready."

In twenty-seven years, I have never been ready for that conversation. I attempted it a few times, those first few years, but she always shut it down. And now . . .

I nod, blinking away tears that I will swear to my dying day are just from exhaustion and stress, and unlock his door. Cass and Watts are waiting at the elevator. They both look blankly at Vic, who just gives them a bland smile and no explanation.

In the lobby, I can see her immediately, sitting stiffly in a chair near the desk, a rosary wrapped around her palm so the crucifix rests on the base of her thumb. I've always remembered her as she was when I was a child; somehow I've never thought of her as being old. Of course she is, she's almost seventy. But as much as she's changed, it's still immediately her, and my heart thumps painfully.

Vic steps to my side, between me and my mother, and as we draw closer, he pushes me along with Cass and Watts, breaking off to stand in front of her. As the three of us walk away, I can hear him address her. "Mrs. Ramirez, my name is Victor Hanoverian. I'm the unit chief for your daughter's team."

Cass gives me an anxious look.

"I'm not discussing it," I whisper. "By the time we get to Manassas, I will be completely focused on Ava."

Watts simply nods. "We're all here for reasons, Ramirez. Just tell me if you need to step away."

That is not something I have ever known how to tell.

Once upon a time, there was a little girl who was scared of her father.

It was only natural; he'd hurt her so badly for so long. But even now, after so many years, he was still her deepest wound, her most visceral nightmare.

She hadn't seen him since the trial, the bits of it for which her presence had been required. She'd sat trembling in the row behind the prosecutor, her advocate by her side, or up in the witness stand, watching her daddy seethe. He'd been so angry. She'd always known to be afraid when he was that angry. When the advocate led her out of the courtroom for the last time, she looked over her shoulder and saw Daddy standing at his table, in one of the nicest suits he wore for work, and he was glaring at her, like it was all her fault.

He hated her, she thought, but it wasn't her fault. It was never her fault.

Mostly she believed that.

Her daddy was in prison, where he belonged, and whatever indelible scars he'd left on her, he could never cause her fresh wounds. She was safe. She was healing. She was okay. It had taken her a long time to get there, but the angel had promised that she was going to be okay, and eventually she was. She was okay.

Then she got a letter from her father.

She didn't recognize the handwriting on the envelope, but it had both her names in the center, and that bolt of fear . . . It had been years since she'd been that suddenly afraid. Then she saw the name in the upper left corner, with the prisoner number and the name of the facility.

It took her four days just to open the envelope.

Another three to actually read the letter.

It started, My Beautiful Angel.

He wanted to apologize in person. There was so much he needed to tell her. Would she come see him?

She didn't want to.

She absolutely didn't want to, and yet . . . and yet . . .

She didn't think either of them were surprised when she finally showed up. He'd always had too much power over her.

He still looked like Daddy. Older, greyer . . . more muscled. He worked out with the boys in the yard, he told her, had him in the best shape of his life. She was so pretty, he told her, but he missed her red hair. She'd looked so perfect with the red hair. He had a look in his eye, one that her tight muscles and hunched shoulders remembered before her mind did.

He was remarried, he told her, to a woman who wanted to save him.

They were expecting a baby, he told her, coming in August, and his lawyer thought there was a chance, given how crowded the prison was, that it might make him seem sympathetic enough to release. He had years—decades—of sentence left, but his lawyer thought he could be out in a few years with any luck.

It was a girl, he told her, grinning. We're naming it after you, *he told her,* my own baby girl again, just like you never left. I do love my baby girl, *he told her, and his laughter clawed in her bones as she ran away.*

Once upon a time, there was a little girl who was scared of her father.

If he got out of prison, her little sister would be scared of him too.

24

Ava Levine is a twelve-year-old girl who practically glows with health, giving us all confused smiles as she sits on the hospital bed with a pair of familiar teddy bears in her lap. Her brown hair is well tended, she's a good weight for her age and height, and she doesn't have a single visible bruise.

But when she follows the doctor's instruction and lies back on the bed, her oversize sleep shirt drapes around the swell of what is either a baby bump or a really bad liver. I don't think any of us actually need the doctor to confirm it's the former.

"Shouldn't my parents be here?" she asks when the doctor has finished her exam and helped her sit up.

Holmes checks her phone. She was definitely called straight from bed, her hair shoved back haphazardly in a clip that doesn't quite manage to hit *contained*. She's in worn jeans and a shirt so faded it's impossible to tell what the lettering used to read, her feet shoved into two different kinds of sandal. "Detective Mignone is almost to your house, sweetheart."

What the shit?

Nancy, sitting in a chair by the bed, looks up at us anxiously.

It's the same bear. It is absolutely, definitely the same bear, and this is very clearly a pregnant twelve-year-old. So why is the rest of it so bizarre?

"Ava," Watts says calmly, standing at the foot of the bed. "Did you know you're pregnant?"

"Well, yeah," the girl answers, still looking politely baffled.

That's not the answer Watts was expecting, but she's too good to show it. "Do you know who the father is, Ava?"

"My daddy."

El mundo está en guerra. Por lo que solo hay que dejar que se queme.

"I've been asking for a little sister for years," she continues, oblivious to the carefully contained reactions of the rest of us. "Mom said she got hurt when I was born, and can't have any more kids in her belly, so I'm doing it." Her brilliant smile falters a bit when we don't say anything. "What's wrong?"

"Your mom knew?"

"It was her idea, but it made Daddy really happy. He called us his smart girls. What's wrong?" she asks again, starting to look a little worried.

Holmes tilts her phone toward me, the screen bright with a new message from Mignone. *Parents are dead. Negative spaces indicate there was only the killer. Tylenol PM packets in the girl's room.*

"Ava, do you ever take anything to help you sleep?"

She nods slowly. "Growing a baby is tiring. Mom says I have to get lots of sleep so my sister and I will both be healthy. She looked it up and everything."

So if a pregnant child took an adult dose of a sleep aid, the killer probably *couldn't* wake her up enough to register what was happening.

"Why is everyone so . . ."

"Ava, what your parents did . . . it's illegal, sweetheart, and it's not healthy."

"No, Mom has been getting me all my vitamins and everything. I'm fine."

Watts shares a look with Nancy, who leans forward in her chair. "No matter what you're taking or how you're eating or sleeping, Ava, your body isn't ready for everything that being pregnant or delivering a baby requires. As you get further along, you're going to be in a lot of danger. And when Agent Watts said it was illegal . . . legally you can't consent to anything like that until you're older. For a parent to do it—"

"No," Ava retorts, clutching the bears tightly. "My parents love me and we're all really happy. We're not doing anything wrong."

Holmes looks exhausted. She's undoubtedly been juggling other cases with this one, which means she probably hasn't had a solid night's rest in weeks.

I cross the room to stand between Watts and Nancy. "Ava, do you remember how you got to the hospital?"

She frowns at that, her fingers running anxiously along the crinkling gold halo of one of the bears. It's strikingly similar to praying a rosary, and it's everything I can do not to close my eyes against the sight, the memory of a string of metal and glass around my mother's palm. "Not really," she says eventually. "I fall asleep to the TV sometimes. My dad carries me to bed."

"You were brought here by a stranger, Ava, someone who knew that your parents got you pregnant and was really angry about it. She brought you here so you'd be safe until you were found, but . . . Ava, I'm really sorry, but she killed your parents."

There is no good way to tell a child that. I don't know if there's a good way to tell anyone that, if it comes to it, but certainly not a child.

She blinks, and stares at me blankly. "What?"

"Detective Mignone went out to your house to find your parents," I remind her gently. "He found your parents dead. Someone had killed them. And because she brought you here, because we recognize the bears she gave you, we know it's the same person who's killed other kids' parents recently."

"No." Her head shakes, increasingly frantic. "No, you're lying. You're lying!"

Nancy and the nurse both rush in to calm her as she breaks into hysterics. No tears yet—the shock is too fresh—but her screams are piercing and pained and the heart monitor is shrieking right along with her.

It's one thing, common and even expected, for kids to deny they've been hurt. But this? To genuinely not even realize? Sympathy stirs for her pain, but I can't bring myself to be sorry her parents are dead.

Her mother's idea? Christ, this poor girl.

The shock triggers a panic attack, and by the time she's finally calmer, she's in an exhausted stupor with the oxygen mask covering the lower half of her face. The nurse strokes Ava's hair, a physical comfort that has the girl drifting off to sleep, the teddy bears clutched to her chest. "I don't think you're going to get anything out of her for a while," the woman says quietly.

Nancy and Cass stay in the room, pulling chairs away from the bed to give some space. The rest of us head into the hallway.

Holmes glances back through the small window in the door, then at me. "Why was she given two bears?"

"One for the baby."

She chokes on that a little.

Watts blows out a frustrated breath that's almost a raspberry. "She didn't wake up enough to be told your name and she hasn't read the note that was pinned to her; if you want to head back to the office, you probably can, Ramirez."

"Do you think there'll need to be a separate warrant for the list of who accessed Ava's file?"

"No; ongoing cases usually garner a little bit of wiggle room. At least for this sort of information. I'm going to send the Smiths to CPS to talk to the clerks. They may be bringing Gloria Hess back with them to question. Ramirez . . ."

"I know. I can't be there if you talk to her."

226

Because talking to the kids is one thing, if it brings them comfort, and if it keeps them calm to answer questions. Because they're given my name. Looking through my case files is research, not investigation. I am an asset to the investigation, but not an element of the investigation itself. Technicalities, as stupid as they can be, protect us. But if suspects are brought into a station or office in an official capacity, I can't participate or even observe.

God damn it.

And I don't actually have a way to get back to Quantico. We came in Watts's car.

I should probably check on the other kids who are still here, but I can't quite bring myself to do it. Maybe this is stepping away, acknowledging that I don't have the strength to do this today.

I head out of the hospital, trying to decide if I remember where my car is. I can call a taxi if it's at Eddison's or Sterling's. But there's also the possibility that it's in the garage at Quantico, and that's a bit more than I want to pay for a ride.

My phone rings in my hand, and I don't want to know, I don't want to know, I don't—why is Jenny Hanoverian calling me? "Jenny?"

"Mercedes," she says warmly. "My husband tells me you might need a ride back to Quantico. The girls are showing Marlene *Magic Mike*, so I'm free as a bird."

Watts, you clever fiend.

"I don't want to inconvenience you—"

"I once had to drive to Atlanta because Holly forgot her running shoes for a track meet; beat that, and we'll talk about being inconvenienced."

Holly is her daughter, though, and I am suddenly very incapable of continuing with any kind of argument, because that is a weird and wonderful and terrifying thought.

She pulls up in her minivan, the front bumper still sporting the blue paint from when one of Brittany's driving lessons ended in a destroyed toy box, and she takes a long look at my face as I buckle in. And then she spends the drive back chatting about her vegetable garden and the war she's waging with the invading rabbits. It's a gift, and there's something about it . . .

It's Siobhan, I realize. When Siobhan and I were together, she'd burble on about things because she didn't want to know about my day or my cases. But Jenny is talking because I can't, and it's strange how something so similar can be so different.

We stop to pick up a late lunch for everyone, bacon grilled-cheese sandwiches and several different kinds of soup, and a quick glance around the office lobby is enough to reassure me that my mother isn't there. Upstairs, Vic gives me a card with an address and a room number on it, a hotel here in Quantico, but doesn't say a word.

I should probably figure out where my car is.

Jenny leaves after lunch, waving off my gratitude. She just kisses us all on the cheek, goes for Eddison's other cheek after he blushes the first time, and walks off laughing.

"If she ever leaves you," I tell Vic solemnly, "I'm marrying her."

He chuckles and leaves us to our research. After all, all three of us have proposed to his mother at various times.

We spend the afternoon digging through my cases, occasionally sending names to Cass to have her analysts do more in-depth research in systems Sterling can't access. Ava, she reports, is with an obstetrician to have an ultrasound. Her mother bought her vitamins, but they weren't specifically prenatal, and she hadn't had any appointments. Of course she hadn't—every clinic in the country would have been required to report it.

"CPS keeps physical and digital files," Sterling says suddenly.

Given that none of us have said anything in half an hour, the abrupt declaration makes me and Eddison blink stupidly. "Right," I say after a minute. "We've got copies of several of the physical files."

"So why are we assuming that the digital files are the only ones the killer is checking? There's a whole file room."

I don't have a phone number for either of the Smiths, so I text Cass, who answers with a promise to have the Smiths poke at it.

And then, an hour later, she calls the conference room extension and demands to be on speaker. "Sterling, you're a fucking genius," she announces.

"Well, yes," Sterling agrees, nonplussed. "Why this time?"

"Because there are files missing from the records room. The administrator has to go through drawer by drawer to match the files to their spreadsheets and what's been checked out legitimately, but we've got three missing from what he's checked so far."

"Ava's?"

"No, it's there, but not quite in the right place. Someone took it out and then put it back wrong. All the kids we've met are accounted for."

"Who reported the Levines to CPS?" I ask.

"A neighbor. The fence between the two houses is chain link and she saw Ava in the pool. Bathing suit."

And a bathing suit was going to make that low belly very evident.

"How far along is she? Do they know yet?"

"Ava wasn't sure, because she's only ever had one period. They couldn't count back. The OB says about eighteen weeks."

Four and a half months. Christ in heaven.

"They've got Gloria down at the station for questioning, and a judge just signed off on a warrant to search her house and car. If she has those missing files . . ."

"And if she doesn't?"

"Then we ask to expand the warrant to the other clerks and administrators. I'll let you know."

We stare at the conference phone in the center of the table. "Does anyone know where my car is?" I ask after a minute.

Eddison snorts, and Sterling smiles. "It's in the garage here," she informs me. "Level four, I think."

"Thanks."

A couple of hours later, when I pack up to head out, Sterling follows suit. "Can I be your DD?" she asks quietly.

"I'm not going out drinking."

"No, but I'm guessing this has something to do with your visitor this morning, and you looked like someone told you there was a killer clown after you."

"A killer cl . . . What?"

"So it's emotional. And something you have to face anyway? I'm asking if I can be your designated driver, because when you're that emotional, driving sucks. And it's hard."

"Who was your DD when you and dickhead fiancé broke it off?"

"Finney," she says with a shrug.

Her old boss, who sent her on to us when we needed an agent because he'd already been promoted out of the field. Vic's old partner, for a long time, and that makes a lot of sense as to why she fits with us so well.

I should say, *No, I've got this.*

"Thanks."

I don't.

So she drives me to the hotel, and I'm willing to bet Vic is paying for the room, because my mother would never spend this kind of money on herself. It's not fancy, not luxurious or expensive, it just isn't twenty-nine dollars a night with a roach chorus. When I was a kid, my mother could barely countenance spending money on herself, and with God only knows how many grandkids now, I can't imagine that's changed much.

I turn the card over and over in my hand, not moving even after Sterling parks the car, brings the windows down, and cuts the engine.

She doesn't ask, or poke or prod or push. She just pulls out a book of crosswords and settles in.

"Do you have any makeup wipes?" I ask.

"Glove box."

It feels strange, wrong even, to strip everything off in the middle of the day, but with the aid of the wipes and the sun visor mirror, I get off every bit of it. I look like hell. The bruises under my eyes, the sallowness of not enough sleep. The scars digging pink-white tracks down my cheek.

"I'm not going anywhere," Sterling tells me, without looking away from her page. "Take as much or as little time as you need."

"Thank you."

Forcing myself out of the car, I head into the hotel and take the stairs to the third floor because the thought of trying to stand still in an elevator right now makes my skin crawl. The door for 314 doesn't look any different from its neighbors: plain white with the heavy lock plate under the handle.

Five minutes later, I still haven't been able to make myself knock.

And then I don't have to, because the chain scratches in its track and the handle rotates, and the door slowly opens to reveal my mother's face.

"Mercedes," she breathes.

My mother.

"You need to go back," I tell her.

Once upon a time, there was a little girl who was scared of the world.

She thought, once, that it could get better, that it could be better. She'd wanted so badly to believe that, and she had for a time.

But the thing with worlds, in the human sense, is that they come crashing down. When a whole world shatters and self-destructs, is it possible to be less than apocalyptic? Wasn't that the very meaning of the word?

She'd had a bad few days after leaving the prison. It wasn't just her daddy's words ringing through her head, not just his wide, triumphant smile. It was all the other things, too, all the memories crashing in. She'd taken a few days off work, trying to get her head around all of it. She'd taken off another few days and checked into a clinic. She just couldn't stop shaking. Or crying. Or panicking.

It was too much. It was all just too much.

All those years of beatings and Daddy coming to her room at night, camera at the ready.

Mama escaping without her.

Those years of the basement and Daddy's friends.

The hospital and the trial and all the foster homes, the parade of horrors too infrequently interrupted by goodness or indifference.

And now her father was going to get out of prison. He was going to have another baby girl. Another daughter that he'd . . .

He'd . . .

But she worked through the fear and sorrow and rage as best she could. It was absurd. If—and it was a massive if—her father was released early, there wasn't a chance in hell he'd be allowed near his daughter. No man with her daddy's history would be allowed near a little girl.

Right?

She returned to work, still shaky but better. A little better. Getting there, maybe. She reminded herself of the good she did. She was helping children, more important now than ever.

But this little boy . . .

Here was this file on her desk, this beautiful little boy with eyes like hers, eyes that were bruised and a little broken and far too honest. There was so much proof that his parents were unfit, and yet, he'd been given back to them. Again. Because there were rules and technicalities and loopholes, because there were too many children in danger and not nearly enough money or homes or people to help.

So this little boy with the shadowed soul and the too-honest eyes would get hurt again, and again and again.

Ronnie Wilkins needed an angel.

25

"Nineteen years, Mercedes, and that's what you have to say to me?" Mama's face creases in still-familiar irritation, and she opens the door all the way. "Get in here."

"No. I'm not here to talk. You need to go back, or go wherever you want, as long as it isn't *to my job*."

"I didn't raise you to be this rude to your mother."

"No, you raised me to be molested by my father."

Her open hand cracks against my cheek, and she stares at her palm, horrified, because it's easier than looking at my scarred face.

"Esperanza told me about the prognosis," I continue after a moment. "She told me about what you all want to do. Bring him to the house, let him die around family. But he's not dead yet and if you think for one moment I will ever even *consider* letting him around children . . ."

"He never hurt any of the others."

"Hurting me was enough. I can't stop you from doing the petition, but I won't be putting my name to it. Not as a victim, not as an agent, and I'll be writing the judge to speak against it."

"This isn't a conversation to be having in the hallway," she frets.

"We're not having a conversation, *Mamá*. I am telling you a thing I will never do."

Her hair is almost entirely silver but still thick and healthy, braided back into a coiled knot low at the base of her skull, single-hair wisps curling away from her scalp as they protest the severity. Her face is creased with wrinkles, her dark brown eyes are the same as I remember. She's her and not her. Even her clothes are nearly the same, an embroidered white blouse and long, multi-tiered colorful skirt, the only things she'd ever buy for herself, because *Papá* fell in love with her in those skirts, she used to tell us. If the necklines are a little higher than they used to be, her arms thicker under the collar ruffle, well. It's been decades.

"Go home, *Mamá*," I tell her, and despite everything, my tone is gentle. Almost kind. "Go home to everyone else and accept the fact that you lost your youngest daughter a very long time ago."

"But I didn't lose you," she insists, tears tracking down her weathered cheeks. "You are right here before me, more stubborn than ever."

"You lost me the minute I told you what *Papá* was doing, and you said I needed to be a good daughter."

"He was your *Papá*," she says helplessly. "He was—"

Part of me recognizes the oddity of her speaking English. English was for school and work and errands. At home we only spoke Spanish unless the older kids were working on homework. The entire neighborhood—literally, the *entire* neighborhood—was family, all the cousins and second cousins and aunts and uncles, the grandparents and almost grandparents, the older siblings who married and moved into houses just down the street or around the corner. Unless it was schoolwork, you didn't hear English until you left the neighborhood and went past the corner stores. Even then, you were as likely to hear Spanish until you got deeper into town.

I take her face between my hands, lean forward, and kiss her forehead. When Vic did it to me, it was support. Now, it's goodbye. "Go home. Your daughter is lost, and she is never coming home. She found a better family on her own."

"That man, that agent," she spits. "He took you away!"

"He rescued me. Once from the cabin, and once from you. Goodbye, *Mamá*."

I turn and walk away, and there's a part of me aware of the sobbing little girl in the back of my mind, the hurt child who couldn't understand why her parents did what they did, why no one else cared. *Be patient,* I want to tell that little girl. *It gets worse, but then it gets better. Then we get rescued.*

Sterling doesn't ask how it went when I get in the car. She just starts it up and pulls out onto the road, headed to Manassas and home.

Home.

"Can we stop by my house?" I ask once we're on the highway. "Something I need to do."

"Of course." She watches me from the corner of her eye, most of her attention still on the road. "Cass called. So far the search of Gloria's house hasn't turned up anything suspicious."

"Are you serious?"

"They're still looking. Watts and Holmes have her at the station, but they haven't questioned her yet. They're waiting for the results."

"This is a terrible day, Eliza."

"Yes."

My house looks the same, my cozy little cottage with its quiet colors and Jason's flowers blooming along the walk and the front of the porch. I'm not sure why I expected it to look different. It *feels* different now. Shouldn't it look different as well?

But it doesn't, and the keys open it same as ever, and aside from the dust that's accumulated over the past eleven days, the inside is also unchanged. Siobhan never kept very much here, just some clothes and toiletries and a couple of books by the bed. Her absence hasn't changed it.

Even the bedroom, the bed still unmade and probably still smelling of her a bit. I haven't been in it since the night Emilia Anders knocked on my door. The black-velvet bear sits on my nightstand, and dozens of relatives line the shelf that wraps around the room.

I've never likened the sight to my family's neighborhood before.

Grabbing trash bags out from under the kitchen sink, I stalk back into the room and pull bears from the shelf, shoving them into the bags. But every last goddamn bear is off the shelf, even if some of them are spilling across the floor. My hand closes around the black-velvet one, with the faded red heart and the smart bow tie, and I . . . I can't.

Clasping him to my chest and trying not to think of Ava holding those damn angel bears the same way, I lean against the wall and sink to the floor, my feet sliding into the space under the bed. After a few minutes, Sterling picks her way between the bears, not stepping on any of them, and moves some aside so she can sit next to me.

I'm not sure how long we sit there in silence. Long enough for the light coming through the windows to shift to dusk, for shadows to stretch across the room and distort perspectives.

"Once upon a time, I was the youngest of nine," I whisper eventually. "I used to share a room with my two next youngest sisters, but when I was five, I got my very own room up in the attic. I was so proud of it. It had a pretty pink canopy princess bed, and a white chest for dress-up clothes. And it had a lock all the way up on the top of the door where I couldn't reach. The night of my birthday party, my very first night in the room, I found out why." I turn the bear so he's braced against my thighs, his worn face more squashed than usual. His stuffing is so old, he doesn't bounce back the way he used to. "For three years, my father molested me, and the rest of the family ignored it. My siblings, all the adults, they knew, but the people of their generations, back in Mexico . . . you just don't *talk* about things like that. So they closed their eyes and turned away."

"Three years," Sterling repeats, her own voice whisper soft. Maybe it's the kind of secret, maybe it's the twisting light vanishing across the bedspread. There's something about the moment that says anything louder will shatter.

"My father also gambled. The family didn't know about that. They would have been less forgiving. All the different pieces of the family relied on each other to get by; his gambling meant he put the whole extended family in jeopardy. He got in over his head with a private group. He couldn't even sell the house to cover it. The entire neighborhood was family, so he would have had to explain. It wasn't enough to cover it anyway."

"So he gave them you."

"He sent me to play in the woods behind the house, and when no one could see me, they grabbed me. They had a cabin deeper in the woods, too deep for anyone to really go."

"How long?"

"Two years." Sometimes I wake up and can still feel the rough boards beneath me, and the manacle around my ankle, hear the heavy chain that rattled across the wood with every movement I made. "There were some other kids there. Collateral, maybe, or winnings. They were never there long, but a couple of the men had taken a liking to me. Said they liked my fear. I'd been there almost two years when I got a chance to escape. The cabin wasn't well-made; the wood wasn't finished. We'd had a wet summer and everything was rotting, and I pulled up the ring-bolt attached to my chain. Wrapped it around me like a feather boa so it wouldn't clank, tiptoed past the men as they were sleeping, and ran like hell into the woods."

"You don't like woods," she says after I fall silent. "Eddison always goes in, if there's a way for it not to be you."

"*Sí*. It was night, and dark, the trees too thick for moonlight. There were little ravines all over. I ran and ran and ran. I fell so often, but I dragged myself back up, more and more scared every time. And I couldn't find a way out. I was too afraid to scream. Maybe it would bring help, but it was more likely to bring the men."

"They found you?"

"In the morning. They came out looking for me when they noticed I was gone. The chain had gotten caught in a root system, and when I tried to work it loose, I fell over the edge of a ravine. The manacle caught and broke my ankle. I was just hanging there. They beat me for trying to escape." Using the bear's soft paw, I trace the scars on my cheek. "Broken bottle."

She leans her head against my shoulder and waits.

"They put me in the root cellar after that. It was stone and the trapdoor had a lot of locks. I don't know if I would have been brave enough to try again, to be honest; it didn't matter. But a few days later, I woke up to yelling. Yelling and gunshots. I was huddled there in the dark, and the locks scraped and the door opened and there was a big man standing there. I was terrified. It could only get worse, right? But someone handed him a flashlight, and he made it dance around my feet, and he came down the stairs and knelt in front of me, and said his name was Victor."

I can feel her surprise, a full-body startle that ends in almost the same posture. "Our Vic?"

"Our Vic. He told me I was going to be okay, that those men were never going to hurt me again. The men had taken the shirt I lived in, so Vic wrapped me up in his jacket while someone brought down tools to take the manacle off. Someone else—Finney, I think—brought a blanket and a teddy bear." I wave at her with the bear's paw and feel more than hear her soft huff of laughter. "Vic picked me up and carried me out into this mess of stand lights, dozens of people milling around. Some of the men who had imprisoned me were dead, but most were injured or handcuffed. And as we passed, there was this momentary . . . hush. A bubble of silence as everyone stopped to stare, and then went back to what they were doing."

"I know our side of that hush."

"There wasn't a road that deep into the woods, no way to drive through. Vic carried me two and a half miles to the closest access point, and the cars had their lights flashing like crazy. He took me to an ambulance, and I didn't want to let go, so he sat in there with me as the paramedics worked on my face and ankle, and all the other wounds. He said he was going to take me home to my parents."

"I can't imagine that going well."

"I started screaming. Told him I couldn't go home, couldn't go back to my *papá* hurting me again. I promised to be good, begged, anything so my *papá* couldn't touch me again. And his face did this . . . I honestly don't know if you've seen Vic when he's about to rain down fire and destruction."

She shakes her head against my shoulder. "I've seen him pissed, but not like that. Saw a hint of it with Archer's fuckup three years ago, but he left that to Finney."

"When the hospital had done all its scans and wrapped and treated everything, he came back in with a social worker and another police officer, and they asked me about my father. My room at the house was still the same; my father couldn't change it because it would look to the rest of the family like he was giving up on my safe return. All the rest of the family thought I'd been kidnapped, even my mother. He was the only one who knew differently. So the police went and they saw the lock, and the dress-up clothes with the blood and semen on them, and the diary I had duct-taped to the back of the headboard. My father was arrested, and the men from the woods admitted I'd been given to them to settle a gambling debt. The family denied knowing anything about him molesting me. Family."

She nods.

"They were furious when the court sent me to foster care. I was supposed to come home. Oh, but they were pissed at me, too, because I should have just said thank you for rescuing me from the woods. Should have come home and kept my mouth shut, because family. I kept getting moved to different foster homes because my relatives would show up and start harassing the adults. My *tía* Soledad tried to kidnap me from school a couple of times. After three years, my social worker got permission to move me to a different city. I've seen one of my cousins a couple times since then, but that was it. But they won't . . ."

"They won't give up on you, even though they gave you up years ago."

"Yes. Yes, exactly. My father has been in prison ever since, and all going as it should, he'll die there. Sooner than expected, maybe, with the cancer."

"That why they're trying to talk to you again?"

"They've never really stopped. It's why I change my number so often. But yes, it's why my mother came out. Esperanza told them I work for the FBI at Quantico, that I'm an agent. Their little girl, look how far she's come. I'm the victim and I'm an agent, and surely if I ask for him to be released so he can spend the rest of his days at home, a judge would do it."

"They're really asking you for that?"

I nod, and can't help but smile as she mutters what sounds like curses into my shirt.

"Did you request Vic's team?" she asks once she's subsided.

"No. Wouldn't have, even if I could; seemed a bit weird, trying to prove myself as an adult agent to someone who'd pulled me naked out of a root cellar when I was ten. When I received the assignment, he took me out to lunch before I even got to meet Eddison, and we sat and talked, to see if we could both do this. He said there was no shame if the answer was no, he'd make sure I got assigned to another team, no stigma, no gossip. At the end of the day, though . . ." The bear is a comforting, familiar brush against my neck, twenty-two years of cuddling and nightmares and triumphs. We were in a car accident once, me and the bear, and I wouldn't let the paramedics touch me until they'd stitched up the bear's arm, even though my own arm was bleeding all over the place. I was twelve. "He was the reason I became an FBI agent.

He pulled me out of absolute hell, and his kindness made me feel like maybe safe was a thing I could be someday. He *rescued* me, *saved* me. And it wasn't about trying to repay him, but just . . . I wanted to do that for others. He gave me my life back."

"And now someone is using your history against you," she murmurs, lightly touching the bear's bow tie with one fingertip.

"I don't think they mean to. I think this is them trying to give that gift to others." We sit in silence until I finally ask the question I try not to ask any agent. "Why are you in CAC, Eliza?"

"Because my best friend's father was a serial killer," she answers calmly. She actually smiles a little. "I told Priya that, three years ago. Archer was being an ass to her. My best friend's father was a serial killer, and even though he murdered grown women, I saw what it did to the kids when the truth came out. I used to have sleepovers at her place all the time. He tucked us into bed. And he did all that. I wanted to understand it. I never have, of course, but it left me obsessively researching criminals and psychology and one day, when I was home from college for winter break, my dad asked me if I was going to make a career out of it."

"You hadn't even thought about it, had you?"

"No. I mean, I had a couple of psychology and criminology classes under my belt, but it was only my sophomore year. I'd only just finished up my gen eds, and was trying to decide on a major. But he got me to realize that I could put that motivation to work helping others. And I chose CAC because I'm still friends with Shira, and I remember how terrible it was when we found out about her father, and I wanted to help kids. CAC lets me do that."

After a while, she gets to her feet and offers her hand to help me stand. We look around the mess of teddy bears on the floor. I don't have any more garbage bags in the kitchen.

"Leave it," she advises. "Come back to it later, decide then. You've been collecting them for years, and this is a really bad time to make important decisions."

"Tossing teddy bears is a big decision?"

"It is when they remind you of why you're here."

"You're a wise soul, Eliza Sterling."

"I think we take turns with it. Given everything else, it would be irresponsible of me to get you drunk, so hopefully this will be enough."

My phone rings. I pull it out of my pocket, but I can't bring myself to answer it. Not if it means another child dead.

Sterling takes it from my hand, checks the display, and thumbs the call to speak. "Kearney, you've got Mercedes and Sterling here."

"Awesome." Cass's voice sounds tinny and distant, like maybe she's using the speakerphone as well. "Burnside went through every single file access in the office the last few weeks and took special note of which ones were accessed without additional information being added, the ones most likely to be superfluous access."

"Okay. Does that point to Gloria?"

"That's where it gets a bit weird."

"How do you mean?"

"For one thing, a lot of the access to our kids' files, among others, was done on Gloria's chemo days. File clerks don't have remote access."

"So someone else is using Gloria's log in. Could it be Lee?"

"If it was, it wasn't from his computer—it's clean, and the clerks probably would have noticed if he'd been out there on Gloria's computer. The really weird part is that there's one search that comes up almost every day that isn't in Manassas CPS jurisdiction. It's over in Stafford, and there is no active CPS file for that address. Can you think why anyone would do a daily search on an address that's not only out of their office's jurisdiction, but also out of their hunting ground?"

"Stafford? Stafford, Stafford . . ." Listen to your gut, Mercedes, it's telling you something. "Run that address against my old cases."

"Let's see . . ." In the silence of the house, I can hear the click of keys over the phone. "Holy shit, Mercedes. Nine years ago, a fourteen-year-old girl named Cara Ehret. Her father beat her, raped her, and prostituted her to his friends. Fuck. You stayed with her in the hospital."

"A guardian angel," I murmur, remembering. "She said she finally had a guardian angel. Her mother drove her car into a tree when Cara was nine or ten. Her father's still in prison—the rest of his life, I seem to recall—so he's not still living in that house. And I doubt Cara is either. We looked at her case this morning but couldn't trace her after high school; where is she now?"

"We'll dig in and find out. I'll call back when we've got it."

"Cara Ehret," Sterling repeats, tasting the name. "She was on our short list. But what's her connection to Gloria? Or to whoever was using Gloria's log in?"

I shake my head, the final threads still just out of reach. "She was blonde as a kid, but her father dyed her hair red when he started renting her to his friends," I tell her, the details I read so recently crowding in on me. "What if we're looking for Cara, but she—"

My phone rings again before I can finish the thought, but it isn't Cass. It's an unfamiliar number. "Ramirez."

"Mercedes," comes a hoarse whisper. "Mercedes, she's here!"

"She's here? Where's here? Who is this?"

"It's Emilia," the girl on the other end of the call whispers. "The lady who killed my parents, she's here at my Uncle Lincoln's!"

26

"We're on our way," I promise immediately, and Sterling has her keys and phones in hand before we even get to the door. She tosses me her keys so she can get the phones ready. "Emilia, are you safe? Are you hiding?"

"No, I have to warn my uncle."

"Emilia, you need to hide." My hands are steady as I jam the keys in the ignition, training beating adrenaline. I can see Sterling texting Cass with one phone and looking up the number for the Chantilly police with the other.

"I can't let him die like my mom did. He's been taking real good care of me. He's nice, and he doesn't hurt me. I can't just leave him."

"Is she in the house?" I ask, pulling out of the driveway. Sterling grabs the phone from my shoulder and switches it to speaker, sliding it into a cradle sticking out of the cigarette lighter.

"No. She's walking around it."

"Is it just you and your uncle in the house?"

"No. His girlfriend's here."

"Okay, Emilia, run to their room if you can do it without being seen through a window. Wake them up. But be sneaky. If they're loud, you could all get hurt. Keep the phone with you."

I can hear her heavy breathing over the line. Mother of God, this girl is brave. Sterling cups her hand around her mouth and the mic on her phone to muffle her conversation with the dispatch officer in

Chantilly. Driving like a bat out of hell, I tap her other phone and make a swirling motion with my finger, the closest I can get to *lights*.

She gets it, though, and starts punching in another text, this one to Holmes, to let her know we're driving like LEOs in a personal vehicle without lights or sirens. She tells the dispatch officer, too, so hopefully we'll be able to get to Chantilly without a well-meaning officer pulling us over for violating a dozen or two traffic laws.

Lincoln Anders's groggy voice comes through the background. "Emilia? What is it, Emi?"

"The lady who killed my parents. She's outside," she tells him, and the phone is right up against her face.

"Did you have a nightmare, sweetheart?" asks a female voice, just as sleep muddled. God, it's later than I thought.

"No, she's here, she's just outside. We have to hide."

"Emilia, put the phone on speaker," I tell her. "Let your uncle hear me."

"Okay," she pants, and I hear the change in the background.

"Mr. Anders, this is FBI Agent Mercedes Ramirez. Emilia called me. If she says the woman is outside, believe her. The Chantilly police are on their way to your address. Is there a cellar or basement where you can hide?"

"No," he answers, suddenly sounding much more awake. "There's a root cellar—"

I cringe.

"—but the entrance is outside. You can't get there from here."

"Do you have any weapons in the house?"

"N-no."

"The address is outside city limits," Sterling whispers. "Dispatch says two cars will be there in ten."

Ten minutes. Jesus fucking Christ.

"Can you get out of the house?" I demand. "Can you get to a neighbor?"

"Come on, Stacia, get up. We'll just—" He cuts himself off, and Emilia whimpers. "She's inside the house," he hisses.

"Get out. Get out now!"

Sterling holds her phone near the microphone, the recording function lit up, and gives me a wide-eyed look.

A gunshot cracks through the silence, followed by a grunt and two screams.

"Emilia, RUN," I yell through the gunshots that follow. Emilia is the only one screaming now. I don't even know if she heard me.

"Stop," a muffled voice commands on the other end. "Stop, you're safe now."

Emilia is sobbing now, and then there's a startled grunt.

"Stop fighting me," the voice snaps. "You're safe now. You're going to be okay."

"Emilia!"

More grunts, and Emilia's screaming again, feral, broken things that must be shredding her throat, and then—

Another gunshot, and a heavy thump.

"No, no, no," whines the voice. "No, it wasn't supposed to happen like this. No. NO. You're supposed to be SAFE! I'm making you SAFE!" She screams, and it tangles off into a choking rasp. I can barely hear footsteps. The time between treads says she's running, and shit, the police aren't there yet, they can't get there in time to stop her!

"Cara!" I yell, wondering if she can hear me. "Cara, it's Mercedes. Do you remember me?"

But the only thing I can hear is the pained groans of someone still alive. Tears running down bloodless cheeks, Sterling tells the dispatch officer to send ambulances.

Too many minutes later, we hear the officers arrive, calling into the house. "This one's alive!" one shouts, and someone steps on Emilia's phone before they say who it is.

I'm doing 110 in a 45, and I wasn't anywhere near fast enough.

When we screech to a halt in front of the Anders house, lights are flashing everywhere, pressing in on wounds that are far more raw than usual. Two ambulances are in the drive, and as we run up to the front door, two paramedics rush out with a gurney.

There's a man on it. Her dad's cousin, Lincoln Anders.

"The little girl!" I snap.

One of them shakes his head, and they push past into the ambulance.

There's an officer at the door, and he barely gives our credentials a glance. "The woman and the girl were dead before they hit the ground," he tells us. "Woman was shot straight through the heart, the girl took one to the head, point-blank."

"We were on the phone with her," Sterling tells him, voice shaking. "She saw the intruder, called us, and went to wake up her uncle and his girlfriend. They were trying to leave the house."

"Why did she call you? Why not the police?"

"Her parents were murdered on the third." I scrub my hands against my cheeks. "She was delivered to my house, and I gave her my number if she needed anything. She saw the same woman outside here."

"You're that one?"

Sterling honest-to-God growls at him, and he flushes.

"I didn't mean anything by it," he says quickly. "Dispatch said the call came from the FBI and we didn't know why, that's all. We saw the story in the paper."

"Agent Kathleen Watts is the lead agent on the case, and she's partnered with Detectives Holmes and Mignone out of Manassas."

"Chief got a call from Watts; she should be just behind you."

"It'll take her longer from—" Sterling stops, watching an SUV with flashing lights slam to a stop behind her car. "She was still in Manassas. Mercedes, she was still in Manassas."

Which means she was still questioning Gloria.

Watts and Holmes run up the lawn. "Cara Ehret," Watts calls before they even reach us. "She changed her name to Caroline Tillerman after she left foster care. She's one of the file clerks. We've got officers on their way to her apartment and an APB out on her car."

Caroline Tillerman. Cass and I spoke face-to-face with her at the CPS office.

I look at Holmes, who's significantly more shaken. "We were on the phone with Emilia."

She closes her eyes, hand rising automatically so she can kiss her thumbnail.

"We all looked at Lincoln Anders when he said he'd take Emilia in," Sterling says. "CPS did their checks, but so did we. He was completely clean. The closest he'd come to trouble was a couple of speeding tickets. Why in the hell would she attack him?"

"CPS received an anonymous complaint this morning."

"Anonymous."

"This morning?"

Watts nods impatiently. "Caller said his girlfriend couldn't be trusted with children, because she killed a boy."

"What?" we both demand.

"When Stacia Yakova was a teenager, she was helping her father clean his guns at the kitchen table, and a neighbor called over to ask her father's help with something heavy. So he told her to put down the gun she was working on and he'd be right back. Her brother came in, high off his ass, and thought she was an intruder. He attacked her with a knife. Got a few slashes and stabs in because she didn't want to hurt him, but when he got the knife to her throat, she grabbed one of the guns they hadn't worked on yet and shot him in the thigh."

"Bled out?"

"No, she called an ambulance, they got him to the hospital, but when they gave him anesthesia for surgery—"

"He was a tweaker."

"The father walked in on the end of the struggle. He was the one to pull his son off of her. It was clearly self-defense so she was never charged with anything."

"If this anonymous complaint turns out to be one of her brother's former friends or girlfriends . . ." I shake my head. "But Cara probably wasn't in any fit state to research it. She heard Emilia's name and decided then and there."

My phone rings, and I swear to fucking God—

Sterling yanks it out of my hands. "It's Cass," she reports, and accepts the call to speaker. "Kearney, you've got Ramirez, Sterling, Watts, and Holmes."

"Emilia?" she asks immediately.

". . . No."

"Damn." She takes a deep, shuddering breath, both inhalation and exhalation clearly audible over the line. "Caroline Tillerman is not at her apartment. Officers found several masks, white jumpsuits, both bloodied and clean, blonde wigs, both bloodied and clean, a box of white angel teddy bears . . . everything in her kit except a knife and a gun, but there are boxes of ammunition."

"Do we know what she's driving?"

"It's a 2004 dark blue Honda CR-V. We found all eight of the files missing from CPS, and have agents and officers on the way to those houses to secure the families."

"What about the address in Stafford?"

"The house is owned by Navy Lieutenant Commander DeShawm Douglass. He lives there with his wife, Octavia, and their nine-year-old daughter, Nichelle. There are no complaints or suspicions of abuse in the household, either in Stafford County or their previous residences."

"Call SPD, get officers out there."

"What are you thinking?" asks Watts.

"Cara just point-blank murdered a kid she was trying to save. She is freaking the fuck out, and if she tries to go to her apartment, she'll see the police. Where do you go when there's nowhere else to go?"

"I go home," Holmes says slowly. "To my husband and daughter."

"Pretend you're twenty-three and single."

"To my parents, then."

"But her mother is dead and her father is in prison. That leaves the house in Stafford, where her father put her through absolute hell. The house where a man is living with his little girl, and she has checked every day to make sure there are no complaints."

"There still isn't a complaint," Sterling points out.

"Do you think that matters anymore to the woman we heard on the phone?"

She shakes her head.

"Burnside is calling Stafford," Cass reports. "He'll give a courtesy call to NCIS after, given that the homeowner is a lieutenant commander. We think we may have identified Cara's initial trigger."

"What's that?"

"A few months ago, her father hired a private investigator to find her. When that was successful, he sent her a letter, asking her to come see him. The letter's still in her apartment, so we called the prison."

"Did she go?"

"Yes. This, though: her father got remarried, and his wife is expecting a baby. She's having a little girl in August."

"You want to tell me how the hell a man in prison for whoring out his daughter gets conjugal visits?" Watts snarls.

"He doesn't, but when there's a friendly prison guard to smuggle out a sperm sample, new wife can go to a fertility clinic for implantation. Guard was fired but it was a done deed."

"And the father who sold her again and again to his friends gets another little girl. I remember interviewing him after the arrest; he probably tracked her down and told her in person just to torture her.

Bastard probably got off on getting to hurt her again. You're right, that has to be our trigger."

"We borrowed Blakey, Cuomo, and Kang's teams so we'd have enough. Hanoverian signed off on it."

"Her endgame is Stafford." My heart beats a rapid tattoo. "She can't help it."

"How sure are you?"

"What do you do when you're lost in the woods?" I ask softly.

Sterling takes a step closer to me, leaning into my side.

"You run home," I remind her. "Everything is on fire and overwhelming, and she's running home, but when she gets there, she's going to remember all the ways she was hurt, she's going to see that little girl, and she's going to see herself."

"Kearney, send the address to Eddison."

"He's still here at the office," Cass says.

"He's what?" Sterling and I ask together.

There's a shuffle and a beep, and then we can hear Eddison's tired grumble. "Where are we going?"

"Fill him in on the way, just get there," Watts orders. "Ramirez, Sterling, go."

"The regulations?" Sterling asks hesitantly.

"Screw them. You're the best chance of talking her down, just make sure Kearney makes the arrest. Give me your keys, take mine; I've got the lights." She holds out her hand. Sterling takes the keys from me and drops them in Watts's hand, scooping up the ring for the SUV.

Sterling had a reputation at the Denver field office for making seasoned agents cry when she drove. Never caused an accident, never incurred damage, but you spend the entire trip praying. Sounds like just what we need. As she peels rubber getting us down the street, I brace myself by my legs, much as I envision sailors must during hurricanes.

"Please let us get there," I whisper. *"Por favor."*

27

The Douglasses' house is painted with flashing red and blue lights when we squeal in. Eddison, standing at the front door with a uniform, checks his watch and shudders.

"She got here first, probably came straight from Chantilly," he tells us. "Mother is inside. Father's on his way to the hospital, but the mother refuses to leave until her daughter's safe."

"The mother's okay?"

"Shot in the arm, a through and through on her side. The paramedics have her bandaged up and they're keeping an eye on her. Kearney's with her. Police are organizing traffic stops and a search back into the woods, FBI is sending more agents to help, and if it becomes a search and rescue, the Marines have offered aid out of Quantico."

"Let's go inside. I need to talk to Mrs. Douglass."

Mrs. Douglass is in her kitchen, both hands wrapped around a glass of water. She's mostly listening to Cass, standing at her side, but she keeps looking out the bay window of the breakfast nook like she'll see her daughter coming down the street. She just saw her husband shot down and her daughter grabbed, and God, I want to be gentle with her, but we don't have time.

"Mrs. Douglass, my name is Mercedes Ramirez, I'm an agent with the FBI. Are there any places for the neighborhood kids to play? Anything that's been here for a while?"

She stares at me. "Sorry?"

"The woman who took your daughter used to live here. Not just in the neighborhood, in this very house. She's not going to get out of Stafford, so is there any place where the kids gather? Something they maybe think is a secret from their parents?"

"Um . . . no, I don't think . . ." She glances at the papers stuck to the door of the fridge and flinches. "There's a tree house! Nichelle drew a picture of it. She and the girls next door found it a few weeks ago. Said it was falling apart, and I . . . I scolded her for going so far back into the woods."

"Did they tell you where?"

"No, just that it was far back."

"You said the girls next door? Which side?"

She points, and I run out of the house to go pound on the door, Eddison sticking close behind me. The door is opened by a round-faced man in a bathrobe. "What's going on?" he demands. "Are the Douglasses okay?"

"Sir, are your daughters home?"

"Yes, but what—"

"Someone took Nichelle Douglass," I tell him bluntly, "and we think the woman may be taking her back to a tree house your daughters found with Nichelle."

"We're not allowed to go there anymore!" pipes up a girl from down the hall. She slips up behind her father and looks at us with wide eyes. "Mrs. Douglass said it was too far."

"I'm not going to yell at you for it, *mija*," I say, crouching down closer to eye level. "I just need to know where it is. Can you tell us how to get there?"

She chews anxiously on her lip. "Is Nichelle okay?"

"We're trying to find her. But we need your help."

"Wait." She races up the stairs, and back down again only a moment later with a piece of paper in her hand. "I made a map." She shoves it into my hands so hard it crinkles, and she smooths it out before pointing. "Go straight back and cross the creek, and then there's a weird rock thing. Go right until the tire stack. Then turn left and go straight for a really long time and the tree house is there. But you can't go up the ladder because the nails are rusty and Mrs. Douglass says that's how we get tetanus."

"This is perfect, sweetheart, thank you." I straighten up, handing the map to her father. "You'll want to stay inside for a while. There are more agents and officers on the way."

"Of course. I hope . . ." He swallows hard and pulls his daughter back into his side. "I hope you find her safe."

Cass meets us between the houses. "Hanoverian's here, he's staying with Mrs. Douglass. Where are we going?"

"We need larger flashlights, and we're going into the woods."

She whistles at one of the uniforms, and in short order we're running into the trees with heavy Maglites and the promise of backup as soon as it arrives. We should wait for it, but one look at my face, and Eddison decides to let us go ahead. Guns drawn and aimed at the ground, we keep the flashlights low as we jog two by two.

It's not the same as the woods back home, where the trees were spindly and needled and stabbed the sky. These are broader, the branches less keen to smack and cling. We don't talk, our huffing breaths filling the space. The noise from in front of the houses floats back, strange snippets of conversation without words. We splash through the creek, shallow but too wide to jump, and ignore the discomfort of squelching in our shoes as we look out for the rock pile the girl mentioned. We've crossed probably a mile before we see it, and we take a right. The tire stack comes up pretty quickly.

Go straight for a really long time, she said, and given how far we've come already, I'm a little worried. We pick up the pace, Eddison and I in the lead, angled in opposite directions so we can have a shred of warning if Cara tries to sneak up on us.

Two miles later, we can hear someone screaming, and another voice yelling. We're flat-out running now, and finally we can see a clearing up ahead. We slow down as much as we dare, trying to be quiet, but there are old branches all around it like a noise trap.

"Don't come any closer!" the woman in white yells, grabbing Nichelle by the neck and cutting her off midscream. Her gun sways back and forth next to Nichelle's face.

Turning off the flashlight, I slide it through the loops on the back of my pants.

Eddison sighs but nods, then motions for Sterling and Cass to each go around a different side. He settles into a crouch behind one of the trees so I can move past him.

"Cara," I call. "Cara, it's Mercedes. I know you don't want to hurt Nichelle."

"I'm making her safe!" she cries, voice still muffled by the plain white mask. "They'll hurt her. They always hurt her."

"Like your father hurt you," I agree, stepping into the clearing. Her gun comes up to point at me, but I don't try to get too close. "I know his new wife is having a little girl. Cara, I promise you, he is never going to get the chance to hurt that baby girl."

"I'm keeping her safe," she insists.

"Cara, can you take off the mask? Let me see your face, sweetheart, I want to make sure you're okay."

She hesitates, but then she steps behind Nichelle, using her as a shield so she can reach up with the hand holding the gun and push back the mask. It falls to the ground, taking the long silver-blonde wig with it. Her natural hair is a slightly dirtier blonde, dark and damp with sweat where it's pulled back into a tight braid. This young woman, with her wide cheekbones and filled-in face, doesn't look much like the broken girl in the photos in the file. She looks healthy, and it's hard to connect her cheerful presence at the CPS office with the child who cried whenever I left her hospital room.

Until she looks up at me, and I recognize the fear.

"There you are, sweetheart. Are you and Nichelle okay?"

The little girl looks at me disbelievingly, tears tracking down her face. I wish I could wink or smile or something, anything to reassure her, but I can't, not with Cara looking at me.

Cara's crying, too, and she shakes her head. "I can't let them hurt her."

"Then let me take her, Cara. You know I won't hurt her."

The gun is abruptly aimed at me again. "You were supposed to keep Emilia safe, but you let her go to that woman! That woman murdered a little boy!"

"No, Cara, she didn't. Her brother attacked her when he was high. She defended herself. He wouldn't have died from the gunshot, it was too minor. The drugs he was on reacted badly with the anesthesia. He died because of the drugs, sweetheart. She didn't do anything wrong."

"No. No, you're lying!"

"I've never lied to you, Cara. Let Nichelle come to me. I'll keep her safe."

"No one can keep us safe," she says gravely. "The world isn't safe, Mercedes. It never has been." Her Tidewater drawl, practically nonexistent when she spoke to us in the office, is thick now in her distress.

"But we're here, Cara. Look at us, you and me. Our fathers hurt us so badly, but we survived. We're helping other kids. You did so good, sweetheart, you worked so hard to get these kids safe. Sarah? Sarah Carter? She's so relieved, Cara, she's safe now. And you did that."

"Her stepfather was a bad man," Cara says, the gun lowering slightly.

"He was. He hurt her. And you stopped him."

Nichelle isn't struggling, but she watches me, wheels turning in her head. When Cass steps on a dry branch, the crack hanging in the air, Nichelle shifts her weight, bringing her foot down on a smaller branch.

Oh, good girl, you brilliant, beautiful girl.

"Cara, I know you're protecting Nichelle, but do you remember when I told you there were rules? I'm not allowed to put my gun away if any other gun is out. Do you remember?"

The blonde nods slowly. "Daddy's friend. He had to put it down."

"Exactly. I know you're keeping her safe, Cara, but you've got a gun. I'm not allowed to put mine away."

"But—"

"Don't you want me to help you, Cara?"

She chose the name Caroline, but Cara is the name carved into her bones, bleeding through her scars. Cara is the name of the frightened girl, the one who wants comforting. The one who trusted me.

Cass and Sterling aren't going to be able to get a shot on her from the sides, not without risking Nichelle. She has to put down the gun.

"I didn't mean to hurt Emilia," she sobs. "I was just trying to protect her."

"I know. I know you were, she just didn't understand. She was scared, Cara. And we do things, don't we, when we're scared? Put down the gun, sweetheart."

Preferably before the helicopter I hear can get any closer and spook you.

But she hesitates too long, and the helicopter comes over the clearing, the searchlight blinding. I squint against it with long practice. Cara screams. "You're trying to trick me!" she shrieks. "You lied to me!"

"Cara, I know you meant the best, but you killed people. There are consequences for that."

Eddison, Sterling, and Cass all step into the clearing, guns up and leveled at Cara. They stay back, trying to let me keep working.

But I've lost her. She stares at me, tears bright in her eyes, her whole body trembling with emotion. "I'm *helping* them, Mercedes. Like you helped me. Why . . . I thought you'd be proud of me. Why are you trying to stop me? Why?"

"Caroline Tillerman," Eddison calls over the deafening thump of the copter blades. "Put down the gun. You are under arrest for the murders of Sandra and Daniel Wilkins, Melissa and Samuel Wong—"

Her face twisted in fury, Cara lunges forward, half-tripping over the resistant Nichelle, and fires. Eddison drops to the ground with a grunt.

Suddenly there's a crack and a black and red rose blooms in Cara's forehead. She takes a breath, tries to take a second, and tips backward to the ground as Nichelle struggles away from her.

I glance to Sterling and Cass, but they're both looking at me.

Dios mío. That was me.

That was my shot.

Sterling races forward to grab Nichelle, kicking the gun away and holding the girl so she can't see. Cara's sprawled across the ground, her eyes wide and startled, mouth open with shock.

A groan behind me makes me spin. Eddison. "Mercedes."

I drop down beside him. He's curled around his left leg, both hands clenched around as much of his lower thigh as he can manage. Blood seeps out, thick and dark, between his fingers. Holstering my gun, so much heavier than I remember it ever being, I yank off my blouse, buttons flying, and start wrapping it around the wound.

"You know," he manages through gritted teeth, "now they're really going to think we're sleeping together."

I yank the first knot tight over the bullet hole, and he growls.

"How is he?" asks Sterling, her voice shaking.

"He'll need to get lifted out. The copter can't land and he can't hike it. That's way too far to carry him."

"Is that your way of calling me fat?"

"It's my way of saying make one more joke and I will leave you to Priya's tender mercy."

That asshole actually grins at me. "I was a model of restraint when she got hurt."

"That doesn't mean she will be."

He grimaces against a throbbing wave of pain, the muscles twitching under my hands. "Point." A Marine in full gear rappels down from the hovering helicopter. "Anyone hurt?" he bellows.

Cass grabs him by the elbow and shoves him our way. The Marine Corps, if I remember correctly, doesn't actually have medical personnel, but most units have corpsmen with some medical training. He gives a quick check under the rapidly soaking-through bandage, then turns his head to speak into the radio on his shoulder. A second Marine drops down with a collapsible backboard and some rigging.

"Oh, fuck no," mutters Eddison.

I flick his forehead with bloody fingers. "You will do it and you will say thank you," I warn him ominously. And then, because he's my brother and we're both scared out of our minds, I scratch along his scalp, fingers digging into his shaggy curls. I don't pull away until the Marines lift him in a smooth, practiced move and transfer him onto the rigged-up board. They carry the board over to the dangling ropes and with a series of knots that seem more fast than safe, to my inexperienced eye, have both themselves and Eddison roped in. Winches in the copter haul them up. The last I see of Eddison is his tired, somewhat mocking salute to the Marines pulling him on board.

Cass grabs my elbow with both hands and yanks me to my feet. "Nichelle," she reminds me as the copter moves away.

Right. Traumatized child, who has absolutely no idea what's going on.

She's wrapped around Sterling, face buried in Eliza's stomach, her shoulders shaking. Sterling rubs firmly between her shoulder blades, giving her a grounding point.

"Nichelle?"

She shifts her head to look at me with one eye.

I crouch down beside her, trying not to touch either of them with my bloody hands. "You are so smart, and so brave," I tell her. "You knew just what we were trying to do, didn't you?"

"Not at first," she mumbles into Eliza's shirt.

"But you figured it out. It was so frightening, but you figured it out and you helped us. Thank you, Nichelle. I'm sorry this happened, and I'm sorry I seemed to make it worse at first. And you know what, your mom is at home, waiting, and she is so worried about you."

She perks up. Not enough to let go of Sterling, but I can see her whole face, at least. "Is she okay?" she asks in a rush. "She was bleeding but I couldn't see how bad."

"She's hurt," I admit, "but she's going to be okay. Once she sees you're safe and sound, you'll both go to the hospital. Your dad is there already. I don't know how he's doing, though. He was in the ambulance before I got to the house."

Sounds start carrying through the woods, yells and calls for us. Cass puts her phone back in her pocket where she's standing guard over Cara's body. "MARCO!" she yells, and there's a ripple of shocked laughter through the trees.

"Stupid fed," someone bellows. "The one *looking* is supposed to say 'Marco'!"

"I can't say 'Polo' if you're not smart enough to say 'Marco' first!"

Nichelle giggles, even as she looks a bit shocked by it.

"Nichelle, we are really relieved that you're okay," I tell her, feeling a little giddy myself. "We might get a little silly. Is that okay?"

She nods with a shy grin.

A small herd arrives in the clearing, mostly uniforms with a couple of agents. A female officer immediately comes over to us and smiles down at the little girl. "Hi, Nichelle. My name is Officer Friendly. Do you remember me?"

It takes her a moment, but then the giggle slips out again. "You spoke at my school. You said your name is really Officer Friendly."

"And so it is," the woman says, pointing to her name tag. "Hannah Friendly. While we were out looking for you, the hospital called your mom. Your dad is going to be just fine. And you'll get to see both of them really soon."

Nichelle looks over to Cara, but a wall of police officers blocks her view of the body. "I . . . I . . ."

"It's okay, Nichelle, you can ask us anything."

"I didn't do anything wrong, did I? She didn't take me 'cuz I was bad?"

"Not a single thing," I answer firmly. "She used to live here when she was a little girl. Her father was a bad man, and hurt her, and when she got really upset about some things, she thought your parents were hurting you, because you were in the same house. You didn't do anything wrong, and neither did your parents. Promise."

She studies my face like she's memorizing it, her dark eyes lingering on the scars I got when I was only a year older than her, and finally nods. "Okay. And I can go home now?"

"Absolutely," says Officer Friendly, offering her hand. Nichelle takes it and allows herself to be led away from me and Sterling. Eliza helps me stand, because my knees are a bit shaky in a way I can't entirely blame on crouching.

And even though I probably shouldn't, I find myself sidling between the officers to kneel down next to Cara, a safe distance away from the pool of blood from what used to be the back of her skull. A thin gold chain peeks above the collar of her white jumpsuit. Finding a sturdy-looking twig, I hook the chain and gently pull until a heart-shaped locket falls out.

"Does anyone have gloves?"

One of the agents from Kang's team kneels across from me, wearing a pair. "Need something picked up?"

I gesture with the twig, setting the locket swaying. "I want to see what's in it."

He catches the pendant and opens it carefully. On on side, there's a picture of teenaged Cara and her plain white teddy bear, red curtains in the back. A photo booth, probably. She's grinning, and her hair is a faded red gold with blonde roots, growing out from the scarlet her father made it. On the other side, there's a newsprint cutout of my face, with a halo drawn in sparkly gold ink.

My stomach churns, and I have to bite down on the urge to vomit. "You can close it, thank you," I rasp.

"Is this healthy?" Cass asks wryly.

The question I asked Father Brendon rolls through my mind. *How do we know when we're doing more harm than good?*

"Mercedes, nine years ago you rescued her, and you tried your damnedest to rescue her again today. What happened in between is not your fault. It's also not your responsibility."

"She got hurt in the system."

"So did you."

I look up at her at that, and she scowls down with an unimpressed glare. "Look, so you've never told me, and I'm not asking now, but I'm not completely unobservant, you know? I know you were in foster care for years, but the only home you talk about is the last one. You think I can't read between the lines that shit happened at the other ones?"

"Only one was very bad," I admit. "The rest of the time I was moved because my family kept trying to take me back."

"Still. You, Mercedes Ramirez, you fucking martyr, are proof that the way she chose wasn't the only way to choose."

"Has anyone told you recently that you're bad at this?"

She shrugs and hauls me up again. "I can't be half as bad as Eddison."

There might be something to that.

"Come on. Let's get back to Hanoverian so you can get to Bethesda and check on Eddison."

I look back at Cara, resisting the pull on my elbow. "I should—"

"Mercedes." Losing patience waiting for me to look at her, she grabs my chin and forces it. "You gave her every kindness you could. Now try to be kind to yourself. No one is going to desecrate her. They're just waiting for the medical examiner. Don't kneel beside her like penance."

But that's exactly what it is, or what it should be. Penance. Vigil, maybe. She needed me to save her. Whether that's fair or not, whether it was possible or not, she needed that from me, and I failed her.

Sterling slides her arm around my waist and joins in the tug-of-war, and the three of us tumble forward, catching ourselves just in time to prevent the Stafford PD from being able to mock us forever.

28

We get back to the Douglass house in time to see Nichelle and her mother ride off in an ambulance. Vic, standing in the driveway, checks over us with worried eyes before yanking all three of us into a hug. The gathered officers and agents laugh at our flailing attempts to regain balance, because Vic doesn't really need to be landing on the concrete, but Vic just as clearly does not give a shit; he is not about to let us go.

Cass wriggles out first, flushed bright pink. She's been loaned to our team on occasion, but I don't think she's ever had a Hanoverian Hug.

Sterling and I shift to settle more comfortably into the embrace, which feels like home. "Eddison got shot in the leg," I mumble into his coat.

"I know. We'll go see him. You just have to give a statement and we can go."

That would mean letting go.

He keeps his arm around my shoulders even when we all finally stand up straight, and Cass calls Watts so we give our statements directly to her. It's pretty no-frills, especially in light of what's to come. An agent discharged a weapon and a suspect died, so IA automatically has to conduct an investigation. The fact that my presence on the scene was borderline not-allowed, requested by the agent in charge but technically against regulations, will make it a bit more complicated. So Watts just has us march through it all together, clustered around the phone like that Mystery Date game we played in middle and high school.

"I'll get Eddison's car back to Quantico," Cass says when the call is done. "You and Watts can trade back in the next couple of days unless you need something right off."

Sterling shrugs. "At this point, even if I did need something I wouldn't know what it was," she admits.

"Do you have an agent you'd trust to drive Watts's car back to the garage?" Vic asks. "That way they can just ride up with me."

"Sure. She's let Cuomo drive it without too much grief, and he's back in the woods. I'll let him know."

Sterling hands over the keys, and we pile into Vic's car for the drive to Bethesda. It's quiet, the CD player crooning one of his favorite Billie Holiday albums. The blood on my hands is starting to itch, but if I scratch or rub, it's going to flake off all over Vic's car. Which, granted, has seen a lot worse from his daughters, but still.

It feels a bit like penance, and Cass isn't here to yell at me for this one.

"Our purses are in my car," Sterling announces suddenly.

"Okay?"

"I drove to Stafford without my license."

I twist around to stare at her in the middle seat. She meets my eyes with a sheepish smile and shrugs.

And suddenly I'm laughing my ass off, trying to imagine explaining to a police officer why we were going 135 without a license, and I can hear her giggling, too, and even Vic is chuckling, because he also knows how Sterling drives when she's determined to get somewhere *now*. It's stupid and ridiculous and *I can't stop laughing*, until the laughter abruptly turns to tears and I'm sobbing into my shoulder so I don't get blood all over my face.

Christ.

Sterling unbuckles her belt and slides up between the front seats as best she can, awkwardly bending over the center console, to wrap me in another hug. She's saying something, her voice soft, no louder than Billie Holiday, really, but I don't know what the words are. It takes me entirely too long to realize that's because she is speaking Hebrew, and I wonder if it's a prayer or a lullaby or a very gentle remonstrance for me to get my head out of my ass.

It's Sterling. It could be any or even all of the above.

When we get to the hospital, Vic parks and pulls a handkerchief from his pocket, wiping my cheeks and throat. I try to help, but he bats my hands away, and yeah, they're covered in blood. For some reason I keep sticking on that.

Eddison, we learn, is in surgery, and they're not sure yet if they need to put hardware in and around his femur. It's broken, definitely, but given that he's an active agent, the surgeon is going to do her best to avoid anything that could keep him out of the field. That's how I remember Bethesda is a military hospital.

Sterling hauls me into a bathroom to wash my hands and face. When we rejoin Vic in the waiting room, he's on the phone with Priya, letting her know about Eddison. I wasn't sure he'd call her so late, but then, this is Priya. Not only is Eddison her brother, but she goes semi-nocturnal during summers anyway. Vic's voice is calm and soothing, the kind of voice we all automatically respond to after so many years. Even Sterling's shoulders loosen a few inches.

At some point, Vic goes off to find coffee and breakfast, leaving Sterling slumped half-asleep against me. I pull my credentials out of my pocket and fold them back to rest badge up on my knee. My badge is ten years old, and it shows in a million ways. The gold is worn and dull at the highest points of the letters, where the metal rubs against the black leather divider of the credentials case. One edge has a chip from getting slammed onto a curb in a takedown, there's a line of dried blood down the inside of the *U* in *US* that no amount of cleaning can seem to get rid of, and the eagle at the top is mostly decapitated because baby agent Cass, with her fear of guns, used to forget that guns have this thing called a safety. The day Cass murdered the eagle on my badge, which had been sitting on the lane's ammo shelf where it should have been safe, was the same day she got the range master as her personal tutor. The range master said it was in the interest of everyone's well-being. Still, blind and burdened Justice stays in stark relief near the center of the badge.

Ideally, our task is to be Justice. Without prejudice or preconceived notions, weigh the information and bring down the sword.

I run a finger along the eagle's wings, tracing the letters that have shaped almost a third of my life.

FEDERAL BUREAU OF INVESTIGATION
DEPARTMENT OF JUSTICE

When I first got the badge, I used to run my finger along the words in almost the same way, tracing them over and over like it was the only way to convince myself it was real. It was new and inspiring and terrifying, and so much changes in a decade.

Some things don't. It's still terrifying.

I knew better than most going into this that the FBI isn't, can't be, anything simple, and yet I still expected it to be easy. No, *easy* isn't the right word. I expected it to be straightforward. Challenging, yes, and sometimes painful, but unwavering. It never occurred to me that I might come to question the good I do.

It's never been a mystery that the system is flawed. My third set of fosters included a skeevy man and his near-adult son who liked to watch the girls when they showered. I learned to skip lunch and shower at school, and the older girls followed suit. The younger ones didn't have showers or gyms, but we could move them through the bathroom at the house pretty quickly with one or two of us standing guard while the men were gone.

But I was also lucky. Most of the homes were safe, and if not all of them were warm, they provided necessities without stripping too much dignity from us in return. My last fosters, the mothers, they were different. Rare, and I think I knew that even then.

How many kids do we rescue who aren't that lucky? How many, who don't have a safe family to go back to, end up even worse than where they started?

How many Caras are out there, one trigger away from snapping and killing others in the course of their spiral of self-destruction?

How many have I helped create?

"You're hurting my brain," mumbles Sterling. "Stop it."

"Trying."

"No, you're not." She reaches up, arm heavy with fatigue, and clumsily pats at my face. "'S'okay. Bad day."

"What do you do to get through an impossible day?"

"Let you and Eddison spend most of it pouring me full of booze."

Okay, there's that.

"Vic is here," she continues after a minute, "because he has the same fears as most of those parents. Eddison is here because he doesn't want any other family to have the weight and pain of always wondering. I'm here because I know how hard these crimes are on family and friends, and want to ease that burden where I can. Of course we're here for the kids. Of course we are. But we also have all those other reasons. You are the only one of us who is here totally and completely for the kids. You're here for them. To rescue them. To help them. You'll help everyone else as much as you can because you're a good person, but the kids are your priority. So *of course* it's going to be hardest on you."

She shifts in her seat, digging her chin into my collarbone for leverage, and resettles with her forehead burrowed into the side of my neck. "I think it makes you a better agent to question the impacts of your actions on others, because it keeps you conscientious. But you belong here, Mercedes. Never doubt that."

"Okay, *hermana.*"

A few hours later, long after Vic returned with a vending machine breakfast for the three of us, the surgeon comes into the waiting room and gives us a broad smile. A knot loosens in my chest. "Agent Eddison is going to be just fine," she tells us, sinking into a chair facing us. "He's in the recovery room, still coming off the anesthesia. Once he's a bit more aware we'll give him all the instructions he's likely to ignore."

"Huh. You really do know his type."

"I operate on Marines; they're all his type. He'll be here for a few days at least, and that number may go up depending on these first days of healing. Mostly it'll be based on how much he behaves himself. Here's where I'll need all of you riding him: We didn't have to put any hardware in, but that doesn't mean someone won't have to go back in and do it if he screws this up. That means abiding by limits, managing his pain, not pushing himself harder than his physical therapist tells him to. He's going to need you to kick his ass."

"Oh, we're good at that," chuckles Vic.

"Normally I'd say you can go one at a time back to the recovery room."

"But?" Sterling asks, pushing herself upright.

"But the first words out of his mouth after surgery were your names, so I think he'd rest better if you were in there with him. Just remember that he needs to rest."

Vic gravely makes promises on behalf of us all, and Eliza and I are too tired to look mischievous, for once. The surgeon herself takes us back to the room, where Eddison is pale and groggy in the wide hospital bed, wires and tubes leading from his chest and hand. He lifts a hand in greeting, and then gets distracted by the sight of the IV.

"He's on the good stuff," Vic says, sotto voce.

"*Vete a la mierda,* Vic," he mumbles.

"I speak Spanish, you'll recall when you're sober. I know what that means. It's only code for Sterling."

"I can't say that to Sterling!" Holy God, he sounds absolutely scandalized. He looks about for Sterling and beckons her closer, groping out with his hand until she steps forward. He tugs her closer, almost face-to-face despite the awkward position of the bed. "I can't say that to you," he earnestly tells her nose.

"I appreciate that," she says in almost the same tone, and drops a soft kiss on the end of his nose.

Vic actually seems startled, and he gives me a curious look. "Did we know about this?"

"You're kidding, right? *They* didn't know about this."

"But you did."

"I may or may not have a pool going with the girls. Priya and I were betting on when; Inara and Victoria-Bliss were betting on no."

"And you didn't think to share?"

I lean against his wide shoulder, smiling as Eddison tries to convince Eliza that he's just fine, really. "I didn't want anyone teasing him until he figured it out. I didn't want him talking himself out of it."

"You do know agents on the same team aren't allowed to date. Fraternization."

"I also know that the friendships we have with the girls are against regulations. We're way too close. We get too involved. But we're one of the best damn teams in the Bureau. We'll make it work."

"Yes. Yes, you will."

We stand near the wall, watching and feeling the warm glow of family, until Eddison gets startled by the IV again and we get to watch Eliza fall off the bed laughing.

29

Jenny brings Priya up to Bethesda later in the morning, after Eddison has been moved to a standard room. Not that Inara and Victoria-Bliss aren't also concerned, but I don't think any of us want to give them ammunition to tease him later. He doesn't entirely remember the hours in the recovery room and he hates hospitals, so he's going to be a bit tetchy for a while.

More so.

"Go home," Jenny orders us, including her husband. "Shower. Sleep. Get in some clean clothes, for the love of God. None of you are allowed back here for at least eight hours."

"But—"

"You are not going to be any help to that young man if you are falling over yourselves. Go."

"But—"

"Victor Hanoverian, do not make me call your mother."

He grins at her and gives her a sweet kiss. "I just wanted to see how long it would take you to pull out Ma."

She returns the kiss with a smile and a hand to his cheek, which becomes the hand twisting his ear painfully as he cringes and follows the movement of her hand to lessen the strain. "Not even a year ago it was you in that bed, Victor, and the doctors weren't sure you were getting out of it in any way but a sheet and a bag. It's going to be a few more years before you get to joke with me in hospitals."

Properly abashed, he gives her another kiss. "You're right, and I'm sorry. It was insensitive."

"Thank you."

Sterling glances at me, her hand in Eddison's, though he's fast asleep. "Relationship goals?"

"Definitely."

Vic rubs his ear with a grimace. "Were you talking about the communication or the abuse?"

"Yes," we answer decisively, and Jenny grins as she returns to shooing us out the door.

Priya takes Sterling's chair beside the bed, feet propped up on the mattress. "Don't worry; if he tries to get up, I'll threaten to yank out his catheter. He'll be so mortified he'll have to behave."

Which is how I half-carry the hysterically giggling Eliza out of the hospital room.

Despite orders from his wife to take us home, Vic does the appropriate thing and drives us back to Quantico. Both our cars are there— I'm assuming Watts brought Sterling's car back—as well as our purses, but there's also something I have to do.

At Agent Dern's desk in Internal Affairs, I hand over my badge and gun, and she swivels away to store them securely in a wall safe. I'm not going to lie—it's painful to see them disappear like that. Usually when my gun is in a safe, I know the combination, whether it's the temporary combo in a hotel room, the date of the Saint Valentine's Day Massacre (Sterling), the date Priya came into our lives (Eddison), or the birth years of Holly, Brittany, and Janey (Vic). Or mine, the date Vic pulled me out of the cabin.

"We're not expecting the investigation to produce any surprises," Dern tells me, handing me a mini bag of M&M's from the top drawer of her desk. "We'll take a few days to get everything together on our end before we call you in. I'd say it will give you time to prepare what you need, but you've kept us in the loop every step of the way, so use the time to rest. I don't imagine you'll be on leave for more than a week or two before we can get your badge back to you."

I'm not sure what my face does, at that moment, because she sits up with interest and concern. "Agent Ramirez? Do you not want your badge back?"

"I . . . I don't know," I confess softly. Despite what Cass and Sterling said this morning—hell, despite what I said to Vic—I'm not sure that I can keep doing this without incurring wounds I'm not strong enough to bear.

The initial surprise in the Dragonmother's expression melts into understanding, and she settles back into her chair. She plucks the reading glasses off her nose and folds them, letting them drop on their chain to sit crookedly against her chest. "Every agent hits this moment, Mercedes," she says gently. "At least every good agent. That you've reached this point in your career without it becoming critical is a testament to you, but also to Hanoverian and Eddison, and the way you all support each other. Questioning your future with us doesn't make you a bad agent. So. You've got some time to think through things."

"Have you ever—" I bite off the rest, but she smiles.

"Forty-one years ago," she answers. "We had an agent who was chasing after a suspect and used lethal force. No witnesses, but his team and the local LEOs he was working with had all commented that something about the case seemed to rub him the wrong way. In the end, our investigation wasn't able to prove one way or the other what actually happened in that confrontation. We recommended suspension and a full psychological evaluation before he could be returned to duty."

"So what happened?"

"He surrendered his badge and gun, went home, took his personal piece out of the closet, and shot his wife and two children before shooting himself."

"Jesus."

She nods, her smile turned sad. "I think you're familiar with the kinds of questions I asked myself over the next few weeks, and even after. Had I caused this? Was I responsible for their deaths? Had I missed something during the investigation that would have told us he would do this? How good could I be at my job if I hadn't realized that could happen? How could I stay in this job with that? This isn't the first time you've asked yourself these questions, Mercedes, though it may be the first time you've had to delineate them so clearly. Whether you stay or not, it won't be the last. Moments like this, questions like this, they become part of you."

"How did you decide?"

"My daughter was worried. If I left the FBI, would I still be Wonder Woman?" She laughs at my startled expression. "My little girl thought all FBI agents were superheroes, and her mom was Wonder Woman, wielding a lasso of truth. I didn't just bring down villains; I protected the other superheroes. She was four. She didn't understand that there was so much more to it. As far as she was concerned, I was Wonder Woman, and Wonder Woman never lets the bad guys win." She shakes her head and pulls out another snack bag of M&M's, spilling some into her palm. "How could I argue with that?"

"Cara Ehret thought I was an angel."

"There have been other cases since then. It isn't one and done, all crises averted. There will be other cases that hit you every bit as hard, and the reasons why may not be the same." She pops the candies in her mouth, chewing and swallowing quickly. "Don't feel bad for taking this time, Mercedes. You are better for it, and the Bureau is better for it."

I nod, brain already spinning on her words.

"How is Eddison?"

"He'll be okay. Weather ache, maybe, and he certainly won't be doing stadiums anytime soon."

Agent Dern shudders delicately. "Even at my best I didn't understand those who do stairs on purpose. Especially at stadiums! Then again, I'm nearly seventy and I still have my original knees, so maybe I was right."

I leave her office laughing, which is probably not the normal reaction for an agent who's just been placed on administrative leave. I get a few baffled looks for it.

For the first time in weeks, I get behind the wheel of my own car and pull out of the garage. Home is waiting, even if I'm not entirely sure it's home anymore, my cozy little cottage stained with the past month and change. I do stop and pick up a box of cupcakes for Jason, and we share them on his front porch as he weeds his flower beds and I sew the buttons back on his shirts and mend some rips, because if there's a sharp edge, he'll catch his shirt on it.

"So it's all done?" he asks.

"All done."

"I'm glad it worked out okay."

I spend the rest of the afternoon puttering around the house, turning on my personal cell for the first time in almost a week and hooking it up to my laptop to move over photos I want to keep. After that, there's a certain satisfaction in taking out the SIM card and beating the shit out of the phone with a baseball bat. I'll get around to replacing it eventually, and this time, I'm not giving the number to Esperanza.

I'm aware, mostly, that I could have just gotten the number changed without killing the phone. It's more fulfilling this way.

Late in the afternoon, I head out to Walmart and come back with a stack of large plastic tubs. The black-velvet bear goes back on my nightstand, safe and sound, but all the rest get layered into the tubs with some mothballs to protect the fabric. The laundry room has a storage closet that's still in range of the AC, protected from the humidity and anything that can happen out in the garage, and when the door closes on the tower of tubs, it feels a little like cutting off a finger.

My bedroom walls look empty, naked even, but maybe that's not a bad thing. I change the sheets and sprawl across the bed, warm with sunlight, and let my mind drift across everything that's happened. I have to make a decision, but Agent Dern says I've got time. Don't rush, because there's time.

That evening, I head back up to Bethesda. According to the nurse at the station, they gave Eddison another full dose of Dilaudid less than half an hour ago, so it's not surprising that he's out cold when I walk in. Jenny's gone, but Priya is sprawled on the tiny couch with a stack of photos and an alarming amount of scrapbooking supplies.

"So, Eddison and Sterling, huh?" she asks.

"He tell you that?" I settle into the chair between her and the bed, on Eddison's right side.

"Sort of? He asked if it would be weird to keep calling someone by their last name after they've kissed you."

"And you said?"

"It isn't any weirder than calling one of your sisters by her last name all the time." She grins at me. "I'm glad you're okay-ish."

"Okay-ish," I repeat, tasting the word. "Yes."

Priya knows okay-ish. She spent five years living with it, and even now, with the healing she's had these last three years, she still has days where okay-ish is the best it gets.

I pull out a book of logic puzzles so I'm not tempted to peek over her shoulder. She'll let us see the pictures when she's ready.

"Ravenna finally made contact," she announces, frowning down thoughtfully at a photo. "She's been staying with a friend in the Outer Banks. They have to go to a different island for Internet access, and she hasn't bothered. She only turned her phone back on today."

"How is she doing?"

"Okay-ish." The grin returns, fleeting but sincere. "She's going to join us in Maryland for the final pictures. After that, she's going to renew her passport and get everything else in order so she can come with me when I go back to Paris. With an ocean between her and her mother, I think she might start doing better."

"I'm a little worried what she may learn from you and your mother."

"There's a ballet studio down the street from the house. I do a lot of their formal pictures, they let me snap rehearsals and classes, and a few staged projects. I think I'm going to take her down there and introduce her."

Because Patrice Kingsley grew up loving dance, and Ravenna danced through the Garden to keep herself going, and ever since getting out, she hasn't known if it was Patrice or Ravenna dancing anymore, dancing for love or for sanity.

"It's a good idea," I murmur, and Priya nods, glues down a strip of paper, and reaches for a sheet of rhinestone stickers.

Around midnight, when Priya is fast asleep with a blanket draped over her, Eddison stirs and looks around. *Hermana?*

"I'm here."

"Get your ass on the bed. My eyes can't focus to the chair."

Snickering, I put the book and pen down and ease onto the bed beside him. His left leg is supported by a shaped foam piece but I don't want to jostle him too much. Fortunately the IV and wires are all on his other side. I settle in against him, head on his shoulder, and we just breathe for a while.

"Did anyone call my parents?"

"They're on a cruise in Alaska with your aunt and uncle. We told them you were doing well out of surgery, and you'd call them once you weren't tripping balls."

"Please tell me you did not—"

"No, we did not tell your mother you were tripping balls," I snort. "We told her you were heavily dosed."

"I don't like it."

"Poor baby."

"Yeah, pretty much." He drifts off again. Eddison's hatred of high-test painkillers has nothing to do with trying to be manly and tough, he just hates being that out of it.

I'm not sure when I doze off. I'm somewhat aware of someone touching my hair, the weight of a blanket over me, but a voice tells me to hush and sleep, and I do.

30

Bright and early Tuesday morning, I sit on the plain wooden bench outside one of the conference rooms in Internal Affairs, thumbs tapping an endless, anxious tattoo against my phone. My knee bounces, and it's only through sheer force of will that I keep my heel from hitting the floor to keep time. I am clearly, visibly, a wreck of nerves, and I can't look away from my hands for fear I'll see the door opening and freeze.

Steady footsteps approach, and I feel someone settle onto the bench beside me. I don't have to look to know it's Vic. Even aside from the familiar sense of his presence, he's been wearing the same aftershave longer than I've been alive. "This is protocol," he says quietly, still trying to preserve my theoretical dignity even though we're alone in the hall. "You've done it before, you'll do it again."

"This time is different."

"It is and it isn't."

Protocol. Because whenever an agent fires their weapon, Internal Affairs investigates the circumstances, makes sure it was the best option, that there wasn't some other way we should have seen. I have done it before, and most of the time, however uncomfortable it is to sit in front of agents from IA and explain every single little thing you've done, it's actually reassuring. Comforting, in a way, to know beyond the shadow of a doubt that not only did you make the right—the only—call, but your agency is holding you and all of its agents accountable to a high standard of integrity and ethics.

Today it is not reassuring, because today it's different.

Vic's hand rests on my knee. Not squeezing, just there. Warm and solid and familiar.

The creak and thump of crutches carries down the hall, and we both look up to watch Eddison slowly make his way around the corner. His top half looks almost work ready, the white dress shirt and black blazer paired with a black tie covered in tiny stained-glass rosettes. Instead of slacks, however, he's in soft black lounge pants and trying desperately to pretend they're professional, and black sneakers he hasn't worn to the office since he was promoted to SSAIC. The pants are loose enough that the bulky bandages around his left thigh aren't particularly noticeable unless you already know they're there.

He looks terrible. The yellow plastic hospital band is still on his wrist, peeking out from his cuffs, and his color is awful beneath the week of dark stubble that's basically a beard at this point. Tight lines around his eyes announce that he isn't taking as much pain medication as he should.

Pendejo got shot a week ago, but damn us all if we try to get him to be sensible. *Dios nos salve de idiotas y hombres.*

"You're almost late," Vic says instead of hello.

Eddison stops in front of us and takes a minute to figure out how to be stationary on crutches. "I think every agent in the building has stopped to talk to me."

"Glad to have you back?"

"Lecturing me to take it easy," he corrects, scratching at his jaw. "Watts says I can't be trusted to take care of myself properly, so everyone wants to see for themselves."

"She's not wrong."

The exchange is familiar, the sound of a million other conversations, and I lean my head back against the wall, closing my eyes to let their voices wash over me. My thumbs keep up their rapid tap-tap-tap against my phone. The repetitive motion is making my wrists ache, but I can't seem to stop.

The front of a sneaker nudges my shin. "Hey," Eddison says. "We've got you."

"I know," I reply, voice a little too high to make it believable.

"You did nothing wrong."

"I know."

"Mercedes." In a trick the dirty bastard learned from Vic, he waits until I look up at him. "We've got you."

I take a deep breath and let it out slowly, then do it again, this time on a count. "I know," I say finally. "I'm just . . ."

"Will this help?" asks a new voice, and Eddison stumbles back with a yelp, catching himself on his crutches almost too late.

Sterling stands beside him with a small smile and a cardboard carrier with four hot drinks.

"Bells," mutters Eddison. "I'm putting bells on you."

"Promises, promises." She hands Vic a cup that smells strongly of black coffee and hazelnut creamer, then hands one to me with the rich scent of chocolate. "I figured you'd be jittery enough," she says with a shrug, "but if you'd rather coffee, we can switch."

"No, hot chocolate is good. Hot chocolate is . . ." The hand not holding the cup is still tapping rapidly against my phone, a little rabbit heart about to burst from fear. "This is good. Thank you."

Eddison eyes the two cups remaining in the carrier. "One of those is mine, right?"

"Yes, black as your soul even. You can have it once we're inside."

"Decaf?" asks Vic.

Sterling shrugs again. "I'd be worried about the caffeine if he was taking his drugs, but he's not, so . . ."

"I am taking my drugs! Vic, don't give me that disappointed look, I am taking my drugs."

"Not all of them," Sterling announces in a singsong voice, and from the beautiful look of disgust and betrayal Eddison gives her, I'm going to guess that she's the one who sprung him from the hospital, and this is her price. I'm also going to guess she didn't tell him that price up front.

"I will take the painkillers when we're done for the day, but I'd like to not be a drooling, incoherent mess in front of IA, thank you very much." He reaches out for the nearer cup, but she pulls it away.

"And how are you going to manage it with your crutches?"

"I've seen you do it."

"You don't have the figure to do it the way I do."

The tips of his ears turning pink, Eddison sends a quick look down both stretches of hallway. "Do you mind? I'm trying to limit myself to one sexual harassment seminar a year."

"Children," Vic rumbles. Eddison glowers, but subsides. Sterling doesn't bother with the glower; even at her most mischievous, she pulls off the innocent look too well to manage anything else well. For the first time, she's wearing color here at work, her blouse a vivid royal blue that makes her eyes pop. It's still a power color, not soft or especially girly, but I'm glad she finally feels comfortable enough to stray from straight black and white.

Does it say anything about me that this is helping me center? If they were genuinely worried about how this investigation was going to turn out, they'd either be very quiet (Vic and Sterling) or blatantly obnoxious (Eddison. Always Eddison). This is business as usual.

Behind the two agents on their feet, the door creaks open. Every conference room on this floor has a door that creaks, no matter how much WD-40 maintenance applies. Rumor has it some enterprising agent went through and put pins in every hinge, so anyone waiting in the hall for an IA deposition or disciplinary meeting has warning when the door opens. I have no idea if the rumor is true or not, but I also know that no agent will ever try to find out.

We're not immune to superstition even if we are supposed to know better.

A young man, probably fresh out of the academy, stands in the doorway and clears his throat. "We're ready for you, agents."

Vic squeezes my knee. "Mercedes?"

I nod, take another minute to breathe, and finally stand up.

Eddison bumps his shoulder into mine, nose pressed into my cheek. "Remember, we've got you," he murmurs. "You're not alone in there, *chula*."

I breathe him in, his familiar scent altered by lingering hospital smells. For ten years, these two men have been my family, and Sterling is part of it now too. I'd have their backs through hell and beyond.

And they've got mine.

31

Two and a half days later, the interviews are basically done, and Agent Dern dismisses us for lunch. The verdict, such as it is, will come down when we reconvene. We retreat to the conference room off the bullpen to wait, and the girls are there, visitor badges clipped to their shirts. They brought the food, insistent on giving us moral support. Inara and Victoria-Bliss actually had to return to New York on Friday, but they came back down last night to be here, and that means a lot.

Eddison pokes at his food. He hasn't had much of an appetite since he got shot, which is normal but still not great. He's almost squinting against the pain, and the muscles at the left side of his mouth keep twitching. As gently as I can, I hook my foot under his and lift his leg until I can discreetly grab his ankle and prop it across my lap. Proper elevation won't make it stop hurting, but at least it's something. He lets out a soft sigh and nudges my elbow with his.

To be honest, I thought we were being wonderfully subtle, but Vic catches my eye and smiles slightly, shaking his head at Eddison's stubbornness.

Priya slides a pair of scrapbooks in front of me, folding her hands on the table. "Vic, Eddison, you have copies coming of the first one, but it felt important to get this one done in time."

I lift up the front cover, aware of Vic and Eddison pressing closer on either side. Sterling smiles and starts cleaning up the boxes. The first picture is of Inara, in those first few days after the Garden, the wings of the Western Pine Elfin emblazoned on her back in pale browns, jewel-like pinks and purples, her sides and hands cut and burned from the glass and explosion. She looks back over her shoulder, slightly, eyes narrowed at whoever else was in the room. On the opposite corner of the page, though, is a newer picture of her, topless and from behind, a few thin scars showing where the wounds used to be, a rainbow mess of full skirts heaped around her as she peeks over her shoulder. She's teasing in this one, the colors of the wings only slightly faded, her arms crossed in front of her with just the tips of her fingers curling over her shoulders. Tiny butterflies and stacks of books decorate the blank corners of the page.

The next page is Victoria-Bliss, the brilliant blue and black of the Mexican Bluewing as dramatic as the rest of her coloring. Like Inara's, the first picture was clearly taken at or just after the hospital, but in the second, she's at a beach, wearing the bottom of a bathing suit, blue ruffled boy shorts, jumping off a squat rock into foaming waves. Her arms are up like she's jumped from a greater height, her feet kicked up behind her.

There's Ravenna, her leg swathed in bandages from a heavy chunk of falling glass, white and palest yellow and orange picked out against her dark skin. In the new one, maybe Ravenna, maybe Patrice, or maybe something wholly new delicately balanced between them, she's dancing *en pointe* in cropped leggings, one arm crossed over her chest, the other arm and one leg fully extended. Strong, graceful, secure in her stance despite the pouring rain. There's hope for her, with luck and the formidable attention of the Sravasti women.

All of the surviving Butterflies, then and now, healthy and mostly happy. Healing. The last of the first set of pages has Keely, just twelve years old when she was kidnapped. She wasn't in the Garden long enough to be tattooed with wings, so unlike the other girls, her current photo is fully clothed. She struggled for a long time with the aftermath, not only with being assaulted and kidnapped when so much younger than the others, but with the widely varying public responses to her. Now, a few months shy of sixteen, she's beaming in the photo and holding up her brand new learner's permit.

This was Priya's project this summer. I continue slowly flipping through pages showing the girls in parts of their new lives, and some where they've clearly gotten together for group shots. There's one of Inara and Keely that makes my eyes burn with tears. Inara protected Keely in the Garden, and did her best to help her afterward, and here they are on the page, sprawled out on a blanket in the sunshine with eyes closed and mouths smiling.

Completely unaware of the water balloon about to land on them. That's . . . that's really a hell of a shot.

But it's so *normal* and healthy, and God, these amazing girls have come so far.

The very last picture has all seven of the survivors, caught midjump in a yard or field, all of them wearing white sundresses and their hair down, with the filmy, brightly colored butterfly wings kids use for dress-up or Halloween catching the sunlight. They're all laughing.

"Some of the others were getting frustrated," Inara says, leaning against Priya. "Sometimes your recovery plateaus, and it was hard to convince them that they were still improving. Priya and I cooked up this idea, so they'd be able to *see* it. But we wanted it for you guys, as well. We've haunted you for a while, and you adopted us, and I think we're the only ones who've been watching to make sure you heal, too."

Victoria-Bliss balls up a napkin and tosses it at Eddison, purposefully shorting it so he doesn't have to grab for it. "We're grateful. We know you haven't seen most of the others since just after the trial, when Mrs. MacIntosh told us about the scholarships she was setting up for us. So we wanted to give you new pictures, so you don't only think of back then."

"This is amazing," I whisper, and I lose the battle with the tears that slide down my cheeks. But Vic has them, too, and even Eddison is trying very hard to look stoic.

"The second one, Mercedes, is just for you," Priya says.

"Does that mean I should open it in private?"

"Up to you. I just meant the boys aren't getting copies down the line." She sticks her tongue out at Eddison's fake pout. "No one else gets vacation photos from Special Agent Ken."

"Although," Inara muses, "his book is going to have a few extra pictures of when Special Agent Ken and my little blue dragon traveled to meet the girls."

He looks both flattered and horrified. "Christ," he wheezes.

All three girls give him wicked smiles.

Stacking the other book on top of the first, I open it and find a picture of eight-year-old Brandon Maxwell, the kidnapping victim in my very first case as an agent. He sits with his parents, teary but beaming, a bright green bear in his lap. Next to that is a new picture, a little grainy like it wasn't entirely focused, of an eighteen-year-old in an orange-and-white cap-and-gown graduation set, beaming with a mouth full of braces and a battered, faded green teddy bear on top of his mortarboard.

"What is . . ."

Every page. Every page has a picture from our case files of one of our rescued children with their bear, and a picture from this summer. The kids range in age from twenties to single digits, and they all . . .

"We got permission from Agent Dern," Priya says as I keep turning pages. "We weren't sure if contacting the families was actually allowed, but she said as long as Sterling did it and no private information was shared, it should be all right."

"Eliza?"

"It's your ten-year anniversary with the Bureau," she says with a smile and a shrug. "I told them we were putting something together for you, and if they were willing, if they still had the bear, would they mind emailing a picture of kiddo with the bear. We probably got about twenty-five percent. Pretty awesome, really. They emailed them and we printed them off."

There are pictures of Priya in there, twelve years old and on the too-skinny edge of a growth spurt, blue streaks in her dark hair. There's one where she's sitting curled around the bear, scowling at the journal in her hands, a never-ending letter to Chavi. There's another one her mother must have taken that perfectly captures Priya's fury, Eddison's shock, and the bear in midair on its collision course for Eddison's face.

Eddison sighs, but it's too fond to be convincing.

And then there's the new picture, Priya at a restaurant table, her shirt cut at an angle below the bust so her tattoo shows bright on her side. The bear sits on a plate wearing a tiny white shirt with red lettering that says "I Survived Dinner with Guido and Sal."

We didn't give bears to most of the Butterflies; they were a bit too old for it, and we didn't want to seem patronizing. We gave one to Keely, though, and she's there in her mother's car, the bear sitting on the dashboard.

There aren't any pictures of the kids from the past month, and I am so, so grateful for that I can hardly speak.

Vic stands up and walks around the table, kissing their cheeks all in a row. "This is wonderful, ladies. Thank you."

I nod, too close to bawling myself stupid to be able to form words.

"Okay-ish?" asks Priya, and I nod again.

The baby-faced agent who's been taking minutes in the IA interviews sticks his head into the conference room. Erickson, that's his name. "Agents? When you're ready."

We stop to put the albums in Vic's office for safekeeping, then escort the girls out. All three give me tight hugs and murmured thank-yous, and if the trip down the elevator had me a little closer to composure, well that just knocks it right the fuck out of the park. Vic hands me a handkerchief without looking.

When we file back into our seats in the conference room, my credentials are on the table in front of what has become my seat over the past three days, the folder flapped back so the badge faces up. I sit down, wrap my hands around the badge, and inspect it.

Someone, probably Agent Dern, managed to get the blood out of the *U*. I've been trying to do that for four years, with everything from Q-tips to needles to dunking the whole damn thing in soapy water, and there it is, finally clean. There's Justice, and the eagle, there's where the gold is dull from being rubbed too many times, surrounded by where it's too shiny from being touched a lot but not yet too much. For ten years, this badge has been a piece of me.

"Agent Ramirez."

I look up at Agent Dern, who regards me with a terrible sort of compassion from the other end of the table. "It is the finding of this investigation that your actions were not only appropriate, but necessary. Though we grieve at the loss of a life, you did what had to be done to protect not only your fellow agents but the child being held hostage, and we thank you for your service. Your administrative leave is lifted, and although we are recommending a set course of counseling to assist with the emotional aftermath, you are cleared to be returned to active duty.

"If that's what you want."

Eddison's mouth disappears behind his hand, and he stares at the table with an expression so blank he has to be hurting himself trying not to scowl. Sterling's hands are folded in her lap, her eyes fixed on them, but those eyes are bright and wet.

Vic . . .

Vic carried me out of hell when I was ten years old, and has carried me so many times since. He meets my eyes and smiles, sad but calm, and nods.

I study the badge in my hands, take a deep breath, and look back at the IA agents on the other side of the table.

"Agent Ramirez, have you made your decision?"

Another slow, deep breath, and all my courage. "I have."

Once upon a time, there was a little girl who was scared of hurting others.

It was strange in context, and she knew that. For so long, the people who were supposed to love her, take care of her, keep her safe, had hurt her instead. She yet bore the scars and always would inside and out. She could trace them with her fingers, with her memories, with her fears.

There's an outer limit to how much you can heal. There comes a point where time just isn't a factor anymore: it's done as much as it can do.

But she survived it, came through it alive even if she was battered, and slowly put together a life for herself. She got away, she made friends, she worked her way into a job she loved.

She just wanted to help people, to help children.

That was all she'd ever wanted, nearly from the moment she'd realized it would be possible. When it finally sifted down through all the years and layers of fears that she had a future, she knew she needed to spend it helping others as she'd been helped.

One night, after years of her being hurt, an angel came to rescue her, and carried her away.

It wasn't the end of her pain—wasn't even the end of her injuries—but it was still a life-changing event. She'd looked into the angel's eyes, kind and sad and gentle, and known that the rest of her life had a path, if she could only get her feet on it.

And she had helped, hadn't she? More than she'd hurt?

Sometimes it was out of her hands. She tried to keep them safe, to get them into better situations, and she'd done that mostly, hadn't she? Or had she been so focused on getting them away, she'd forgotten—her, of all people—that where they were going to was just as important?

She wasn't sure how the scales balanced. Had she helped more than she'd harmed?

But Mercedes knew—she hoped, she prayed, she knew—that the fear made her a better agent. It made her care about what came after, not just what came before. There were children she'd failed and children she'd saved, and children she had yet to save (children she had yet to fail), and she'd be damned if she was walking away from any of them.

There was another scared little girl who chose a different path, but Mercedes chose this one, and she'd choose it again and again.

ACKNOWLEDGMENTS

Every book has its own challenges, and breaks your brain in a different way, and this book was no exception.

So, massive thank-yous to Jessica, Caitlin, and the incredible Thomas & Mercer team, you guys are amazing and supportive and an absolute hoot, and I still can't believe you met the please-don't-hate-me email with laughter. Agent Sandy, who laughed twice as hard, and I'm starting to think this may say more about me than I intend it to.

Thank you, Kelie, for letting me steal your tattoo for Mercedes, and for you being generally you, and to Isabel, Pam and family, Maire, Allyson, Laura, Roni, Tessa, Natalie, and Kate for continuing to be the amazing people you are.

To the family, for being supportive and cheerful and so, so proud of me. It means a lot and keeps me going even when I want to set the draft on fire, and I am very grateful. And thank you for not minding when I carved out a few hours away from the mass arrivals and prewedding festivities so I could work on edits. Specifically, thank you to Robert and Stacy for giving me a place to land when I was so caught up in trying to finish the book on time that I couldn't look for a place to live.

Thank you to Kesha, whose new album fueled half the draft and edits, and Mary Balogh, whose books keep me sane when I'm stressed, and the Yankee Candle Company Mountain Lodge candle, because the smell of lumberjack Chris Evans is surprisingly helpful in keeping calm to work. Thank you to the tenth anniversary live-in-concert *Les Misérables*, the 2015 live-action *Cinderella*, and *Shrek: The Musical*, for being the things I can have on in the background while I'm editing.

Finally, thank you to all of you, all my readers, all my chatterboxes who talk the book up to others, to the bloggers and crafters and artists who share the word in their own way. Thank you for your support, for your time, thank you for your responses, thank you for making it possible for me to continue doing this wacky thing I love.

ABOUT THE AUTHOR

Photo © 2012 Arabella Blizzard

Dot Hutchison is the author of *The Butterfly Garden* and *The Roses of May*, the first two books in The Collector Trilogy; as well as *A Wounded Name*, a young adult novel based on William Shakespeare's *Hamlet*. Hutchison loves thunderstorms, mythology, history, and movies that can and should be watched on repeat. She has a background in theater, Renaissance Festival living chessboards, and freefalls. She likes to think that St. George regretted killing that dragon for the rest of his days. For more information on her current projects, visit www.dothutchison.com or connect with her on Tumblr (www.dothutchison.tumblr.com), Twitter (@DotHutchison), or Facebook (www.facebook.com/DotHutchison).